A MESSAGE FROM CHICKEN HOUSE

I couldn't wait for the next rip-roaring adventure in Maz Evans's totally magnificent series. Not only is the second instalment just as funny and exciting as the first, it's also the best kind of sad – the kind of sad that makes you fiercely protective of your heroes. Full of wonder, adventure and a divine sense of humour, *Simply the Quest* is just about everything a book should be . . . brilliant!

BARRY CUNNINGHAM
Publisher
Chicken House

P.S. There's a really useful 'What's What' on page 363!

Maz Evans

SIMPLY THE QUEST

2 Palmer Street, Frome, Somerset BA11 1DS
chickenhousebooks.com

Text © Mary Evans 2017

First published in Great Britain in 2017
Chicken House
2 Palmer Street
Frome, Somerset BA11 1DS
United Kingdom
www.chickenhousebooks.com

Lines from 'Y.M.C.A.', words and music by Henri H Belolo, Jacques Morali
and Victor Willis, copyright © 1978, are used by permission of
Scorpio Music/EMI Music Publishing, London W1F 9LD.

The paper used in this Chicken House book is made from wood
grown in sustainable forests.

1 3 5 7 9 10 8 6 4 2

British Library Cataloguing in Publication data available.

PB ISBN 978-1-910655-51-1
eISBN 978-1-911077-57-2

For my Dilly

*Heroes come in all shapes and sizes.
Mine is dinky and blonde and would eat
chocolate for breakfast if I let her.*

I love you, my little Hercules.

Also by Maz Evans

Who Let the Gods Out?

1. Mortal Peril

The scream tore through the dawn like a razor blade through toilet paper. Elliot Hooper was the first to respond – if you can call burbling 'whargihghplfm?' a response.

Before he entirely knew where he was – or even who he was – another scream shattered the February morning.

Elliot sat up in bed and scratched his head. He caught his reflection in the bedroom mirror. His blond mop of hair was wayward at the best of times, but at this hour, the twelve-year-old sleepyhead thought he resembled a slightly used toilet brush. His fuzzy brain told him that it was early, although he had only just put Mum back to bed for the umpteenth time. It had been another bad night. Nowadays, they nearly always were.

A third scream forced him into reluctant action.

It definitely wasn't Mum, he knew her screams too well. Were they under attack from Thanatos, Daemon of Death? No – Elliot had squashed him in the Underworld. With a sigh, Elliot realized that this was the third big problem in his life . . .

He rolled out of bed in his school uniform – why change into pyjamas if he was only going to wear the same clothes the next day? – and stumbled towards the bathroom.

He reached it just as his immortal Greek housemates – Zeus, Athene, Aphrodite, Hermes and Hephaestus – were hurtling (flying in Hermes's case) up the stairs. They were greeted by another soul-splitting shriek.

Elliot pressed his ear to the bathroom door.

'What in the name of thirty thermal thunder-bolts . . . ?' roared Zeus.

'It's nothing, it'll just be—' Elliot began, but was slammed against the wall by the two Goddesses, who formed a protective barrier around him in their full battle-armour and fluffy slippers.

'Don't worry – we're here,' said Athene, Goddess of Wisdom.

'Are you OK, Elly?' panted Aphrodite, Goddess of Love, drawing her crossbow.

'I'm fine,' said Elliot, crushed behind Athene's enormous silver shield.

If Elliot wasn't panicking, it was because living with a family of ancient immortals had made him no stranger to drama. From the moment Virgo, a Constellation from the Zodiac Council, had crashed into his cowshed three months ago, Elliot had:

- accidentally freed Thanatos, Daemon of Death
- borrowed Queen Elizabeth II's Imperial Crown
- nearly been expelled from Brysmore Grammar School
- learnt how to swear in Latin, Ancient Greek and Satyr.

'Open up!' boomed Zeus, hammering at the bathroom door. 'I command you!'

He was answered by another brain-melting yelp.

Zeus signalled to Hephaestus, God of the Forge.

'All o' you – stand back!' yelled the blacksmith, heaving his gigantic bronze axe with surprising strength from a hunchback the height of a nine-year-old. 'We're coming in!'

'Wait! Let's just try the—' cried Elliot as the bronze axe smashed the wood to matchsticks. 'Handle,' he said, pushing open the remains of the unlocked door.

The Gods bundled into the bathroom with a ferocious cry, weapons aloft . . .

But all they found was Virgo, rocking on the floor with a towel over her head.

'Babe? What gives?' asked Hermes, after an admiring glance at his reflection.

''Ere we go again,' grumbled Hephaestus.

'Whatever's the matter, dear girl?' said Zeus, sheathing a thunderbolt. 'I haven't heard a furore like that since I dumped Henrietta the Harpy on Valentine's Day.'

'It's . . . it's hideous,' snuffled Virgo.

'Is it a curse?' asked Athene.

'Is it a plague?' asked Aphrodite.

'Is it that fringe?' asked Hermes. 'Babe, I warned you. Totes off-trend . . .'

'No . . . It's . . . it's . . . it's . . .' Virgo slowly lifted the towel from her head.

The Gods gasped.

Elliot just stared.

'I don't get it,' he said, disappointed that Virgo

hadn't grown a second head or an elephant's nose. 'What's wrong?'

'WHAT'S WRONG?!' Virgo shrieked, pulling her hair. 'LOOK AT IT!'

Elliot did. Still nothing.

'Boys . . .' muttered Athene as Aphrodite hugged Virgo.

Elliot shrugged at Hermes.

'E, mate!' the Messenger God whispered. 'Her hair. It's, like, totes *brown*.'

'Isn't it always?' Elliot asked.

'Mate . . .' laughed Hermes with a head-shake.

'My beautiful silver hair!' Virgo cried. 'IT'S GONE!'

'Oh, yeah!' said Elliot slowly. Now he thought about it, she did look a bit different.

'Did you dye it?' said Aphrodite, running her fingers through Virgo's long tresses.

'Babe – never dye your own hair,' said Hermes. 'I tried it once – ended up with a head like a cress plant.'

'I haven't touched it!' squealed Virgo. 'Why would I? It was perfect! I just woke up like this! What's happening to me?'

Elliot caught Aphrodite and Athene exchanging knowing glances.

'It's just your body adapting to being a mortal,'

said Athene. 'It actually quite suits you . . .'

'SUITS ME?!' squealed Virgo at a pitch that could start a football match. 'Have you forgotten about *today*? My trial?'

'Fat chance, with you banging on about it,' mumbled Elliot, pushing past the crowd to reach his toothbrush. He was never a morning person, and five hours sleep certainly wasn't enough for immortal dramas.

'You have got to stop getting in such a state,' said Athene, giving Virgo's shoulders a reassuring squeeze. 'If there is any justice, today is the day you'll get your immortality back.'

'Listen to Boffin Butt — that kardia's yours,' chirped Aphrodite, helping herself to a spray of perfume. 'Besides, it's only a trial. The Zodiac Council like to waggle their clipboards around to feel important. Look at Christmas Day . . .'

'We do not mention Christmas Day!' snapped Zeus.

'Exhacshly,' spat Elliot through a mouthful of foam. 'Sho schill out. Itsch not vat wig a weal.'

'Not that big a deal?' breathed Virgo menacingly. Everyone instinctively stepped back.

'Uh-oh,' whispered Hermes. 'She's gonna blow.'

'NOT THAT BIG A DEAL!' screamed Virgo. 'For weeks I've had to endure mortality! I've suffered hunger, tiredness, every tedious mortal emotion and some toxic reaction in my trousers whenever I eat beans! It's degrading, it's unjust and it's TOTALLY PANTS!'

Elliot spat his toothpaste down the plughole. 'So I shouldn't mention that zit on your chin?'

'What?! Arrrrrrrrghghgh,' screamed Virgo as she wrestled free from Athene and attacked Elliot with the nearest available weapon, which happened to be a giant pink loofah.

The Gods scrambled to protect Elliot again. Aphrodite held the flailing girl back so Hermes could disarm her. Athene and Zeus grabbed Elliot's arms to drag him to safety as Virgo screamed a curse that could boil an egg.

' . . . and then you can bake it in a pie and CHOKE ON IT!' she screeched.

'Elly, have you watered the plants?' peeped an agitated voice behind them.

Elliot turned to see his mum, Josie, standing in the broken doorway, confused and upset. These days, she always was. He tried not to think of his bright, funny Mum who used to cartwheel home from school. She had changed so much in the past year. Everything had.

'Elly?' she asked again. 'You must water the plants. You know what Grandad's like about his

7

tomatoes. Have you done it?'

'Yes, Mum,' said Elliot, who had given up on difficult truths in favour of easy lies. Although he wasn't sure if Mum really understood either anymore.

The last few weeks had seen a lot of changes in Josie and none of them good. Despite Elliot's best efforts to care for her, she wasn't getting any better. She barely remembered anything that had just happened, her moods were getting really unpredictable and she often struggled to find the right words to express herself.

Elliot ignored the dark voice inside his head.

She's getting worse. Fast, it said.

'Good boy,' said Josie. 'Grandad will be . . . What happened here?'

'Nothing to worry about, Josie – just children being children,' said Athene kindly, turning the frail frame of Josie Hooper discreetly from the broken door. 'Why don't I poach you an egg for breakfast?'

Josie wriggled free from Athene and held Elliot's hand. 'Elly will do it, thank you,' she said warily.

Elliot sighed. The Gods tried to help with Josie's care, but increasingly she'd only allow Elliot to put her back to bed, bathe her or make her food. It was tiring, but Elliot didn't mind.

Yes, you do, his dark voice insisted.

'Well let's go downstairs and lay the table,' said Athene, shrugging an apology at Elliot.

'OK,' said Josie cautiously. 'Have you watered the plants?'

Elliot watched Athene gently guide Josie downstairs. Would today be a good day he wondered? A day when Mum remembered people and places, and stayed happy and calm? Or a bad one, when she became very confused, or angry, or obsessed over a tiny detail, or couldn't recall a conversation from five minutes ago? Elliot hoped for a good day. They hadn't had one for a while. Nor a good night.

Aphrodite smiled and pinched his cheek in a way that would really annoy him if she were anyone but a beautiful love Goddess. Elliot surveyed the carnage around him.

'Sorry, mate,' said Hermes. 'We're all just a bit stir-crazy. Y'know, being, like, totes grounded since Christmas Day . . .'

'We DO NOT mention Christmas Day!' Zeus roared.

'Fine,' said Elliot. 'I'd better get started on breakfast . . .'

'Breakfast!' said Virgo, instantly brightening and

9

bounding downstairs. 'Excellent. I'm famished. Then I'm going to get my immortality back, reunite all my socks with their partners and finally understand long-division!' She leapt from the bottom step. 'It's going to be a super-optimal day!'

Elliot rolled his eyes and headed slowly after her. Girls were so incredibly weird.

2. Postal Strike

'**M**ortal education is highly sub-optimal,' Virgo announced in the kitchen a short while later.

'Tell me about it,' yawned Elliot as he dropped two eggs into a pan of boiling water and set his pocket watch.

Hephaestus had been kind enough to modify his father's watch when it was smashed by a flying train last year. One of the most useful settings was announcing when eggs were perfectly cooked, although Elliot looked forward to trying the 'Controlled Explosion' function too. He couldn't help but glance at the Earth Stone, the diamond

Chaos Stone he kept in the watch. He must never use it – Zeus had told him that – but he still had to find the Air, Water and Fire Stones if he was to defeat Thanatos. But vengeful death daemons would have to wait. Right now, Elliot was too tired to save the world.

Elliot yawned and looked around the kitchen for the bottomless satchel Hermes had given him for Christmas. He spied it on a chair and tipped the contents on to the kitchen table. The symbols of his normal – and not so normal – lives piled together: the Queen's Imperial Crown, his maths book, the wishing pearl, some fluff, Zeus's thunder-bolt pen (he'd not used it since a mishap in the school chemistry lab), some more fluff, Hypnos, Daemon of Sleep's magical trumpet, three pen lids, two pens (not matching) and finally, Aphrodite's box of potions.

He opened it up – Tickling Potion, Bazooka Fart Brew, Bad–Hair–Day Remedy . . . Ah – Wake-Up Juice. He took a big swig and immediately felt a zing of alertness.

'I mean,' Virgo continued, 'we've barely returned to school after Christmas, yet we are having another week away.'

'Great, isn't it?' grinned Elliot, revitalized by the potion and the prospect of half-term that afternoon.

'I do not understand your reluctance towards school,' said Virgo. 'Mortals without formal education are most likely to endure unemployment and daytime television.'

'Sounds all right,' said Elliot.

'It does not!' huffed Virgo. 'The consequences could be calamitous. You could end up—'

'Relax,' Elliot sighed. 'It was a joke.'

'I cannot comprehend this joking,' said Virgo, wrinkling her brow. 'It is far more efficient to say what you mean.'

'Not as much fun, though,' grinned Elliot. 'Knock, knock.'

'Identify yourself,' said Virgo.

'Ivor.'

'Specifically which Ivor?' asked Virgo. 'Statistically, there must be thousands.'

'Ivor sore hand from knocking!'

Elliot sniggered. Virgo did not.

'I see,' she said. 'Did Ivor receive medical attention?'

'You are so weird,' muttered Elliot, returning to the breakfast as his watch chimed.

An agitated Josie wandered into the kitchen, running her hands through her hair. 'Have you watered the plants?' she said quickly. 'We mustn't upset Grandad.'

Elliot sighed. This could go on for hours. His Mum had started endlessly repeating a single worry. No matter how much he reassured her, on a day like this, Josie would become increasingly frantic, forgetting the answer to a question she had asked only moments before. It was horrible to watch.

And kind of annoying, said his dark voice.

'Did them this morning,' said Elliot with a strained smile, putting her poached eggs in front of her. 'Eat up.'

'Oooh – my favourite,' smiled Josie, the plants wiped from her mind.

A bike bell outside signalled that the postman was waiting at the gate. Elliot darted to the kitchen door, feeling the familiar guilty gratitude at an excuse to leave for a minute. He walked out into the crisp February morning.

'All right, young Hooper – how do?' called the postie.

'Morning, Reg,' said Elliot, opening the magical gate that protected Home Farm. 'How's everything?'

Reg Hyatt had delivered the post for ever. His favourite pastime was telling everyone in Little Motbury the importance of confidentiality in his job. His second favourite was gossiping about everyone in Little Motbury.

'Not too bad,' sighed Reg. 'Better than Mrs Moppett down the village shop. Just delivered a letter from her husband's divorce lawyer.'

'Didn't know she was getting divorced,' said Elliot sympathetically.

'Neither did she,' said Reg. 'You didn't hear it from me, mind . . .' He handed over the post. 'Take care, boy – best to your ma,' he said, cycling down the path.

Elliot meandered back to the kitchen, rifling through the usual jumble of bills and junk mail.

'Perhaps Ivor should call in advance?' Virgo was saying thoughtfully. 'This would ensure someone was there to open the door . . .'

But Elliot didn't answer. An unusual envelope had caught his eye.

'Mum?' he said. 'There's a letter for you.'

He looked at the handwritten address before handing it over. Not a bill or a bank statement then – this was personal. Who was writing to his mum? He watched Josie open it and begin to read . . .

'Elliot? Elliot?' said Virgo impatiently. 'Is your hearing optimal? I doubt it, with all the wax building up between your ears.'

'At least there's something between my ears,'

said Elliot. 'You are such a—'

'Lock the door!' Josie shouted suddenly, jumping from the table with the letter crumpled in her hand.

'Mum?' asked Elliot.

'Where are the keys?' She rushed to the kitchen door, her face contorted with panic. 'We need to lock the door!'

Elliot and Virgo shared bewildered looks as Josie ran around the kitchen searching for the keys.

'HELP ME!' she screamed.

'Wh-what's the matter?' Elliot asked. Mum often got upset over little things, but he'd never seen her this distressed. This was scary.

'Are you quite well, Josie-Mum?' asked Virgo.

'Here — here they are,' said Elliot, pulling his own keys from his coat pocket.

'Lock it!' panted Josie. 'Lock it now.'

'O-OK,' said Elliot, turning the keys in the kitchen door. 'It's locked. Everything's OK, Mum.'

'Good. Good. We must keep it locked,' said Josie urgently, yanking on the door handle. 'We must stay safe.'

'Who's that from?' Elliot asked, trying to take the letter. 'Let me see it . . .'

'You are not to leave this house,' shouted Josie,

16

snatching the letter away and clutching it to her chest. 'You stay inside! Always! Do you hear me, Elliot?'

'Mum – I can't be here all the time!' Elliot laughed. 'I've got to go to school . . .'

'DO AS YOU'RE TOLD!' screamed Josie, making Elliot jump. She hardly ever shouted at him. 'YOU STAY HERE!'

There was a painful silence.

'Josie-Mum,' said Virgo softly. 'Your breakfast will get sub-optimal. Yours too, Elliot.'

But Elliot didn't want his breakfast. He remembered refusing to go to school when he was little. Josie had threatened to carry him there in his pyjamas.

Josie came back to the table, the letter already forgotten now it was stuffed in her pocket. Elliot and Virgo looked at one another. What had just happened?

The door handle jiggled frantically.

'E! V! Mate! Babe!' shouted Hermes from outside. 'Peg's getting proper chewy – reckons the air traffic's gonna be a nightmare if you don't motor . . .'

Elliot unlocked the door, not taking his eyes from his mother, who was now happily eating her eggs.

'Morning, J-Hoops!' called Hermes. 'Looking good, babe!'

Josie grinned at Hermes. He always made her smile.

'I'll stay with her,' said Athene, walking into the kitchen and putting a reassuring arm on Elliot's. 'You go and be star witness – Virgo needs you.'

'It would be far more optimal if you could come,' Virgo called to Zeus outside. 'I think that Christmas Day . . .'

'WE DO NOT MENTION CHRISTMAS DAY!' Zeus hollered so loudly he made the ground shake. The King of the Gods blushed sheepishly. 'I mean, er . . .' he mumbled, 'you don't need us – you've got Themis. She's a bang-up lawyer. Used her for my last seventeen divorces – top hole. Good luck, old girl.'

'You too, Elly,' said Aphrodite. 'Sock it to 'em.'

'Much as I'd love to join the cheerleading,' drawled Pegasus, 'I appear to have left my pom-poms in my other saddle bag. If you wish to attend your trial before the verdict, however, I suggest we leave now.'

'And shut the ruddy gate!' Hephaestus yelled across the paddock.

'Come on!' said Virgo, grabbing her coat and running out of the door.

'Nothing to worry about, kids,' said Zeus. 'You'll be back home in twenty minutes for a cup of tea. Toodle-pip!'

Elliot looked over at Josie, calmly eating her breakfast and reading the paper. What he would have given a year ago to be banned from attending school.

But as Elliot Hooper was fast learning, a lot could change in a year.

3. Trial and Error

Three hours and forty-seven minutes later, there was no sign of home, nor a cup of tea. Virgo was feeling decidedly sub-optimal. She stared forlornly out of the window at the paradise that used to be her home. She'd had so many happy times here in Elysium. At least three.

The glass pyramid of the council chamber had been arranged like a courtroom for her trial. The Zodiac Council's red sofas were in a semi-circle around the golden table, facing Virgo in the dock before them. On the evidence table between them lay Virgo's crystal kardia, the heart within a flame that made her immortal. Would she ever get it back?

'And that concludes the prosecution testimony for 5.01 p.m. to 5.04 p.m.,' droned Aquarius, the water bearer, who was Council leader in February. 'Who has 5.05 p.m.?'

'Where is Themis?' hissed Virgo to Elliot in the gallery nearby. Her lawyer still hadn't arrived. 'As a mortal, I only have a life expectancy of 81.2 years . . .'

' . . . and it is further alleged that at 5.05 p.m. and 23 seconds, Virgo, a *junior* Constellation, absconded from Elysium with the flask of ambrosia for Prisoner Forty-two – with neither permission, paperwork, nor any indication where the pencil sharpeners are kept – and went AWOL to Earth, before disobeying a string of Council rules,' pronounced Capricorn, the half-goat, promptly eating his notes.

Virgo had heard enough. In this, as in all things, she was right. She just needed to help everyone to realize it.

'Look, if I could just explain—' she blurted.

'No need!' interrupted a triumphant voice as the chamber doors burst open in a flash of golden robes. 'I have all the proof we need right here!'

'Themis!' exclaimed Virgo in delight.

The Goddess of Justice charged through the

21

court, waving a piece of parchment. Virgo looked hopefully at her kardia. She could almost feel it back around her neck.

'Sorry I'm late,' Themis whispered as she passed the dock. 'Got a bit held up. That's the last time I agree to defend a chicken. Or an egg. I forget which came first. Right – I've got this sewn up tighter than a Titan's swimming trunks.'

Themis took a moment to adjust her golden robes and fix her curled, white barrister's wig, which Virgo realized was, in fact, her own hair.

'This whole trial is a farce!' cried Themis, approaching the Council's golden table. 'Here is the piece of paper that proves my client is innocent!'

Virgo tried to stop a smug smile. She failed.

'This not only proves that she didn't commit the crime,' said Themis, walking slowly around the Council, 'but she is also really nice to kittens and overdue a Girl Guide embroidery badge.'

'Let me see that!' snapped Cancer, the crab, snatching the parchment from Themis with a pincer. 'Whatever are you talking about? This has nothing to do with Virgo. This is a receipt for a prawn vindaloo with extra chillies!'

'Ah,' said Themis, as the Gemini twins tore the parchment up and aimed the scraps at Capricorn's snoring mouth. 'Well, that solves the Case of the

Exploding Bottom . . . But my client still didn't do it!'

Themis sidled up to Virgo.

'Remind me what you did again?' she asked out of the corner of her mouth. 'You opened Pandora's box? No – you gave mortals fire? Ah – that's right, you smelt it AND dealt it?'

'She's the one who released Thanatos,' sighed Sagittarius, the centaur. 'Allegedly. The Council denies all knowledge of knowing anything.'

'Ah, yes!' shouted Themis. 'My client pleads not guilty to all charges!'

'There is only one charge,' yawned Leo, adding another sugar cube to his tall tower.

'Then she's not guilty of all the ones you don't know about!' the lawyer declared. Virgo worked out the statistical probability of getting her kardia back now. It was, as Elliot might conclude, "pants".

'Perhaps you'd like to call a witness?' bleated Capricorn.

'Absolutely. Tip of my tongue,' smiled Themis. 'What should I call them?'

'Elliot,' coughed Virgo. 'Elliot Hooper.'

'Quite right,' shouted Themis. 'I call upon . . .'

'*Elliot. Hooper,*' whispered Virgo loudly.

'Mr . . .' Themis continued, leaning so close to

Virgo that the former Constellation could see right down her earhole.

'E-L-L-I-O-T H-O-O-P-E-R,' Virgo hissed.

'Got it,' whispered Themis with a wink. 'The defence calls . . . Mr . . . SMELLIEST POOPER!'

The gentle thud of Virgo's head hitting the table was the only sound in the chamber.

Elliot stepped into the centre of the pyramid. He winked at her and mouthed, 'I've got this.' Virgo hoped this referred to his confidence, not his bodily odour.

'Hello again, Mr Hooper,' said Aquarius with a thin smile.

'Hiya,' said Elliot, fiddling with something in his pockets.

Virgo had observed that mortal boys did this a great deal. She made a note to investigate what unsolvable puzzle they kept there.

'Mr Hooper, why don't you tell us what happened – in your own words?' asked Scorpio.

'Objection!' yelled Themis. 'My witness – I'll ask the questions!'

Scorpio held his pincers up as Themis cleared her throat.

'Mr Hooper,' she began grandly. 'Why don't you tell us what happened – in your own words?'

'Er . . . well,' said Elliot. 'See, it was like this.

Virgo crashed into my cowshed in a big pile of poo. I thought she was mad – still do, actually – so I took her home to find her parents, but she kept saying she was a constellation, which sounded crazier than a box of sugar-high frogs, so I didn't believe her until she went underwater for, like, ages. Anyway, she wanted to take this ambrosia stuff to a secret prisoner who, it turns out, was Thanatos – weird, right? So, we went to Stonehenge and I was going to leave, but I got chased by this fat security guard and ended up under the Heel Stone with her, but Thanatos did all this, like, Jedi mind-bending stuff and I believed him, so that was kind of my bad – he tried to tear Virgo to bits so I said he couldn't have his ambrosia, he tried to kill me, he couldn't, then Virgo whooshed us out of the cave in her star-ball thing . . .'

'It's a constellation!' hissed Virgo.

'Yeah – that,' said Elliot, 'and then we came here and you said she couldn't use her powers any more. Then we got the Earth Stone, then I went to Thanatos, then she used her star-b— constellation – to get me back to Earth, then I'm alive again, then you made her mortal and now she wants her kardia back.'

The chamber fell silent again as everyone looked quizzically at Elliot. Virgo distinctly

25

remembered telling Elliot exactly what to say. Clearly Elliot did not.

'Think that's about it,' he added quietly.

'Is that so?' said Pisces, piecing the story together. 'And where is Thanatos now? Not that he was ever anywhere. We know nothing about that.'

'He's squished beneath a heap of stalactites in the Cave of Sleep and Death,' said Elliot. 'But it's only a matter of time before…'

'How convenient,' sighed Taurus. 'So the truth is …'

'YOU CAN'T HANDLE THE TRUTH!' yelled Themis, slamming her hand down, sending Leo's sugar-cube tower clattering across the golden table. She leant into Virgo with a whisper. 'Remind me again – what was the truth?'

'The truth is,' said Elliot, rolling his eyes, 'if I'd let Virgo do her job, none of this would have happened.'

'So what are you saying?' asked Aquarius.

Elliot released a reluctant sigh. He appeared to have something deeply distasteful in his mouth. Virgo presumed he'd eaten the contents of his nostrils. Again.

'What I'm saying is …' he said eventually, 'it was all my fault.'

Virgo felt her favourite sensation flood her body.

She was right.

Surely this changed everything! She looked hopefully at the Council.

'Well, this changes everything!' said Aquarius with a smile. 'You know what this means?'

Virgo could barely breathe with anticipation.

'This means,' Aquarius continued, 'it's not *our* fault! WHOOPEEE!'

The Zodiac constellations bounced from their seats and started whizzing gleefully around the room as showers of stars.

'Not our fault!' squealed Sagittarius, reforming on his sofa. 'Wow. That's not happened since 1352 – this is a wonderful day!'

'Marvellous!' said Themis, accepting a celebratory sausage roll from Aquarius on her way out. 'My work here is done. I'll send you my bill . . .'

'Er, Themis! Er . . . excuse me!' Virgo called over the hullabaloo. 'What about my kardia?'

'Ah, yes, that,' said Aquarius, calling the trial to order again. 'You don't deny that you broke Council rules and travelled to Earth without the proper authorization?'

'Well, no, but . . .'

'Nor that you revealed your immortality to a

27

mortal, expressly contradicting your conditions of employment?' said Scorpio.

'OK, I shouldn't really have done that ...'

'Nor that you used your constellation powers in defiance of this Council?' asked Cancer.

'That's unfortunate, but, as Elliot says, he was mostly to blame,' Virgo said desperately. 'Please. Please give me one more chance.'

The councillors looked doubtfully amongst themselves.

'I'm sorry, Virgo,' said Aquarius gravely. 'You have failed to provide any compelling evidence that you are worthy of your kardia ...'

'But ... I ...' wailed Virgo desperately.

'So if there's nothing further, I declare the defendant g—'

'Please!' begged Virgo, extending her clasped hands towards Aquarius. 'I can't stay like this! Mortals are irrational! Mortals are unpredictable! Mortals grow hair in their armpits! Surely I don't deserve that?'

The councillors looked unconvinced. Virgo stared helplessly at Elliot, hoping her silent pleas for him to speak out made it through all that ear wax.

The mortal boy rolled his eyes and belched slightly. Eventually, he stood up and turned to address the Council again.

'Look,' said Elliot. 'Apart from the fact that I really need you to take her back because she's an epic pain in the butt – seriously, how long does one person need in the shower? – it's not fair to punish her for . . . for saving me. Thanatos nearly killed me. And if he ever escapes and gets his hands on the Chaos Stones, he's going to kill loads of people. Virgo's not the bad guy here, Thanatos is. She risked everything to save my life. In fact, if you look at it in kind of a weird, twisted, really annoying way . . . she was a hero.'

Aquarius raised an eyebrow. 'A hero, you say?' he said. 'Interesting . . .'

Virgo smiled gratefully at Elliot, which he appeared to reluctantly accept. He had tried. And she could always arrange a presentation of all the things he did wrong later.

The councillors huddled together in a whispering frenzy.

'All right,' said Aquarius at last, as the councillors returned to their seats. 'Virgo, we will grant you the chance to earn your kardia back.'

'Yeeeeesssss!' squealed Virgo. 'I'll do anything – you name it. I'll alphabetize Cancer's classical music CDs. I'll clip Scorpio's dodgy toenails. I'll do Taurus's laundry after Fajita Friday – anything,

29

anything at all . . .'

'The punishment should fit the crime,' said Aquarius. 'The child is right. Your reckless behaviour *might* have placed the mortals in terrible danger.'

'Not that we know anything about that,' added Leo.

'*If* Earth is indeed an endangered realm, the mortals will need someone who is prepared to undergo unthinkable perils to protect them,' said Aquarius. 'They'll need someone who will lead the fight against evil. They'll need someone who will risk their very being to ensure their survival. If you want your kardia back, you really do need to give the mortals a hero.'

'Great,' said Virgo confidently. 'Who?'

'You,' said Aquarius casually.

'Me!' exclaimed Virgo. 'How am I supposed to do that?'

'I'm afraid that falls under Directive 7408c: Your Problem,' said Aquarius, bringing down his golden gavel. 'Prove yourself a hero or kiss your kardia farewell. Case dismissed.'

4. To the Letter

Sharing his farm with Virgo and the Gods, Elliot had learnt to expect the unexpected. Over the past few months, his breakfast cereal had made him sing opera, his PE socks had been sacrificed on the barbeque to encourage a good harvest and a community of gorgons had claimed asylum in his downstairs loo.

But as Pegasus, Elliot and Virgo touched down at Home Farm, Elliot wasn't expecting to see the King of the Gods throw a rusty tractor across the paddock.

'Aaaaaaaaaargh!' Zeus puffed as the vehicle sailed over their head.

'Must be Friday,' sighed Pegasus, trotting back towards the shed.

'AND THIS TIME – STAY OUT!' bellowed Zeus, storming back into the farmhouse, barging past the faintly familiar figure at the front door. Elliot had only seen her once before.

The lady – Elliot instinctively felt she should be called a lady – took a deep breath and lifted a pale white arm to tuck a stray hair back into her immaculate dark bun. She turned her cool gaze on Elliot and Virgo.

'Hello, children,' she said, with a voice like a crystal dagger. 'How nice to see you again.'

'Your Highness,' said Virgo, raising her right hand to her left shoulder in greeting. 'What an unexpected honour. We haven't seen you since . . .'

'Christmas Day,' said Hera.

Elliot had only briefly met the Queen of the Gods – Zeus's ex-wife – when she knocked on his door that day. But she had made quite an impression.

'To what do we owe the pleasure?' asked Virgo.

'I meant to come sooner, but my role as Chief Investigator of Immortal Conduct keeps me rather busy . . .' said Hera grandly. 'Just this week the Maenads have caused havoc on their rugby tour and as for Silenus's stag night . . .'

'You still here?' roared Zeus, bursting out of the kitchen window and holding a thunderbolt aloft. 'I said – GET OUT!'

'It's always so lovely to drop in on the family,' said Hera with a small smile, elegantly side-stepping the thunderbolt that exploded at her feet. 'I've been trying to deliver this to the prisoners . . . the *probationers* . . .' she went on, handing a small golden box to Virgo. 'But I'm having a little difficulty. Would you kindly pass it on? And if you could remind Zeus and his children that they are still expressly forbidden to leave Home Farm until their assessment has been completed. In order to help, I am deactivating all their transport.'

Great, thought Elliot. The Gods had already been grounded since Christmas Day and they'd been going beserk. Now they'd be going even . . . beserker.

'Hera – babe!' said Hermes, fluttering over from the shed and kissing the Goddess's hand. 'Not being funny, but you look hotter than a taco in Tartarus.'

'Charming as ever, Hermes,' said Hera, losing her battle with a coy smile. 'Could you kindly fetch Pegasus for me? The Council have decided to send him to a time-management seminar. He needs to leave now – it's over a day's flight away.'

'For you, babe,' winked Hermes, 'anything.'

'Thank you,' said Hera. 'I've been impressed with your attitude to your probation. Consider all restrictions on your movement lifted. You are free to leave.'

'And that,' said Hermes, bowing in mid-air before jetting off, 'is why you are one awesomely authoritative mega-babe. Boom!'

'Pardon me, er, Ma'am,' said Elliot, 'but when do you think they'll be able to get out again?'

'When their assessor is satisfied that they won't run around Earth trying to steal Crown Jewels, fly commuter trains and fight Beefeaters,' said Hera with a cool smile. 'A full report will be filed to the Zodiac Council, who will decide how to proceed. Until then, they remain under house – farm – arrest.'

'And who's their assessor?' asked Virgo.

'Well, now,' said Hera with a satisfied smile. 'That would be me.'

'I'M WARNING YOU!' Zeus yelled again, this time from an upstairs window. 'You have to the count of three! One ...'

'Well, I'd better be off,' said Hera calmly as Pegasus flew down beside her. 'Dionysus is holding a poker night and we know how those end ...'

'Two ...'

34

'Come along, Peg,' she said with a smile.

'I fail to see an issue with my time-management,' huffed Pegasus. 'Why, only today, I'd scheduled a facial, hoovicure and wing wax.'

'You'll return Friday morning,' said Hera. 'Goodbye, children. See you soon.'

'Three!'

And Hera calmly led Pegasus down the path and out of Home Farm, just as an enormous thunderbolt exploded inches behind her.

Virgo and Elliot shrugged at each other.

'So I'm guessing it wasn't a friendly divorce?' said Elliot.

'You might say that,' chortled Virgo. 'But then you might say that the Trojan War was a neighbourly squabble!'

She laughed, clearly expecting Elliot to join her. He did not.

'The Trojan War was in fact a protracted conflict between two embittered enemies that lasted for a decade,' she explained. 'I am obviously going to be highly optimal at joking.'

'Let me know when you start,' said Elliot.

'Father, you have to calm down!' they heard Athene say as they approached the back door. 'Don't let her rile you like this.'

'That simpering shrew!' barked Zeus. 'This –

this is why our marriage ended!'

'Dad – not being funny,' said Hermes, whizzing into the kitchen ahead of them, 'but your marriage ended because you ran off with Sheila.'

'Yes, I did!' roared Zeus. 'Sheila was my true Goddess!'

'Sheila was your cleaner!' Aphrodite said, then spotted Elliot and Virgo in the doorway. 'Kids! You're home!'

'So babe – how did the trial go?' asked Hermes.

'Virgo'll be off scot-free,' said Zeus. 'That Themis has a brilliant legal mind.'

'Shame she didn't bring it with her,' said Elliot.

Virgo handed Hera's parcel to Athene. 'As Elliot would say, "she sucked".'

'So?' asked the Goddess of Wisdom. 'What happened?'

Elliot related the trial in as much detail as he could remember – and Virgo seemed more than happy to fill in the bits he couldn't. And most of the bits he could.

'So if I'm to regain my kardia, I have to prove myself a hero,' said Virgo. 'But how?'

'I'd research the greats,' said Athene, swapping two spices in the spice rack so they were in alphabetical order. 'Hercules, Theseus, Jason – what made them the heroes we still celebrate?'

Elliot could almost see the light bulb illuminate over Virgo's head. She pulled out her *What's What* and scuttled away.

'We should go up to that bally Council and blast them into the middle of next week!' roared Zeus, with a wave of his arms, sending the spice rack flying across the kitchen. 'The ruddy nerve of them – I've got a good mind to—'

'LOCK THE DOOR!' Josie suddenly screamed behind them, running to secure the open kitchen door. 'Where are the keys?'

'Mum!' said Elliot, slightly more impatiently than he meant to as she threw the orderly kitchen into disarray. 'Mum, it's OK – we'll find the keys . . .'

'Here you are, Josie,' said Athene, transforming a nearby ball of wool into a set of house keys. 'Shall we lock the door together?'

'Yes,' said Josie, calming slightly as Athene turned the key in the lock. 'We must keep it locked. At all times. We must keep the bad man out.'

'What bad man, babe?' said Hermes kindly.

But Josie had already wandered to the other side of the kitchen. Hermes shot Elliot a questioning look. Elliot just shook his head. He didn't

feel like talking.

'Why don't we go and do some more patch-work?' suggested the Goddess of Wisdom, leading Josie gently into the other room. 'I'll make us some tea.'

Elliot's heart sank. Today clearly wasn't a good day either. He turned to the Gods.

'Guys. We can't keep having this conversation,' he said. 'You've got to chill out. I get it. It must have been hard since all that Hera stuff on Christmas Day . . .'

'WE DO NOT MENTION CHRISTMAS DAY!' roared Zeus.

'Sorry!' said Elliot, putting his hands up. 'But all this drama, all the time – it gets Mum all . . . y'know.'

'Quite right,' said Zeus more calmly. 'I'm sorry, old chap. It's just being stuck in here while Hypnos is out there . . .'

'I know, but . . .' Elliot began.

'We have to find that feathery fruitcake,' Zeus muttered for the millionth time. 'Only he knows where the bally Chaos Stones are and if he gets to you or them before we do, I shudder to think . . .'

'Dad – I'm on it like a car bonnet,' said Hermes. 'I've got Uncle Hades on the case – he's got eyes everywhere. The second Hypnos shows his crazy kisser – bosh!'

'We have to stay on our guard,' Zeus said. 'Hypnos could be anyone. Like that chap who charged at you brandishing that huge grenade . . .'

'That was Steve the milkman,' said Elliot. 'The "grenade" was a pint of semi-skimmed. And he was charging because you turned his milk float into a Challenger tank and fired it at him . . .'

'Or that fella who tried to melt your mind with his daemonic incantations?' Zeus insisted.

'That was my local MP, campaigning to turn the local library into a gym,' said Elliot. 'You turned him into a two-headed slug. Although that was quite funny . . . The point is that you can't keep being so over-protective. I have a life . . .'

'Which we're trying to protect, sweetie,' said Aphrodite, sashaying over for a cheek-pinch.

'And people are going to get suspicious,' Elliot pointed out. 'I can't have people sniffing around here. If anyone finds out about Mum, they'll split us up.'

'We're just trying to look after you, old boy,' said Zeus softly.

'And I appreciate that,' said Elliot. 'But you "looking after" me has cost three doors, two sofas, that unfortunate incident with Bessie's dungheap, and no one will deliver milk. I am surrounded by

Hephaestus's magic fence that attacks any stranger who tries to enter. How much safer can I get?'

'Who left the ruddy gate open?' Hephaestus bellowed from across the paddock.

'Message received loud and clear,' said Zeus. 'Brains in. Noses out.'

'Deal,' said Elliot. 'Listen, I'd better ...'

He trailed off and stared at an envelope the floor. It was his mum's letter. It must have fallen out of her pocket. He should really give it back to her ...

Elliot slowly put his foot over it. Surely a quick peek wouldn't hurt? No one needed to know ...

'You'd better what, mate?' Hermes grinned. 'Finish your sentence?'

'Er ... tie ... my ... shoelace!' said Elliot, bending down and pretending to fiddle with his shoe, quickly scooping the envelope up into his pocket. 'And check on Mum. Back in a minute.'

Elliot raced into the hallway before anyone could speak. Checking no one had followed him, he pulled out the letter.

His conscience made one last feeble protest. Opening someone else's post was invasive. It was rude. It was wrong.

But since when had any of those things bothered him?

Elliot opened the crumpled envelope and withdrew a single sheet of paper. The brief letter was written in a scruffy biro scrawl.

As Elliot read, the words started to swim in front of his eyes. It sounded like . . . but that was impossible . . . He searched for the signature at the bottom to prove himself wrong. His heart punched against his ribcage. It was the first time he'd ever seen that name handwritten. The letter couldn't possibly be from . . .

But it was.

'Elliot?' said Virgo, suddenly appearing in the hallway with his satchel. 'Time to go. What's that?'

'Nothing,' said Elliot quickly, scrumpling the letter back in his pocket. 'It's . . . my . . . I . . .' He had no idea how to explain what he had just read, let alone lie about it.

'Elliot?' asked Virgo again. 'Are you optimal?'

'Sure,' said Elliot, his whirring mind racing his manic heartbeat. 'I just . . .'

'Come on, children, you need to get back to Brysmore this afternoon,' said Athene, popping her head around the door. 'I told Mr Sopweed you had an eye appointment, but that wouldn't take all day would it Elliot . . . Elliot?'

But Elliot was replaying the words now tattooed on his brain. So that's why Mum had lost it this morning. Because of . . .

'Elliot?' said Athene softly, putting her hand on his shoulder. 'Are you all right?'

'Er . . . yeah . . .'

'OK – well, off you go, then,' said Athene. 'Try not to worry, Elliot. Josie will be fine. I'll find out what's upsetting her.'

Elliot nodded dumbly as he stumbled out of the door. The question wasn't what was upsetting his mum.

It was what on Earth Elliot was going to do about it.

5. School's Out

Graham Sopweed, headmaster of Brysmore School, was feeling all right. Not great, you understand – there was always the risk of injury, death or his mother-in-law – but Friday was ... OK.

The school governors had been right. The Management Assertiveness Course they had sent him on had done a power of good, especially the seminar 'How to Stand Your Ground and Give Nothing Away'.

He hadn't quite stood his ground and had given the headmistress of Privel Ledge Prep School his right sock, his annual pass to Hedgehog World and his car. But Graham knew that a journey of a thousand miles begins with a single step. Especially if you've just lost your car.

'Stand up for yourself, you pathetic excuse of a spineless moron!' the ballet mistress from St Mary's Primary School had yelled at him.

'You can Call Me Graham,' he'd whispered back.

But when Call Me Graham had walked over the fire pit to celebrate his more confident self, he'd felt ready to take on the world.

(It was just a shame he hadn't felt ready to take off his shoes. Those burning coals had ruined his favourite brogues.)

Yes. Even though his wife had threatened to destroy his ceramic badger collection unless they went caravanning in Skegness, Call Me Graham was doing fine.

Until he looked in his diary and saw his next meeting. Mr Boil.

A quivering Graham tried to remember his 'How to Stop Being a Doormat' tutorial.

'You mustn't let people take advantage of you,' the tutor had insisted. 'Now be a love and fetch me a decent coffee from Latte Shack. Shouldn't take you more than an hour.'

The door flew open and Mr Boil stomped in.

'I am in control,' Graham chanted under his breath as his legs started to shake. 'I am a strong, brave, independent woman.' (He'd accidentally wandered into the wrong classroom on Day 3, but rather enjoyed discovering his 'Warrior Woman Within'.)

'Hello, Mr Boil,' whimpered Graham. 'Won't you take a—?'

'Get a move on,' groaned Boil, slumping into a chair and folding his arms over his gut. 'Whaddya want?'

'Right . . . well . . . as you know, we regularly give pupils questionnaires rating their teachers,' said Graham. 'I feel it would be . . . beneficial to discuss your results.'

'That makes one of us,' spat Boil.

'Let's start with student satisfaction,' said Graham. 'You averaged a score of 5.6.'

'Sounds all right,' said Boil.

'It was out of 1,000,' whispered Graham. 'When asked, "Is Mr Boil approachable?" 99.6 per cent of students answered "No", with several adding, "Only with a gas mask".'

'This is what happens when you let children have these stupid things,' muttered Boil.

'Questionnaires?' asked Graham.

'Opinions,' sneered Boil.

'Finally your students were asked, "Do you feel safe in Mr Boil's classroom?" Let's focus on the positives – 46 per cent answered "Yes—"'

'See!' said Boil.

'"Until he walks through the door",' Graham read. 'It seems we could brush up your student welfare.'

'They're children,' shrugged Boil. 'Who cares about their welfare?'

Graham sighed. He thought about his 'Who Wears the Trousers?' role play, but could only remember his partner giving him a wedgie.

'We have an inspection from our child welfare officer after half-term,' said Graham. 'I suggest you think about pupil safety.'

'Lock them in a cupboard?' suggested Boil. 'That should keep me safe from pupils.'

'I mean it, Mr Boil,' said Graham more force-fully, slightly breaking wind with the effort. 'I need to see your duty of care.'

'Or you'll do what?' jeered Boil.

'Or I will recommend some staff training,' said Graham. 'There's a course called "Feeling Your Way Around Feelings" that would help. You'd work with over one hundred disadvantaged children . . .'

'And why would I do that?' spat Boil.

'Because if you don't, I will be forced to review your employment at Brysmore,' whimpered Graham. 'Under my management, this school has been deemed "Barely Adequate". I won't see you undermine that achievement. Please. If you don't mind.'

'Fine,' seethed Boil, attempting to free his bottom from the chair, but it was stuck fast. He hobbled out of the office, chair and all, leaving Graham trembling at his desk.

'I did it!' the headmaster whispered to himself. 'I stood up for myself! There's nothing I can't do!'

With a triumphant flourish, he picked up the phone and called his wife.

'Lilith?' he said. 'I've made a decision . . . We are *not* going to Skegness . . . yes, it *is* my final word . . . oh . . . great . . . so pleased we agree, dear. What's that? You've made a decision too? Well, super . . . you're going to what? No . . . no, you can't do that . . . we only took those photos to get a closer look at that funny lump on my . . . no . . . you don't have the password to my Facebook account . . . OK, maybe you do, but you . . . Lilith, don't you hang up this phone . . . Lilith . . . LILITH!'

That afternoon, Elliot's head was still swarming with the contents of his mum's letter. Every time half a thought formed in his mind, another jumped across it. His brain was one big tangle of ideas and feelings. What should he do?

'HOOPER!' roared Mr Boil. 'Repeat what I just said!'

Elliot tried to pluck a single word out of Boil's history lesson. He had nothing.

Virgo's hand shot up. It usually did.

'If I might assist,' she began, 'you were informing us about historical regulations regarding pavement height.'

'I didn't ask you!' spat Boil.

'Sorry, sir,' Elliot sighed. 'I was just . . . thinking.'

'Unacceptable!' Boil snapped. 'I will not have students thinking in my class!'

'Yes, sir,' said Elliot, sinking back into his seat.

The bell signalled half-term to a whoop of excited cheers as everyone shot out of their chairs.

'Sit down!' commanded Boil.

The students begrudgingly returned to their seats.

'As you'll be aware, you will not attend school for one week,' Boil spat at the sea of happy faces.

A chorus of excited whispers erupted around the room.

'But to ensure you don't fall behind with your

studies, you *will* be required to research our topic "Historical Town-Planning Regulations" during half-term.'

Elliot groaned and Virgo shook her head disapprovingly.

'Your attitude towards education is as woeful as your bathroom habits,' she whispered. 'Seriously, is it *that* hard to flush the toilet?'

'And to ensure you don't miss this invaluable opportunity,' Boil continued, leering at Elliot, 'I have left a register with Mr Simpson the librarian, which you will be required to sign. Anyone failing to visit the Local Studies section and research Little Motbury's Drainage System in the Inter-War Years will spend the next term in detention. With me.'

Elliot rolled his eyes. How could one man have so little life?

'Class dismissed,' muttered Boil reluctantly as his students sprinted out of the classroom towards their half-term break.

'So I've been doing extensive research on *What's What* about the great heroes – they make a fascinating study,' said Virgo, showing Elliot the magical scroll of parchment that she consulted for guidance on everything from politics to pants.

49

She was going to get her kardia back, she just knew it. And Virgo was never wrong.

'Great,' groaned Elliot, jumping the stile towards Home Farm.

He was in a most peculiar humour, Virgo thought.

'Where are you going?' she said. 'We assured Athene we would go to the shop for some groceries. And Zeus gave me some money for a publication he enjoys – although what more he needs to learn about models in swimsuits, I do not know. He said we can purchase some sweets.'

'Great.' Elliot muttered again, but turned back and followed her along the lane that led to Little Motbury.

Virgo was confused. This was highly irregular – the boy would normally eat his own toenails for the promise of sweet goods. Or without.

She carried on anyway.

'According to *What's What*, there are differing definitions of a hero in the immortal and mortal realms. An immortal hero is defined by a "quest". So that's it! I need to undertake a quest!'

'Great,' said Elliot once more. He was clearly not listening.

'Will you stop saying that!' snapped Virgo.

'OK . . . fascinating,' said Elliot, wiping his nose

on his sleeve. Had no one informed mortal boys about tissues?

'*Hercules's quest was to complete twelve impossible labours, risking his life to obtain forgiveness,*' Virgo read out. 'What is this forgiveness? It must be very important.'

'It's when you say it's OK that someone did something wrong,' sighed Elliot. 'Like . . . "Virgo, you're really annoying, but you're forgiven." Except you're not.'

'Not annoying?' said Virgo. 'I'm perfectly aware of that. *Theseus's quest was to solve the labyrinth, risking his life to slay the Minotaur.* But this is illogical. Why would you risk your life?'

'Great hero you're gonna make,' said Elliot, removing a piece of paper from his pocket. He'd been looking at it all afternoon, Virgo had noticed. Curious. Elliot rarely read anything and never more than once.

'*Jason,*' she continued, '*went on a quest to retrieve the Golden Fleece, risking his life to find a priceless treasure* . . . Again, the risking of life. This seems highly excessive. Why would anyone want to harm me?'

'Because they met you?' Elliot suggested.

'So if that's the immortal definition of a hero, what's the mortal one?' she continued. 'Ah – here it is . . . *Mortal hero: anyone who has won a reality television contest.* So if I'm going to be a hero, I need to be on constant alert for my quest. Maybe I must perform an impossible task? Maybe I must solve a labyrinth? Maybe I must find a priceless treasure? Maybe . . .'

Her phone bleeped a text.

'This could be it!' she squealed, taking a deep breath to read it out loud. 'My quest to become a hero and regain my immortality is: *Babe – don't forget to buy more loo roll. I'm stuck in the bog with guts like a gorgon – Hermes.*'

She stopped outside the shop.

'I fear it would be life-threatening to reject this quest,' she said to Elliot. But he was leaning against the shop window re-reading the piece of paper. A look passed over his face that Virgo had observed before, but not conclusively analysed. Occasionally, it was an indication that Elliot was feeling sub-optimal. More frequently, it was a warning of impending wind.

'What is that?' Virgo asked, trying to grab the piece of paper. She caught a glimpse – it looked like a letter.

'None of your business,' said Elliot, snatching it away. 'Let's get those sweets.'

Virgo eyed him curiously. She had learnt that

'none of your business' was mortal code for something of great interest. Athene had explained that mortals highly valued the right to privacy. This was fascinating, but deeply unhelpful when all she wanted to do was read that letter.

A plan started to form in her perfect mind. It might not get her kardia back. But Virgo's first quest was to find out precisely what was in that letter.

6. Two for the Price of One

Patricia Porshley-Plum thought she'd survived her worst nightmare when she lost her fortune last December. Stripped of her wealth, her dignity and her biggest house, she truly believed that she'd hit rock backside (she refused to use the other word, which was only for oiks and Shakespearean actors).

But in the weeks since, matters had become far, far worse. Patricia had been degraded. Patricia had been humiliated. Patricia had sunk to a new low.

Patricia had got a job.

Spendapenny was Little Motbury's budget supermarket. Patricia had been unaware it existed

– she understood all food simply arrived in a hamper. Spendapenny represented everything that Patricia loathed: it was cheap, it was popular and it allowed poor people to eat.

But desperate times called for desperate measures. Although her illegal tax haven had saved one of her smaller properties – the shame of having only the five bedrooms was intolerable – she still needed money for life's essentials: food, bills and society magazine *What-Ho!*

And so Patricia now wasted her days selling gum and lottery tickets to people who actually bought their own groceries. It was unbearable. The only thing that cheered her soul was encouraging customers to spare some change for charity. It felt so good to empty that tin into her purse.

The one thought that dragged Patricia through every soul-destroying day was getting her own back on the Hooper boy. Elliot had cheated her out of what was rightfully his. She was going to make him pay.

'Revenge is a dish best served cold,' said the boy she'd bullied at school when he left her on their wedding day. He had a point. Which is why Patricia had waited a whole year before planting fake evidence for an unsolved murder in his car, then calling the police. Patricia Porshley-Plum would have her revenge. All she had to do was wait.

A regular approached the kiosk.

'Hello, Betty, how are you, sweetie-pops?' said Patricia, almost pleasantly. Patricia had a lot of time for the elderly. They might leave her something in their wills.

'Well . . .' said Betty, as a moth flew out of her overcoat. 'Me hip's giving me bother, me knees ache like billy-o in this damp, and as for me dodgy bladder . . .'

'How delightful, sugar plum!' Patricia grimaced. 'What can I do for you?'

'Please could you check me numbers?' said Betty, handing over a crumpled lottery ticket with shaking fingers. 'I'd do it meself, but I don't have a telly.'

'Ooooh – how exciting!' said Patricia as she scanned the ticket. 'What will you buy with your millions? A yacht? A plane? A mansion?'

'A telly,' said Betty.

Patricia scanned the ticket into her machine and looked at her flashing screen:

No Match.

'Sorry, lovey,' Patricia pouted, 'not your lucky day.'

'At my age,' smiled Betty, 'every day's a lucky day.'

'Not for anyone downwind,' muttered Patricia as the little old lady hobbled away.

'*Trisha to the self-service checkouts please! That's Trisha to the self-service checkouts!*' chimed the supermarket intercom. *Patricia* shuddered as she trudged towards the self-service area. A fat, balding man whose eyes barely fit behind his glasses, let alone his posterior into his trousers, was cursing at the till.

'Welcome,' said Patricia flatly. 'How may I help you Spendapenny?'

'This idiotic machine keeps asking me to place my bags in the bagging area,' grumbled the man. 'Can you see that I have already done so, or are you as stupid as this device? Your gadgets are ridiculous! A trained ape would do a better job.'

'They're recruiting on the fish counter if you're interested,' muttered Patricia, swiping her staff card. 'There you are. Sir. Enjoy your visit to Spendapenny. We're your Number One!'

'Hmmmm.' The customer glowered as he scanned his tripe, pickled herring and pig livers. Patricia hurried away from this objectionable buffoon. His blue shirt smelt like three-week-old cream of vegetable bisque.

'*Approval needed*,' the machine intoned as the man placed a tin of poison in his bag.

'It'll be a cold day in hell before anything here gets my approval,' said the man to Patricia's back. 'You! Get back here and sort this out!'

Patricia felt anger prickling the back of her eyes. She clenched her fists and returned to the checkout.

'Certainly, sir,' she said, punching the keypad. 'Are you over eighteen? Years, I mean. Not tonnes.'

'How dare you!' spat the man.

'May I ask why you require this poison?' said Patricia, as the tedious rules required.

'What do you think?' hissed the customer. 'Because I need to get rid of a pest.'

'Rats?' asked Patricia.

'My neighbour's kitten,' said the man. 'The old biddy next door can't be bothered to fetch it. Like it's my fault her wheelchair can't get up my front steps.'

Patricia authorized the purchase with an approving nod. The gentleman poured a shower of copper coins into the machine.

'*Please wait for assistance*,' it replied.

'Assistance?' he shouted. 'I'll be waiting for ever

in this dump . . .'

'Now listen here,' said Patricia. 'If you speak to me like that one more time, you impudent knave . . .'

A familiar figure burst through the automatic doors of the supermarket. Patricia ducked out of sight. So did her customer.

'Hooper,' she and the man whispered simultaneously, as the Hooper boy and the strange girl headed for the sweet counter.

'You know him?' they both said.

'I'm his history teacher,' muttered the man. 'Vile child.'

'I used to be his neighbour,' moaned Patricia. 'Repulsive boy.'

The man paused for a moment as he eyed Patricia up and down more appreciatively.

'Boil,' he said, offering his fat fingers. 'But you can call me Lance.'

'Porshley-Plum,' she answered, reluctantly taking the edge of his pudgy pinkie. 'But you can call me Mrs.'

'*Please scan your next item*,' the checkout requested.

'So you had to live near Hooper?' said Boil. 'You have my every sympathy.'

'I deserve it.' Patricia pouted. 'He stole a house

from me.'

'The nerve of the boy!' roared Boil. 'Not that I'm surprised. That child is an utter delinquent.'

'*Please scan your next item,*' the checkout asked again.

'Well – what do you expect with a mother like that?' said Patricia.

'The fashion photographer?' said Boil. 'Never met her. Can't say I want to . . .'

'Fashion photographer!' Patricia laughed. 'Is that what the lying little swine told you? She couldn't take a picture from a toddler . . .'

'What do you mean?' said Boil.

'*Please scan your next item,*' the checkout repeated.

'SHUT UP!' Patricia and Boil yelled in unison.

'The mother – Josie Hooper,' said Patricia, circling her right ear with her finger and whistling. 'She's completely cuckoo. Batty as a cricket match. Mad as a March Hare with a parking ticket. She has totally lost her mind. Didn't you know?'

'I did not.' Boil grinned unpleasantly. 'So that's what Hooper's been hiding. What about this family of his?'

'I lived next to the Hoopers all my life – that's forty-six . . . er . . . thirty-seven years,' said

Patricia. 'First I've ever seen of them. They are about as likely to be related as I am to adopt an orphan.'

'I see,' leered Boil. 'Tell me, Mrs Poorly-Tum—'

'Porshley-Plum!' snapped Patricia.

'Would you prefer the Hoopers to ... relocate?'

'Does a politician have two houses?'

'And I feel that Hooper would be better off ... elsewhere,' said Boil. 'Just imagine if our school welfare officer found out that a young boy was having to care for an incapable mother! After all, I *do* have a duty of care to my pupils ...'

Patricia's eyes flashed like a faulty fire alarm. She grasped the checkout for support before sitting on Boil's shopping.

'*Unidentified item in bagging area,*' the machine groaned. '*Checking item weight.*'

'She'd need to go into an institution,' gasped Patricia. 'They'd have to take her away.'

'And if these relatives are as fake as you say, social services would have to take Hooper into care,' grinned Boil.

'Home Farm would be up for sale ...' gasped Patricia.

'Hooper would be out of my hair ...' exclaimed Boil.

The pair looked at each other breathlessly.

'Wait a minute,' said Patricia more calmly, rising to her feet. 'We can't just go to the authorities and split up a defenceless child and his mother.'

'You're right,' said Boil. 'We need evidence.'

Potential ideas floated around Patricia's mind.

'Do you have a large net, long-range telescope, mantrap and tranquillizer gun?' she asked.

'Don't be ridiculous, I'm a school teacher,' sniffed Boil, peeling his squashed shopping off the checkout. 'Of course I do.'

'*Have you swiped your loyalty card?*' the machine asked. '*Next time, Spendapenny on us!*'

'Then meet me at Home Farm on Sunday night,' said Patricia. 'I think it's time we took some snaps for the Hooper family album.'

The pair ducked down again as Elliot and Virgo left the shop, rising slowly like sewer fumes as they watched the children leave.

'Tell me,' said Boil. 'What do you know about Hooper's father?'

Patricia pulled a face as though she had just tasted supermarket-brand caviar.

'Don't you know?' she scoffed. 'Hardly surprising. The grandparents did their best to hush it up at the time – caused quite the scandal.'

'Scandal?' gasped Boil, licking some crusty

spittle from the corner of his mouth.

'Oh, yes,' grinned Patricia. 'There's good reason you've never heard of Elliot's father. David Hooper has spent the last ten years in prison.'

7. Mail Shot

On Saturday morning Elliot picked up the letter for the hundredth time, hoping that this time his brain might make sense of it.

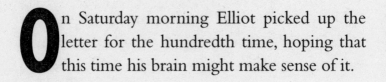

My darling Jo,

I hope this finds you and Elliot really well. I'm sorry I haven't written sooner, especially when you were kind enough to let me know about Mum and Dad. It's taken me a long time to figure out what to say. I'm sorry I couldn't come to their funerals and that you had to carry that burden alone. There's so much that I'm sorry for, Jo, I don't know where to start.

But I hope I might have the chance. I'm going before the parole board and they say I have a really strong case. If the hearing goes my way, I could be a free man very soon. I know what I said and what we agreed – it seemed right at the time to let you get on with your life without me. But thoughts of my beautiful wife and son are the only things that have dragged me through these past ten hellish years.

I have got so much wrong. Apart from you two. I want to come home, Jo. I want to come home to you and to Elliot. Is there any hope for us? Is there any hope for our family?

After everything I put you through, I will understand if you never want to see me again. But please give Elliot a kiss from his old man. And if you'll accept it, save one for yourself.

All my love – for it belongs to you both,

Dave xx

Elliot mouthed the words as he read them. For so long he'd wanted to know what had happened to his dad. But then Mum had always told him to be careful what he wished for.

Josie stomped into the kitchen and slumped into a chair. Great. She was in one of those moods today. Just what he needed.

Elliot looked at his scowling mother and tried not to be angry. Why hadn't she . . . ? Why hadn't *anyone* told him? He shouldn't have found out like this. His dad was alive. His dad still loved them.

His dad was in prison.

Elliot shoved the letter in the bread bin and

65

picked up Josie's breakfast.

'Here you go, Mum,' he said. 'Your favourite.'

'Don't like poached eggs,' pouted Josie.

Elliot took a steadying breath. This was one of his mum's latest and least welcome changes. Every so often, she would behave like a stroppy toddler for a few hours for no reason at all. Elliot found it hard to handle on the best of days. And today certainly wasn't one of those.

'Come on, Mum,' he said, his voice far too high. 'Tuck in.'

'I said I don't like it!' huffed Josie, pushing the plate away.

'Fine,' snapped Elliot. 'I'll eat it.'

'Give it back!' snarled Josie. 'It's mine.'

He slammed the plate back down a little too hard. He knew it wasn't her fault.

It's not yours, either, said his dark voice.

'So explain again why this chicken feels the need to cross the road?' asked Virgo, striding into the kitchen. 'A lone farm animal is statistically most unlikely to survive a road-traffic situation.'

Elliot groaned. He'd already spent half an hour that morning explaining how Doctor Doctor had been allowed to graduate from medical school.

'Has anything arrived for me during my absence?' Virgo asked for the millionth time as she sat at the table. 'A herald from a distressed king? A message via rainbow? I must be ready to respond to—'

The sound of Reg's bicycle bell rang through the kitchen.

'My quest!' gasped Virgo, jumping up with a piece of toast stuck to her arm.

'Give it up,' grumbled Elliot, peeling the toast off her and replacing it. 'That flyer for crochet classes at the village hall wasn't your quest. The man asking where the nearest toilets were wasn't your quest. Me telling you you're an idiot wasn't your quest. Although you should respond to that.'

Virgo suddenly gasped.

'Maybe the chicken is on a quest!' she cried. 'It undertakes the perilous journey to "cross the road", risking its life to reach "the other side"! I knew I could understand jokes! Now explain again how the bubble gum becomes attached to its foot?'

'Shhhh!' hissed Josie as she stabbed at the eggs on her plate. 'I'm eating my breakfast.'

Elliot stifled his irritation and headed outside to meet Reg, his mind still spinning with a carousel of questions. Why was his dad in prison? What had his parents 'agreed'? And why hadn't anyone told him the truth?

'Morning, young Hooper,' Reg called across the paddock.

Elliot silently took the post from him.

'Lovely day,' said Reg, raising his face to the sun. 'Makes you feel good to be here. Not as good as Martin Houseman's gonna feel tomorrow, though – you going to his bash?'

'No,' said Elliot distractedly.

'Well,' said Reg, leaning in conspiratorially, 'you didn't hear it from me, mind – but his missus has spent six months organizing a massive surprise party for his sixtieth! Sworn everyone to secrecy! And loads of people from the village are going. I told him all about it this morning. Cheerio, then.'

A thought suddenly struck Elliot. Reg had lived in Little Motbury for ever. Perhaps . . .

'Reg,' he began cautiously. 'Did you know my dad?'

The postman stopped in his tracks.

'Before he went to prison, I mean,' said Elliot quietly.

'So your ma's finally told you, then?' said Reg, pushing his bike back towards the farm. 'I thought she might when I saw that letter t'other day – I never forget a person's handwriting. None of my business, mind . . .'

'So did you?' Elliot pushed. 'Know him?'

'Know him!' Reg laughed. 'The whole county knew your pa! He was a local legend!'

'Was that a good thing?'

'Most of the time,' winked Reg. 'He and my son used to knock about when they were kids. Caused some havoc, nothing too bad. I'll never forget the Little Motbury County Fair – must have been fifteen year ago now. My Gary bet your dad a hundred quid that he couldn't hit all the targets on Farmer Belbow's shooting gallery. Your grandad went near mad!'

'Why?' said Elliot. 'That's not so hard.'

'My boy only bet Dave he couldn't do it blindfolded!' Reg laughed. 'Your pa took the bet! With respect to your grandparents, may they rest in peace, they didn't have a hundred pound no more than I've got a third leg.'

'What happened?' asked Elliot.

'So not only does your dad take the bet, not only does he put on the blindfold – the daft beggar only bets Gary double or quits he can do it backwards!'

'That's impossible,' said Elliot.

'So my son thought!' Reg guffawed. 'He's happy as Larry thinking he's got two hundred quid in the bank, your grandad's shouting blue murder while your nan tries to calm him down, and by now half of Little Motbury is standing round old Belbow's stall!'

'Did he do it?' said Elliot, his heart picking up pace. 'My dad, I mean – did he win the bet?'

'So Dave starts swinging his gun all over the shop like he's never seen one in his life,' said Reg. 'He's got the crowd screaming and carrying on – he always was a bit of a showman, your pa. Finally he turns around, holds the gun over his shoulder, takes aim and . . . Bam!'

Elliot jumped.

'First target straight through the middle. He lines up the second. Bam!'

Elliot jumped again.

'True as an arrow,' said Reg. 'Third one he takes his time . . . then Bam! Bam! Hits three and four in less than a second. Now he's only got one left. I swear you could have heard a flower grow in that field.'

'And . . . ?' said Elliot, leaning in further. 'Did he make it?'

'Your dad sways from side to side,' Reg whispered. 'He makes the sign of the cross. He tells your nan he's sorry. And then . . .'

'Yes?' gasped Elliot.

'BAM BAM BAM BAMAMAMAM!' shouted Reg. 'Blow me if your pa hadn't shot a bloomin' smiley face into the last target! The crowd went nuts! Your grandpa stormed off! And my Gary had to take three summer jobs to pay me back that two hundred pound! It was the talk of the village for weeks!'

As Reg wiped the tears of laughter from his eyes, Elliot processed this new information about Dave Hooper. His dad sounded reckless. His dad sounded irresponsible.

His dad sounded kinda cool.

'Yeah – he was a one-off your dad, that's for sure,' sighed Reg. 'Besides, this mysterious new beauty had just arrived in Little Motbury and your dad went completely cuckoo over her. I'm sure he only did it to impress her.'

'Did it work?'

The postman winked. 'You wouldn't be here if it hadn't. Yep – your pa could shoot the petals off a daisy by the time he was knee-high to a donkey. That's what made it all so sad really . . .'

'Made what so sad?' asked Elliot.

The postman looked guiltily around him. 'I'd best be getting on,' he said, getting back on his bike. 'You go ask your ma.'

'I can't,' Elliot blurted suddenly.

The postman eyed him quizzically.

'I mean, she gets really upset whenever we talk

about it,' said Elliot quickly. 'I don't want to stress her out.'

Reg took a deep breath and stared at Elliot. Elliot really wanted to know whatever was on the tip of the postie's tongue.

'Go to the library,' Reg said eventually. 'You'll find some answers there.'

'Thank you,' said Elliot, trying not to look disappointed. How was he going to find out anything about his dad at the library?

'My pleasure. You didn't hear it from me, mind. Now I'd best be off. Mrs Jeffery from the bakery can't lose "Thirty Pounds in Thirty Days" without her fitness DVD. Mind you, between you and me, she'll only lose thirty pounds if she drops her purse down the loo . . . Cheerio, young Hooper – best to your ma.'

'So this is your location?' said Virgo, finding Elliot on a hay bale in the top field. She knew he'd be keen to hear her latest thoughts. He often sat in rapt silence when she spoke.

'No one's seen you since breakfast. I'm still awaiting my quest. I was hopeful when Aphrodite said she required vital assistance. But she only wanted to know which jeans were optimal for her backside. Hermes has been entertaining your mother with something Athene disapproves of on the internet. Why the protracted absence?'

'I wanted to be by myself,' said Elliot quietly.

'I quite understand,' said Virgo, sitting down next to him. 'I have some joking for you. What do you call a camel with three humps?'

'Dunno.'

'A freak genetic mutation!' laughed Virgo. 'Camels have a maximum of two! I made it up myself!'

Elliot didn't mock her. She found this most irregular.

'Explain something to me,' she said, producing the letter that she'd accidentally found in the bread bin while searching the kitchen. 'Why have you never mentioned that your father was imprisoned?'

'Give me that!' Elliot shouted, snatching the letter from her. 'It's private!'

'Your anger is predictable,' Virgo nodded. 'According to *What's What*, mortals are easily upset by secrets of which they are ashamed. It advises behaving with tact and sensitivity. This difficult issue could make you prone to irritability and even worse hygiene.'

'Stay out of it,' said Elliot, stuffing the letter into his pocket. 'It's none of your business.'

There was that code again. She knew this letter was significant.

'*What's What* also suggests that talking to a sympathetic individual can help,' Virgo continued. 'From your sullen mood and strong, unwashed aroma, I conclude that you were unaware of your father's situation. Why were you not informed by Josie-Mum?'

Elliot was silent for a moment. Eventually, he exhaled deeply. This gave Virgo two pieces of data. Firstly, he had decided to take her into his confidence. Secondly, he had neglected to clean his teeth for at least seventy-two hours.

'I don't know,' shrugged Elliot. 'Trying to protect me, I guess.'

'I am confused by families,' said Virgo, tucking her brown hair behind her ears. '*What's What* says they are a close-knit group of relatives who support each other at all times – unless they support opposing football teams or play a board game on Christmas Day.'

Elliot shrugged.

'And yet what I observe of the Gods suggests that families are prone to intense dislike and threats of unpleasant biological consequences,' she continued. 'Yours mystifies me also.'

'You're not the only one,' said Elliot.

'If he is released, will you allow your father to return?' asked Virgo.

Elliot paused. 'No,' he said eventually.

'What do the Gods advise?' Virgo asked.

'I haven't told them,' said Elliot quickly. 'And you're not to either. I need to think about this without all their . . . stuff.'

'I'm sorry, Elliot, I cannot agree to this,' said Virgo. 'I would be failing in my duty as your appointed companion and vast superior if I did not inform them of this—'

'If you tell them, I'll tell Zeus that *you* ate his secret biscuit stash,' said Elliot.

'This is a wild accusation!' said Virgo. 'You have no proof!'

'Who else would eat a whole packet of chocolate digestives?'

'Actually, they were custard creams and there were barely any . . .'

Elliot's triumphant smile suggested that her negotiating position had weakened.

'All right,' she said reluctantly. 'We should respect each other's privacy. I felt strongly about this when searching through your dirty laundry. But I am surprised about your father. You are nosier than Pandora's nasal hair. Are you not curious about him?'

'Couldn't care less,' said Elliot.

Virgo was unconvinced. Mortals often said something inaccurate in order to mask the truth. Especially politician mortals.

'What crime did your father commit?' asked Virgo. 'Did he slay his brother in a duel? Did he steal another man's wife and start a war? Did he wear salmon pink trousers? Hermes assures me this is a most serious offence.'

'It could be anything,' said Elliot. 'Lying. Stealing. Murder . . .'

'All those misconducts have the same punishment?' exclaimed Virgo. 'You are imprisoned?'

'Sure,' said Elliot.

'But they are so different,' said Virgo. 'Mortal justice is sub-optimal. A liar is not as dangerous as a killer.'

Elliot appeared to consider her words more carefully than usual. It was about time.

'You might be right,' he said after a pause. 'That feels weird.'

'I am *always* right at least three times before lunch,' Virgo said. 'My point is, perhaps it would influence your decision if you discovered the precise nature of your father's crime?'

'You're freaking me out now,' said Elliot. 'That's two good points you've made in one conversation. Stop it.'

'You're welcome,' said Virgo, congratulating herself on remaining humble in the face of her brilliance. 'Listen, why don't we go to the library and perform Mr Boil's task? We may as well get it out of the way.'

'The library,' said Elliot thoughtfully. 'You're right ...'

'You see,' smiled Virgo brightly as she followed him through the field. 'That's the third time. And it's not even midday.'

8. Local History

Elliot hadn't been to the Little Motbury library for ages. He and Mum used to come every week to choose a book. There was one about a burping frog he'd taken out a million times, just to hear her champion belches. But that seemed a long time ago. He'd never wanted to come on his own. Besides, there wasn't much to do there. It was just full of books.

'Local studies is on the second floor,' said Virgo, reading the sign in the entrance hall.

They climbed a creaking staircase to a small room at the top of the building. Elliot caught a musty waft as he opened the door. If old had a smell, this room was it.

'What an extraordinary collection,' said Virgo, surveying the leather-bound volumes crammed on to every shelf.

Elliot glanced over the books of council minutes and planning applications. Reg had said he'd find answers about his dad here. How would any of this help?

'Why would anyone keep this stuff?' Elliot said under his breath.

'So people can find it,' said a sharp voice behind him.

Elliot turned around sheepishly. Sitting behind a desk Elliot hadn't noticed was a middle-aged man with a thin beard and even thinner glasses. His left eyebrow was raised not unpleasantly as Elliot fished around for an apology.

'Sorry,' he muttered.

'Felix,' said Virgo, reading his name badge. 'That's a pleasant name.'

'How kind,' smiled Felix. 'How can I help?'

'We're from Brysmore School,' explained Virgo.

'Ah – your history topic?' said Felix, pulling out a piece of paper. 'Sign in here, please?'

Virgo wrote her mortal name, Anna Hooper, on the paper and Elliot scribbled his carelessly

79

underneath. Felix stared intently at the names, then peered at them through his glasses.

'Hooper?' said the librarian with his eyebrow raised even further. 'Of the Home Farm Hoopers?'

Elliot nodded cautiously. Was that a good thing?

'Your family goes back a long way around here,' Felix reassured. 'I've archived many documents about you all. I was sorry to hear of the loss of your grandparents.'

'Thanks,' said Elliot softly.

'What are you looking for?' asked Felix.

'Something about drains?' said Virgo.

'Lucky you,' smiled Felix. 'Follow me.'

Felix picked up a black cane from beside his desk and used it to stand. He led them to what looked like a computer's great-grandfather, his cane tapping the wooden floor with each slightly uneven step. He switched the enormous machine on and it slowly whirred to life.

Elliot watched as Felix removed four small cardboard boxes from a nearby drawer. Each one contained a spool of shiny black ribbon.

'What's that?' asked Virgo.

'Microfilm,' Felix explained. 'On these rolls are photographs of every single edition of the *Little Motbury Gazette*, put there by hand.'

'Wow,' said Elliot. 'What saddo did that?'

Another raised eyebrow gave Elliot his answer.

'Oh,' said Elliot with a blush. 'Well done.'

Felix loaded the film in the machine, wound the end around a second wheel and put the film under the glass panel in the centre of the machine. A wonky photograph of an old edition of the *LMG* popped up on the screen.

'So if you press these here,' said Felix, pointing to some red buttons with arrows in opposite directions, 'you can move forwards and backwards through the paper. All of Little Motbury's history in one collection. From cake sales to crime sprees. Although I'm pleased we've had rather more of the former.'

Crime?

A thought suddenly lit up Elliot's mind like a lightning storm. What if the local paper had reported on Elliot's dad going to prison? Perhaps there would be a record of his father's crime? That must have been what Reg had meant.

'So these newspapers have everything that ever happened in Little Motbury?' he asked.

'Pretty much,' said Felix.

Elliot suddenly felt nervous. Did he really want to know what his dad had done? What if it was really horrible? There were some things you

81

couldn't unsee. He knew that from the time he'd seen his PE teacher, Mr Meaner, wearing Speedos at the leisure centre.

'OK,' said Elliot. 'So how would I search for a name?'

'You use your eyes,' said Felix.

'No, I mean where do I put someone's name in to search for them?'

'You don't,' said Felix. 'You have to look through every single page until you find what you want.'

'You're kidding!' said Elliot. 'That'll take hours!'

'We close at six,' said Felix with a slight smile, returning to his desk.

Elliot slowly dropped into the chair in front of the computer, as Virgo switched on the one next to his.

'Hours of poring over decades of information,' sighed Virgo. 'What an optimal day.'

Elliot didn't share her enthusiasm. Over the next few hours, he read dozens of copies of the *Little Motbury Gazette*. He learnt about people bathing in custard for charity, and the time a soap star fused the Christmas lights. He became an expert in the controversy surrounding zebra crossings, and everyone who ever turned one hundred. But by mid-afternoon, there was still no mention of his dad.

An irregular tapping interrupted his concentration.

'Here you go,' said Felix, putting glasses of water on the table next to Elliot and Virgo. 'Drink these. Otherwise you'll dehydrate and then I'll have to dust you up as well.'

Elliot gratefully accepted the drink as he exhaled with frustration.

'How's it going?' Felix enquired.

'Tremendously,' said Virgo, shuffling her copious notes. 'Little Motbury's drainage system is fascinating. The Great Hair Blockage of 1964 was quite something . . .'

'How about you, young man?' Felix asked Elliot.

'It's impossible,' said Elliot despondently.

'Perhaps I can help?' said Felix. 'I've lived here my whole life and archived many people's. I have a good memory. What are you looking for?'

'I don't know,' grumbled Elliot.

'When did it happen?'

'I don't know.'

'So you're searching for you don't know what, you don't know when,' said Felix, turning to leave. 'Good luck.'

'It's my dad,' said Elliot quickly. 'He . . . He did something. Something bad. I'm trying to find out what.'

'I see,' said Felix.

The librarian studied Elliot curiously.

'How much do you already know?' he asked.

'Nothing,' said Elliot.

'I see,' said Felix again. He gestured to Elliot to stand and took his place at the computer. 'I remember your father's story well. Small town like this, the big news stands out.'

'Undoubtedly,' said Virgo. 'The 1979 Summer of Soap Scum must have been exhilarating.'

'It was around my fortieth birthday,' said Felix, whizzing through newspaper pages at speed. 'So that makes it November, ten years ago. He was front page news.'

'Why?' said Elliot nervously. 'What did he do?'

'It would have been . . . here,' said Felix, expanding a page on the screen. 'There. Why don't you read for yourself?'

The librarian stood up silently, allowing Elliot to see the page he had loaded on the computer. Elliot looked with a heavy heart at the first picture he had ever seen of his father: being hauled away in handcuffs by the police.

'He looks just like you!' Virgo gasped.

She was right. The man in the photograph could be Elliot's future self. As his stomach churned with fear, curiosity and anticipation at discovering his father's crime, Elliot hoped that his own future would be very different.

He read the article, splashed across the front page.

LOCAL FARMER GUILTY AFTER FAILED JEWEL HEIST

A Little Motbury farmer has been found guilty of attempted robbery, grievous bodily harm and possession of a firearm at the Crown Court.

David James Hooper, thirty-four, pleaded guilty to all charges relating to the attempted robbery of Kowalski Gems on 26 November, in which Constable Simpson was seriously wounded by a shot fired by Mr Hooper. Hooper was sentenced to twelve years' imprisonment. His accomplice, Stanley Johnson, remains at large.

Hooper said nothing as he was led from the court, watched by his wife, Josie, and parents, Wilfred and Audrey Hooper.

Elliot slumped into the chair. So that was it. His dad was a violent criminal. No wonder his family had disowned him. No wonder Mum was so scared. He must be the bad man she was trying to lock out.

'That can't be easy,' said Felix gently.

'What happened to Constable Simpson?' asked Virgo.

Elliot held his breath. He didn't really want to hear the answer.

'That was the end of his police career,' said Felix eventually. 'But he healed in time. Gave him a new lease of life, in fact. Realized he didn't want to waste a moment. He went back to university, got the education he never had and went on to a whole new career. He always felt that, in a funny way, your dad did him a favour.'

'Doubt he felt like that with a gun in his face.'

'No,' said Felix quietly. 'I doubt he did.'

'Who is this Stanley Johnson?' Virgo asked. 'His name frequently appears in the newspaper.'

'Back in the day, he was Little Motbury's one-man crime wave,' said Felix. 'A very troubled individual who caused a lot of individuals trouble.'

'Why was my dad mixed up with him?'

'You'd have to ask him that,' said Felix quietly.

There was a heavy pause as Elliot looked miserably at the screen. He had always feared his dad might be dead. Somehow, this felt worse.

'Would you like me to print it out for you?' asked Felix.

'Sure,' said Elliot. 'I can hang it in the Hooper Hall of Fame next to my first letter suspending me from school and my most recent report card.'

Felix fiddled with the buttons on the front of the screen and an aged printer churned the page out, burning the image of his criminal father on to Elliot's mind.

'If this job has taught me anything,' said Felix, putting the paper into an envelope and handing it over, 'it is that the past is not black and white. It's far more complex than words on paper.'

Elliot turned the article in his hands as he choked back the shame and disappointment rising from his gut. How could a single sheet of paper in an envelope feel so heavy?

'This past looks pretty clear to me,' he said, putting the article in his satchel.

'That's only one side of the story,' said Felix. 'In my experience, there are always at least two.'

'This is true,' said Virgo. 'You should hear Aphrodite's and Athene's conflicting opinions on optimal clothing.'

'People aren't always as they appear,' Felix continued. He walked over to a creaking stand that held some yellowing leaflets. He picked one

out of the rack and handed it to Elliot. 'You might find this useful.'

'*How to Contact a Prisoner*,' Elliot read. 'Why would I want to do that? He shot a policeman. He's a loser.'

'You're looking for answers,' said Felix. 'Your father would be able to provide them. Think on it.'

Elliot noticed a petition on the librarian's desk asking people to oppose the redevelopment of the library into a gym. He added his name to the short list of signatures. This place was actually pretty useful.

'I appreciate that,' said Felix with a warm smile.

'Thanks,' said Elliot.

'My pleasure,' said Felix, his eyes twinkling. 'We saddos always welcome a little excitement.'

9. If the Zap Fits . . .

Once he'd finally assured Mum that the door was locked, back in his bedroom, Elliot's mind was buzzing with the day's discoveries. How did his dad go from troublemaker to violent criminal? Why was he robbing a jewellery shop? Why did he risk everything he had with Mum?

Why did he leave you? said his dark voice.

He tipped his satchel out on to his bed and found Felix's leaflet. It said that if he wrote to a prisoner, the letter would be given to them. It was then up to the prisoner if they replied.

Elliot turned it over in his mind. His angry self said his dad could rot in prison – he'd never

bothered to write to Elliot, so why should Elliot write to him?

But a different voice said that maybe his dad had good reason. His letter had suggested that he and Josie had agreed not to communicate – perhaps his dad didn't feel he could get in touch? Perhaps he was sitting in prison even now, hoping for some word from his only son? Perhaps he missed Elliot and wanted the chance to apologize?

'Nothing comes from nothing,' Mum always used to say. He could really use her wisdom right now. Elliot looked at all the magical gizmos on his bed. If only one of them had the answer. He pulled out a notepad and started to write.

Dear Dad,

He stopped and looked at the page. He had never used that word before. It felt very strange – and this complete stranger didn't deserve it now. Elliot screwed the paper up and tossed it over his shoulder.

Dear Dave,

Now he had a problem. Which name should he use? Dave? Or David? This was stupid. He didn't know what to call his own father. He screwed up the second piece of paper and threw it at the first.

Dear Dad,
I hope you are well.

Well? His dad had been in prison for ten years. Of course he wasn't well. Elliot threw his third effort away.

He stared at the empty page for what seemed like an eternity before picking up his pen once more.

Dear Dad,

This is a really weird letter to write and it must be a really weird letter to read. I am your son, Elliot. I only just found out where you were because no one told me. I know you're in prison and I know what you did. But I'd like you to explain why you did it. I want to hear your side of the story. I think what you did was wrong. But then lots of people think the stuff I do is wrong. Sometimes they're right. But not always.

I am twelve — you should know that — and I like eating, hate school and don't care what I do when I grow up, but I hope I never have to wear a tie. I hope you'll answer my letter because only you can answer my questions. I still live at Home Farm with Mum.

I hope prison isn't too rubbish and that the food is OK.

Elliot

He wondered if he should mention Mum's illness, but something stopped him. He didn't know this man – he had no right to their business.

Elliot put the letter in an envelope and addressed it as Felix's leaflet instructed. He stared at it. Would his dad write back?

A wild banging on his window startled him.

'Mate! You gotta come up to the shed,' laughed Hermes, hovering beyond the glass. 'Not being funny, but you *have* to see this . . .'

Elliot thought about Mum. He should really spend some time with her, but . . .

She's being a real pain today, his dark voice whispered.

'Hermes – could you do me a favour?' he said as he opened the window.

'Mate – name it, it's done, boom!' said Hermes with a fist-bump.

'Could you fly this down to the postbox, please?' Elliot asked, handing him the letter. 'It's for a school project.'

He coloured slightly at his half-truth. But until he knew what the whole truth was, he wasn't ready to share it. He stuffed everything back in his satchel and headed for the door.

'On it like a siren's sonnet – see you in the shed,' yelled Hermes over his shoulder, already whizzing over the fields.

Elliot's mind was a blizzard of his dad's words as he walked across the paddock towards the shed. *There's so much I'm sorry for . . . I could be a free man . . . I want to come home.*

Should he let his dad come home? After all, Dave Hooper was no more than a stranger to Elliot. What if he really was a bad man? What if he came home and upset Mum? What if Elliot opened their door to a dangerous criminal? What if they got hurt?

But then again, Elliot thought – what if he wasn't? Dave Hooper wasn't a stranger to his mum – she had loved him. What if his dad was a changed man? What if his dad going to prison had made Mum sick? What if he came home and she got better? What if they fell in love again? What if they became a real family? What if . . . ?

What if you weren't always stuck with looking after her? his dark voice taunted.

'Elliot?'

Virgo's voice yanked him out of his own head as he walked into the shed. 'Are you optimal?'

'I'm fine,' said Elliot reflexively. He wasn't sure how he felt about sharing his thoughts. He wasn't sure how he felt about anything.

'It's an absolute bally DISGRACE!' roared

Zeus, perched on his golden throne, wrestling with something on his leg. From the outside, Elliot's cowshed looked like any normal farm outbuilding. But after some immortal interior design from Hestia, Goddess of the Hearth, the inside of the Gods' dwelling had the grandeur of an ancient Greek palace. What had once been a rundown shelter for Bessie, the cow he had raised from a lame calf, now sported marble floors, rows of verdant olive trees, a fountain and the Gods' luxurious bedchambers. Elliot patted Bessie on his way past her luscious meadow in the corner of the shed.

'Daddy, you need to calm down,' said Aphrodite, pulling at a small silver box on her ankle. 'There has to be a way to get them off . . . OH, SNORDLESNOT!'

'What's occurred?' said Virgo.

'We opened . . .' Athene began.

'*You* opened,' snapped Zeus, yanking at his ankle. 'I wanted to put a thunderbolt to anything that witch has laid her evil fingers on . . .'

'Fine − I thought *someone* should open the package that Hera left yesterday,' Athene explained, pulling at the identical device on her leg. 'These boxes flew out and attached them-selves to our ankles.'

'Oh my days! Hold tight — I'll just shut this up . . .' yelled Hermes, his iGod ringing as he flew into the shed. 'Not being funny or anything, guys — but you've all been ZAPPED!'

'Zapped?' asked Elliot.

'Zillion Amp Power-Preventing Electrical Devices,' Hermes explained. 'They're normally dished out to rowdy satyrs after a stag night. Dad, you really don't want to—'

'Ruddy ridiculous name!' bellowed Zeus, pulling a small thunderbolt out of his pocket and aiming it at the box on his ankle. 'Why would anyone call it . . .'

ZAP!

'Aaaargh!'

As the thunderbolt left his hand, Zeus leapt from his throne, clutching his considerable backside.

'The bally thing just bit me in the bot!' he boomed, rubbing his sore bottom.

'How come you don't have one?' Virgo asked Hermes.

'You can't tag the H-bomb!' posed Hermes, flexing his biceps and kissing them both.

'But you can kiss Hera's shrivelled old bum,' said Aphrodite. 'I can't believe she's let you off. You always were her favourite stepchild.'

'Er, sis, not being funny,' said Hermes, 'but I wasn't the stepchild who turned her into a hairy pig.'

'You were the only stepchild who noticed the difference, though,' grumbled Athene. 'Let's just apply some simple logic. Perhaps I can change it into something easier to remove . . . I'll try a rubber ring . . .'

ZAP!

As her magical touch made contact with the box, the Goddess of Wisdom's hand quickly snatched to her bottom with a yelp.

Aphrodite laughed as her sister tried to maintain her dignity while rubbing her backside.

'Your problem,' said the love Goddess, 'is that you don't think out of the box. Elly? Please may I have the wishing pearl? Elly?'

But Elliot was in a world of his own. A world where he had a mum, a dad and a normal life.

'Earth to Elly?' Aphrodite cooed while stroking his chin. Elliot snapped back to the room.

'Are you sure you're all right, Elliot?' asked Athene. 'You seem very distracted.'

'Just . . . stuff,' said Elliot. 'What did you say?'

'The wishing pearl, please, sweetie,' said Aphrodite with a cheeky smile.

Elliot rummaged around in his satchel and

pulled out the heart-shaped wishing pearl. It only worked once a day for seven minutes. But when those seven minutes were spent flying, being invisible or eating an ice cream the size of the Statue of Liberty, they were pretty epic. He'd learnt over the weeks that you could only make each wish once – but during a night on the toilet after wishing for the world's hottest curry, he'd decided that was no bad thing.

'Have you used it today?' Aphrodite whispered.

Elliot shook his head. He needed more than a wishing pearl right now.

'Perfect,' smiled the Goddess of Love. 'So . . . I wish to take off all our zappers . . .'

ZAP!

ZAP!

ZAP!

The moment the words left her beautiful lips, Aphrodite, Athene and Zeus all received a personal prod in the rear.

'What did you do that for!' Athene shouted. 'I only just got over the last one!'

'If you'd all just listen . . .' shouted Hermes, pulling out his ringing iGod. 'Mates. Babes. You mustn't use your powers. And no one should use their powers on you. Otherwise, not to put too fine a point on it, you'll have a bum like a

97

sunburnt baboon. Epic non-bosh. Hello?'

'OH, FOR GOODNESS' SAKE!' roared Zeus, as he changed into a snake, a mouse, a duck and a bee to shake the box off, each transformation earning him a zap, making him hiss, squeak, quack and buzz.

'I was applying your precious logic!' yelled Aphrodite at her sister.

'Sorry Uncle H, I can barely hear you,' said Hermes, fluttering away from the chaos with his iGod on his right ear and his finger in his left.

'Well, stick to applying your lipstick,' shouted Athene back. 'Your powers are useless!'

'Oh, yeah?' said Aphrodite, producing a small phial from her pocket. 'Well, let's see how useless you find a dose of my extra-potent Burping Brew – TAKE THAT!'

ZAP!

But when Aphrodite went to throw the potion at her sister, she was zapped again, throwing her aim, and the bottle, off course. It flew through the air, discharging its contents over the nearest person – who just happened to be Virgo.

BUUURRRRP!

An ear-shattering belch burst from Virgo's lips.

'What was THAT?!' she cried.

'Maybe it's your quest,' said Elliot, trying not to

laugh as the Gods clasped their backsides, every attempt to use their powers for themselves or on each other resulting in a zapping.

'That can't be right,' shouted Hermes over the chaos. 'Sounded like you said . . .'

ZAP!

'You pig!'

OUCH!

'You witch!'

QUACK!

'Snordlesnot!'

BURP!

'I never ate that . . .'

'WILL EVERYONE JUST SHUUUUUT UUUUUP!'

The shed fell silent as Hermes shot into the air to make himself heard. Virgo stifled another almighty gastric eruption with a cushion.

'Right. OK. Gotcha,' said the Messenger God. 'We'll be there.'

'Well, who the devil was that?' said Zeus, transforming an apple into an ice-pack and getting a zap for his troubles.

'That was Uncle Hades,' said Hermes. 'He wants to see us.'

'Well, he can't,' grumbled Zeus. 'We're stuck here. He'll have to wait.'

'Dad, not being funny, but this one won't wait,' said Hermes, looking worriedly at Elliot. 'Uncle H says I need to get E to the Asphodel Fields. Pronto.'

'Why?' asked Athene, instinctively moving to Elliot's side. 'What's wrong?'

'It's Thanatos,' said Hermes grimly. 'Someone's set him free.'

10. Long Time No See

Thanatos had no idea how long he had lain beneath the rubble of stalactites in the Cave of Sleep and Death. It could have been days. It could have been weeks. It had in fact been over two months. At least it wouldn't be for ever, he thought, hauling his bruised and bleeding body on to his throne of bones.

He stared intently into the dark green eyes of his rescuer.

'Why now?' he asked after a long pause.

'Because you need me,' she replied.

'I needed you for two thousand years beneath Stonehenge,' said Thanatos.

'You wanted me then,' she said with neither emotion nor apology. 'You need me now.'

To anyone but the Daemon of Death, his saviour would have been a truly terrifying vision. Her face and torso had the allure of a beautiful woman, her long black hair cascading down the curves of her tawny skin. But then there were the spiky black wings protruding from each shoulder blade, the clawed feet tucked beneath her feathered legs and the blood-stained talons where her hands should have been. The expression painted on her beautiful face was like staring straight into the heart of fear. A single flash of her lurid green eyes warned you that this creature could inflict unimaginable pain. And that she would enjoy every second.

The only sound in the cave came from Thanatos's long bony fingers drumming on the arm of his throne.

'Where have you been?' he asked at last.

'In hiding,' she replied. 'Zeus killed your father and imprisoned you. I did not wish to share either fate.'

'I was cheated . . .'

'You were weak,' she hissed, stepping closer. 'If it weren't for your brother . . .'

'If it weren't for my brother, Zeus never would

have defeated me!' shouted Thanatos, leaping from his throne. 'Hypnos stole my Chaos Stones. He betrayed me . . .'

'You betrayed yourself!' she said firmly. 'Your failure cost everything.'

'But I . . .'

'SILENCE!' screeched the creature, unfurling her wings in fury.

Thanatos drew an angry breath, but said no more. He knew better than to argue.

'For two thousand years I have lived in the shadows,' she continued. 'I have watched. I have waited. And now it is time.'

'Time for what?' said Thanatos.

'To claim your father's legacy!' she shrieked. 'Now you are free, it is time for you to earn what he laid down his life for. It is time for you to rule the world!'

Thanatos limped back to his throne. 'Don't you think I've been trying?' he said. 'Don't you think that's how I ended up here?'

'At the hands of a mortal child!' she cackled derisively. 'What would your father say? You should be ashamed to call yourself—'

'He has the Earth Stone,' said Thanatos.

'I know,' spat his tormentor. 'Why do you think I'm here? If the Gods reunite the Chaos Stones, all hope is lost. We have to get to them first. Where is your brother?'

'I have no idea and care even less,' growled Thanatos.

'We need to find him. Hypnos should be here with us.'

'Never!' shouted Thanatos. 'He's a traitor, a loose cannon and a fool.'

'He won his freedom and you lost yours.' She laughed. 'You tell me who's the fool!'

Thanatos glowered on his throne.

'You leave Hypnos to me,' said the visitor more calmly, folding her wings back down her spine. 'The Gods will find him. I'll be there in the shadows when they do. But what are you going to do about the Earth Stone?'

'I can't touch the boy,' said Thanatos. 'So I need to get inside his mind. I need him to give me that stone of his own free will . . .'

'You are a disgrace to your father's name!' she spat. 'Do you think the mighty Erebus would have wasted time with the child's mind?! No – he'd reach inside his body and rip out his beating heart for his Chaos Stones!'

'And what use is this?' roared Thanatos. 'The prophecy is clear! I can't kill him!'

The Goddess of the Night tossed her head

back with a joyful howl, letting ragged tendrils of black hair slither down her body, unfurling her jet black wings to their sharp tips before wrapping them around her body like a shroud.

'But I can!' she cried with a laugh like blood dripping.

She turned to leave the Cave of Sleep and Death, her talons scratching on the stony floor.

'Without your stones you are weak,' she said, spreading her wings to take flight. 'Stay here. I will fetch your brother. I'll be back before dawn.'

'I'm afraid the days of you telling me what to do are long gone,' said Thanatos, rising to his full height. 'I will do as I please. Your plan will fail. Mine will not. And as for my brother – Nyx, I'm warning you …'

Nyx swivelled at the cave's entrance and stared hard at the Daemon of Death.

'I don't respond well to threats,' she warned. 'And Thanatos?'

'What?' snapped Thanatos, rubbing his bruised body.

The Goddess of the Night smiled coldly. 'That's "Mother" to you.'

11. Inferno

Hades's casino was fashioned like a vast rocky cave, lit by blazing multi-coloured torches. Over the entrance, the casino's name, scorched brightly into the Asphodel gloom in huge burning letters, greeted the stream of immortal gamblers trying their luck:

INFERNO
WHERE SINNERS ARE WINNERS!

After a slow voyage on the Ship of Death – made considerably longer by Charon, the immortal boatman's views on the Zodiac Council's new congestion charge along the River Styx – Elliot,

Virgo and Hermes leapt from the wooden boat and hurried through the casino's enormous gambling floor, past whirring fruit machines and excited dice throwers, around spinning roulette wheels and tense card games.

'I CAN'T TALK! I'M PLAYING POKER!' yelled a fairy on a mobile phone at a nearby table. 'NO, I'M BLUFFING! THESE CARDS ARE RUBBISH!'

'Elementals . . .' scoffed Virgo. 'Gambling is for the sub-optimal.'

'Babe – you must be a right laugh on a night out,' said Hermes.

Elliot let out a big yawn. He had spent another sleepless night considering the latest bombshell that Thanatos was on the loose. The Gods hadn't been at all happy with him leaving Home Farm, but Hades had insisted that Elliot needed to come with Hermes. Besides, Elliot wanted to know the score.

His mind flashed back to the Cave of Sleep and Death.

I can give you your mother back, Thanatos had promised.

Elliot's hand went to his father's watch in his pocket, the watch that contained the Earth Stone he'd nearly given the Daemon of Death. Thanatos had told him that he could heal Josie if Elliot gave him the four Chaos Stones.

Elliot pushed the thought away. Thanatos was free. Surely he'd be coming straight for him?

But if Thanatos is free, his dark voice said, *he can help Mum.*

At the back of the casino was a huge black door, covered with small sculptures of men and women. In bronze letters across the middle were the words:

ABANDON ALL MONEY, YE WHO ENTER HERE
STAFF ONLY

The door was guarded by a burly security centaur in a tuxedo.

'Mate. Let us in,' panted Hermes.

'Nah. Mate,' came the centaur's reply. 'This area is restricted.'

'Seriously. Mate – I have to see my Uncle Hades,' Hermes grunted, trying to squeeze past the half-man–half-horse mountain in his way. 'So do us a solid and shift, yeah?'

'Mr Hades ain't seeing no one today,' said the guard, holding Hermes's head at arm's length. 'And that includes you. *Mate.*'

'I hear you. Friend,' said Hermes, through gritted teeth, 'but we need some face time. It's urgent.'

'Sure,' said the guard, 'you've spent your life savings. I see it all the time. Not my problem. Maybe you should phone a . . . friend.'

'Not being funny or nothing, but we don't have time for this,' said Hermes.

With lightning speed he grabbed Elliot and Virgo, lifted them off the ground, flew over the centaur's head, kicked the door open and slammed it quickly shut behind them all.

'Ouch,' moaned Virgo as she pulled herself off the floor. 'That was uncomfortable.'

'That was epic,' said Elliot admiringly, just as Hermes threw his hands above his head.

'Uncle Hades! Don't shoot! Seriously!' he yelled.

Elliot spun round, instinctively raising his hands too. A bulky man in a black suit was sitting in a red velvet chair, a pistol aimed in their direction.

Virgo pulled her *What's What* out for guidance.

'HOIMES!' Hades bellowed in delight, replacing the gun in the drawer with a sigh. 'Geez, Louise, I haven't been that scared since I saw my last lawyer's bill. How ya bin? It's bin for ever, get over here!'

Relieved, Elliot watched the two Gods hug.

'And who are these skinny drinks o'water?' asked Hades, winking at Elliot and Virgo.

'I am Virgo, Constellation of the Zodiac Council . . . well, sort of . . . and Guardian of the Stationery Cupboard. Almost,' said Virgo clumsily.

'Geez,' laughed Hades. 'That ain't gonna make your business cards easy. And you are?'

'Elliot Hooper,' grinned Elliot, shaking Hades's hand. He could tell he was going to like the God of the Underworld.

'So what's the deal with Thanatos, Uncle H?' asked Hermes. 'How do you know he's out?'

'Cos I know people, who know people, who used to be people,' said Hades. 'Nothing happens in the Underworld I don't know about. Used to be my 'hood. Don't know where he is. Don't know what he's doin'. But no doubt about it. He's free. So you need to watch ya back. And ya front. And all the stuff in between.'

'You're not wrong,' said Hermes, looking over at Elliot.

Elliot returned his anxious gaze. 'If Thanatos is out, we need to find the rest of the Chaos Stones,' he said.

Yes, you do, said his dark voice. *For Mum*.

'To stop him, and save the world from his Daemon army,' Elliot added firmly.

'Too right, mate,' sighed Hermes. 'But the only way to find the Chaos Stones is to get our mitts on Hypnos. He's the only geezer who knows where he hid them. And he's harder to find than flattering Lycra. Boom, bosh, back to square one.'

'Well, that's where you come in, short stuff!' said Hades.

'Me?' said Elliot.

'Yoos,' said Hades. 'I got some good noos for ya. It's a long story, so take a load awf.'

Hermes dropped into a chair, but immediately sprang up again as a desperate banging started beneath him.

'Shut! Up!' he yelled from three feet in the air.

'You gotta be kiddin' me,' sighed Hades, guiding Hermes to another chair before rolling away the rug to reveal a trapdoor in the floor.

'Scuse me,' said Hades to his guests as he lifted the hatch. 'Hey, Benny!' he shouted down the hole, 'you don't like your new digs, maybe next time you'll keep your hands outta my till, you thievin' joik.'

He slammed the trapdoor back down on the dirty fingers that had clutched the edge and listened to the falling wail, until it hit the ground with a whimper.

'Sorry 'bout that,' said Hades, running a hand over his receding slicked black hair. 'Staff training . . . So here's da ting . . .'

Without warning, the door to his office blasted open again and an ageing showgirl, decked out in a sequined leotard with pink and yellow feathers, hurtled towards Hermes armed with a silver stiletto.

'You leave him alone, you . . . Oh, Hoimes, it's you! What you doing here, dollface?'

'Persephone! Babe!' said Hermes, accepting her kiss on his cheek. 'Look at you! Boom!'

'Aw – you old charmer, you . . . Nice to meet you, kids, I'm Mrs Hades,' Persephone said to Elliot and Virgo as she adjusted her tail-feathers. 'I heard y'all from my cabaret show. That's one crowd ain't never gonna know what happened to Lola at the Copacabana. But what you gonna do . . . ?'

'Sweet cakes, why don't you go fix us a drink and let us get back to business, eh?' said Hades to his wife.

'Don't you tawk to me like that, you big lug,' said Persephone indignantly. 'I'm your business partner! You're only awn a six-month contract and don't you eva forget it!'

'She's been saying that for three thousand years,' whispered Hades to Elliot. 'That dame can't get enough o' me. But we got other fish to fry here. Come with me, shortie. I got someone really

112

wants to see you.'

Elliot looked quizzically at Hermes, but the Messenger God was as clueless as he.

Hades turned to the huge bookcase behind him, which contained volumes of leather-bound novels.

'Now, where is it?' he asked as he ran his fingers along the middle shelf. 'Ah, got ya.'

He pulled out a copy of *The Great Escape*, which automatically turned sideways and opened up to reveal a small keyboard. Hades used his right middle finger to play the first few notes of the funeral march, which split the bookcase lengthways down the middle, creating a door that led to a dark tunnel.

Hades ushered everyone through the gap and grabbed a torch and a set of keys from the wall. They walked downhill through a long, dingy corridor until they reached a small door.

'This is where we keep guests who gamble on credit, but struggle to pay their bill,' he said, unlocking the door. 'I call it the "Money Soon Suite". In here.'

Elliot, Virgo and the immortals ducked through the narrow doorway into a gloomy cell. Elliot's eyes took a moment to adjust to the dark, damp cave into which they stepped. But when they did, he saw that huddled in the corner was a young woman with white-blonde hair, filthy and shivering in a torn dress. She ran to Elliot and fell to her knees.

'Please – help me!' she cried. 'He's holding me here against my will! I haven't done anything wrong!'

Hermes looked aghast. 'Mate!' he gasped. 'Seriously?'

'Is this a joke?' Virgo whispered to Elliot. 'Because the professional challenges facing Waiter Waiter were more entertaining . . .'

'Knock it awf,' Hades said to the prisoner with a yawn. 'I'm not fallin' for that load o' baloney again. Drop the act before I smack you round the kissa.'

'Wh-wh-what do you mean?' said the woman. 'Please, sir, just let me go home to my children. They'll be starving . . .'

'Uncle H, you do *not* talk to babes like that,' said Hermes. 'You are in serious danger of a proper bosh-not . . .'

'She ain't no lady, bro,' said Hades. 'And she ain't an old guy trying to buy a new kidney, an injured soldier saving orphans, an aid worker trying to raise money to buy pencils for starving children or any of the other bull my dealers have swallowed while this joik runs up a debt the size of Mount Olympus.'

'I . . . I don't understand,' said the woman, her eyes brimming with tears. 'I'm begging you – just let me go home to my babies. They're all alone.'

'Sure they are, sweetheart,' said Hades. 'You nearly got away with it too. If it wasn't for CCTV.'

'Closed Circuit TV?' said Hermes.

'Cyclops Catching Tricksy Varmits,' said Hades. 'Caught this joker dissembling out the back . . .'

'Dissembling?' said Virgo. 'But apart from Zeus and Hermes, the only immortals who can dissemble are . . .'

'Daemons,' said Elliot as the realization hit him. 'So this must be . . .'

'Well, you can't blame a girl for trying,' said the woman innocently as a pair of wings sprang out of the side of her head. 'Hi, honey. Heeeeeeeeeere's Hypnos!'

And with a cackle, the woman's face melted into the wild features of the Daemon of Sleep. Elliot's breath caught in his chest at the sight of the daemon who had tried to kill him three times already. He hoped this wouldn't be the fourth.

'Voilà,' said Hades, folding his arms. 'I believe you've been looking for this piece of woik?'

'Yeah, we have!' said Hermes, slapping his uncle on the back. 'Bosh boom bonanza!'

'Well, isn't this super!' squealed Hypnos. 'I must say the entertainment here is tremendous. Even you, Persephone, darling . . .'

'Whatcha doing here, freakazoid?' asked Persephone.

'Going on the biggest losing streak since Prometheus lent the mortals a match,' said Hades. 'He owes me over fifty large.'

'So what? You're loaded,' said Hermes to the Daemon.

'Not since I bet it all on a coin toss with that Texan oil baron,' sulked Hypnos. 'I'm utterly broke. But if you just let me back on the roulette wheel, my luck's about to change, I can feel it . . .'

'There's as much chance of that as Persephone winning *Immortal Idol*,' said Hades.

'You shut your mouth!' said Persephone. 'When I sing "Can't Smile Without You", the whole room cries.'

''Cos their tickets are non-refundable, doll,' said Hades, cracking his fist. 'So I'm tawking to this joik, telling him he can pay me what he owes me, or he can meet my friend Knuckles . . .'

'It's not fair,' huffed Hypnos. 'It's so much harder when everyone stays awake. If I just had my beautiful trumpet . . .'

'And he tells me he's got something you want,' Hades continued. 'But he ain't saying nothing until he can tawk to the kid.'

'And here you are!' said Hypnos, clapping his hands like a deranged toy monkey. 'Have you still got my baby?'

'You mean this?' said Elliot, producing Hypnos's sleep trumpet from his satchel. Hypnos had dropped it at Buckingham Palace when the Queen kicked his butt.

Hypnos shrieked with glee. 'My trumpet!' he squealed, swiping for it. 'I want it back!'

'Not likely, mate,' said Hermes, whipping it from Elliot's hand.

'I guessed you might say that,' giggled Hypnos. 'So d'ya fancy a swapsie?'

'You're in a highly sub-optimal position to trade,' said Virgo. 'Statistically, you are most likely to leave here in an ambulance.'

'Too right, babe.' Hermes nodded. 'Not being funny, but other than the teeth that Uncle H is going to knock out of your head, what have you got for us?'

Hypnos's crazy eyes widened. 'I thought you might like to know where I hid one of the Chaos Stones,' he whispered naughtily.

Elliot's pulse thundered through his body. Another stone. Another chance to stop Thanatos.

Another stone, his dark voice whispered. *Another chance to save Mum*. An image of Josie cartwheeling down the street burst into his mind. He pushed it away.

Hypnos took a moment to delight in the bombshell he had just dropped.

'You tell us where all three of them are,' said Hermes. 'Then we can start talking.'

'Two,' said Hypnos.

'Tree,' said Hades, stretching his neck as he pounded one first into the other.

'Two-and-a-half,' said Hypnos.

'Three,' said Hermes, twirling the sleep trumpet like a baton.

'Oh, all right,' pouted Hypnos. 'But I want all my gambling debts written off. Now. Do we have a deal?'

Hermes looked at Hades. Elliot willed the God of the Underworld to agree.

'Uncle H?'

Hades looked murderously at Hypnos. 'Anything to help the family,' he said darkly. 'Although if he ever sets foot in here again, I'll snap awf his—'

'Nice one!' yelled Hermes, holding his hand up

for a high five. It wasn't returned. 'Right, Hypnos – spill.'

'Well, now here's the thing,' said Hypnos. 'I don't want to tell you.'

'Seriously, pal, you are really getting up my . . .' said Hades, picking Hypnos up by his winged head.

'I want to tell . . . *him*,' giggled Hypnos. He waggled a finger at Elliot.

'Me?' said Elliot.

'Elliot?' said Hermes. 'Why?'

'Because,' squealed Hypnos conspiratorially, 'it will drive my twin brother crazy when he finds out that the mortal boy knows where his precious stones are! He was mean to me. And I love watching him squirm . . . it's a brother thing. Elliot knows something Thanatos doesn't know. That'll teach him. . .'

'You haven't told Thanatos where they are?' Elliot asked.

'If I tell him, he'll rip me into teensy tiny little pieces,' grinned Hypnos. 'My lips are sealed.'

'And they need to stay that way. You have to swear you won't tell anyone else,' said Hermes. 'And that you'll keep your mitts off our Elliot.'

'Well, that's a little awkward,' said Hypnos. 'You see, Thanatos and I agreed that I'd, sort of, kill the child. Blood *is* thicker than water and Thanatos gets rather stroppy if he doesn't get his way ...'

'Mate. So do we,' said Hermes, as Hades cracked his knuckles. 'Swear on the Styx that Elliot will be the only person you blab to and that he stays safe. Or we can just leave you to Uncle H's hospitality.'

'But what if I ...' Hypnos whined.

'Listen, pal,' said Hades, with an irritated sigh. 'I ain't a patient man. But I'm a man who can make you a patient. Take the oath, tell the kid, bada-boom, bada-bing, that's life.'

'I wonder how strong this is?' said Hermes, going to snap the trumpet over his knee.

'All right!' Hypnos squealed. 'I swear on the Styx not to harm the child, nor tell any other living soul where I hid the Chaos Stones. Happy now?'

'Boom!' said Hermes. 'So go on, then. Start talking.'

Hypnos beckoned for Elliot to come closer. Elliot hesitated. This was a huge responsibility. Zeus had warned him that the Chaos Stones were a heavy burden to bear. And Zeus had no idea what Thanatos was offering for them.

I can give you your mother back.

Should he say about Thanatos's deal?

No, said his dark voice decisively.

'Go on, mate,' Hermes prompted kindly. 'We've got your back.'

'And ya front,' said Hades forebodingly, punching his fist into an open palm. 'And all the stuff in between.'

Elliot gingerly leant towards the Daemon of Sleep, who slowly brought his mouth to Elliot's ear.

'BOO!' he shouted, making Elliot scream. The Daemon collapsed into a hysterical fit.

'OK, that's it!' said Hades, picking Hypnos off the ground by one wing and shaking him.

'Where's . . . your . . . sense . . . of . . . humour?' giggled Hypnos between shakes. 'OK, OK. Seriously this time.'

Hades dropped Hypnos to the floor. Elliot put his head tentatively forward again.

'So . . .' said Hypnos, 'the Fire Stone is . . .'

He whispered the secret in Elliot's ear.

'How am I supposed to get that?!' Elliot asked. 'That's impossible . . .'

'I never said it was easy.' Hypnos shrugged and grinned. 'The Water Stone? Well, that's . . .'

'I don't even know where that is,' said Elliot.

'And as for the Air Stone, that one is . . .'

'What's the Duke of Devonshire Emerald?' said Elliot.

'That's what the mortals called it,' said Hypnos. 'I hid it in Columbia – now there's somewhere that knows how to party – but it found its way to a Brazilian Emperor, who gave it to some English Duke. Lost track of it since. The mortals think it's a priceless emerald. They have no idea.'

'A priceless treasure . . .' whispered Virgo.

'There,' said Hypnos. 'I've given you what you want. Now gimme my trumpet back.'

Hermes and Hades exchanged a glance.

'If you even think of using that in here, you'll have your teeth for breakfast,' warned Hades.

'Fine,' huffed Hypnos. 'You're no fun. Now hand it over.'

With a reluctant sigh, Hermes returned the trumpet to the Daemon of Sleep.

'Yipppeeeee!' screamed Hypnos, flying up and blowing a fanfare from his trumpet. 'See ya, sleepyheads.'

And with a whoosh, he whizzed out of the cell and down the dark tunnel to freedom.

'What a freak,' said Hades.

'We'd better get back to Dad, like, now,' said Hermes. 'Hades – can you call us a cab?'

'I can do better than that,' said Hades. 'Yous

need a set of wheels. Follow me.'

They walked further down the tunnel until they came to a door that led to the rear exit of the casino. Standing in the gloom was a huge black chariot drawn by four magnificent black stallions.

'Now here's what I'm gonna do,' said Hades. 'My chariot here is so fast it can outrun death. Which, given the coicumstances, is really quite convenient. My boys can take you wherever you need to go. Take it – sounds like you guys need all the help you can get.'

'We could use you, Uncle H,' said Hermes as he settled himself inside the chariot. 'You're proper scary when you want to be. I remember that time Dad gave you reindeer socks for Christmas . . .'

'Get outta town,' laughed Hades, slapping his nephew on the back so hard he fell out of the chariot. 'I gotta business to run. But I got eyes and ears everywhere – I'll let you know if I hear anything that could help.'

'You take care now,' said Persephone. 'And remember – it's OAP night in the cabaret on Toosdays. Tell all your friends.'

'Yeah – remind 'em to switch their hearing aids awf,' said Hades, to a hefty punch from his wife.

'Thanks, Hades. Thanks, Persephone,' said

Hermes, fist-bumping all round as the four horses turned the chariot to face one of the tunnels. 'We'll be in— Aaaaarghghgh!'

At a slap from Hades, the horses charged so fast into the fog that no one noticed the Goddess of the Night hiding in the shadows, holding a writhing Hypnos bound and gagged in her wings.

12. Questions

'No, I promise – I'll understand it,' said Virgo as she and Elliot climbed out of Hades's chariot that evening. 'Tell me again.'

'This is absolutely the last time, OK?' said Elliot. It had been a long ride home.

'I swear it on the Styx.'

'Right,' sighed Elliot. 'Knock, knock.'

'Who's there?'

'Interrupting cow.'

'Interrupting cow wh—?'

'MOOOOOOOOO!'

Virgo stopped and put her hands on her hips. 'You've done it again!' she huffed. 'How can I possibly understand mortal humour when you don't even let me finish my sentence!'

Elliot stifled a yawn. His lack of sleep was starting to catch up with him. Last night, when he hadn't been thinking about ways that Thanatos might rearrange his body parts, he'd been endlessly putting Mum, who was convinced the bad man was at the door, back to bed. His thoughts slipped back to his dad. If he came home, perhaps he could do some of the night shift. Elliot couldn't remember his last night of unbroken sleep.

His tired eyes struggled to take in the scene that greeted him in the shed.

'Snordlesnot!' cursed Zeus, peeling a scorched shirt with an iron-shaped burn in the centre off the ironing board. 'This bally contraption is the devil's own work!'

'Daddy, you suck at mortal housework,' Aphrodite laughed as she hoovered the wallpaper.

'I must say, I'm finding a degree of satisfaction in going about tasks without our powers,' said Athene at her desk, unaware that she had knitted a scarf into her own hair. 'Ah – you're home!' She gathered up her huge sheaf of notes and handed them to Zeus. 'I've been researching the Duke of Devonshire Emerald.'

Hermes had called on the way back to fill her in but Elliot had to hand it to her. Even without her powers, the Goddess of Wisdom was quick.

'The Air Stone – the Duke of Devonshire Emerald, as the mortals believe it to be – is in the Natural History Museum in London.'

'But where?' said Elliot, recalling Mum pretending to be a dung beetle in the Creepy Crawlies room. 'We'll never find it, that place is like a maze.'

'A maze . . .' said Virgo with a frown. 'Or a labyrinth . . .'

'Fortunately for us, it's a prize exhibit,' explained Athene. 'It's housed in the Vault, a high-security area where the museum's most precious artefacts are kept.'

'Brilliant,' said Aphrodite. 'Another stupid Chaos Stone in another stupid place. This is impossible . . .'

'An impossible task!' shouted Virgo suddenly, leaping up and knocking over Zeus's ironing board. 'A priceless treasure, hidden in a labyrinth, that's impossible to obtain! This is it!'

'This is what?' asked Elliot, picking up the iron before it set fire to Zeus's shirt.

'THIS IS MY QUEST!' Virgo shrieked.

The shed fell silent and listened to the echo.

'Mate,' Hermes whispered to Elliot. 'What's she banging on about now?'

'She's trying to be a hero,' Elliot whispered back. 'Just go with it. It's better than her trying to be a comedian.'

'Nice one, babe!' Hermes shouted. 'I'm in. So all we need now is a plan full of mega-boom to get it back. We've done it before, we'll do it again. Bosh, boom and an extra portion of bang! There's no great rush. Hypnos told us that Thanatos doesn't have a Scooby where to find it – we'll figure something out.'

'If only it were that simple,' sighed Athene, reading from her laptop. 'The Vault is closing this Thursday for a year for refurbishment. Who knows where the Air Stone will be put then? We have three days.'

'And *some* of us don't have any powers,' grumbled Aphrodite. 'And *some* of us are stuck here.'

'And even if we weren't, *all* of us have the same problem – even you, Virgo,' said Zeus. 'We can't steal it. We're still bound by the Sacred Code.'

Elliot's mind raced. The Sacred Code forbade the immortals from committing a mortal crime. And from using yellow toothbrushes during cloudy days in April. It was weird. Yet all the immortals had sworn a sacred oath on the Styx to abide by it. So they were stuck.

'But I'm not,' said Elliot quickly. He knew he had to do whatever it took to get the Chaos Stones. If Thanatos got them, he planned to cull mankind with natural disasters before enslaving the survivors. If Elliot got them, he could save the world.

Or save Mum, shouted his dark voice. But maybe he could do both? He'd figure something out. *After* he got all four stones.

'Out of the question,' said Athene immediately. 'With Thanatos *and* Hypnos now at large, you're in terrible danger. You must stay here at all times.'

'Quite right,' agreed Zeus. 'That fence is enchanted with the most potent magic we possess. It's powerful. It's protective. It will keep you safe.'

'ONLY IF YOU SHUT THE RUDDY GATE!' hollered Hephaestus from outside. They all heard the gate slamming shut.

'They're right, Elly, you need to stay put,' said Aphrodite. 'The Daemons can't hurt you here.'

'Actually, the Daemons can't hurt me anywhere,' Elliot insisted. 'Thanatos can't touch me and Hypnos just swore on the Styx that he won't.'

'But we can protect you here, old boy,' said Zeus.

'No disrespect, but you can't even protect the laundry,' said Elliot, looking at the scorched clothing around the shed. 'You guys don't have your powers. I'm safer with Hermes.'

'But you'd be breaking a serious mortal law,' Athene insisted. 'You could be taken away – from your home, from us . . . from your mother.'

Elliot considered this. Trouble with the law was the last thing he needed.

'Well, what choice do we have?' he said. 'You need the Air Stone. I'm the only one who can get it for you. I have to go.'

He felt one of Zeus's soul-searching stares.

'You're right,' said the King of the Gods at last. 'It has to be you. But you bally well don't have to do it alone. If we can't help you, you need someone who can.'

Virgo puffed up with pure smug.

'We need someone strong . . .' said Zeus.

Virgo gently flexed her puny muscles.

'Someone brave . . .'

'Did I mention that I have been to the lavatory three times after Elliot today?' said Virgo.

'Someone accustomed to perilous adventures . . .'

'I organized the Zodiac Council Secret Santa,' said Virgo. 'Trust me, nothing's more perilous than that . . .'

130

'We need a hero!' roared Zeus, warming to his theme.

'YES! Yes, you do!' Virgo roared back. 'So I am of course delighted that you've chosen . . .'

'Hercules!' shouted Zeus. 'They don't come more heroic than my boy! If anyone can help us, he's the chap!'

'Er – Dad? Have you seen Herc lately?' asked Hermes.

'Not really – he's been busy with that new business of his,' said Zeus. 'Why do you ask?'

'No reason,' said Hermes quickly, punching a text into his iGod.

'But this makes no sense,' said Virgo. 'Just like the gentleman with a pigeon on his head, who happens to be called Clive.'

'It's a seagull and he's called Cliff!' sighed Elliot. 'What do you call a man with a seagull on his head? Cliff!'

'Ah,' said Virgo. 'Mine was better . . . But I need to be the hero. I have to get my kardia back. *I* am doing the quest.'

'Of course you are, sweetie,' said Aphrodite, putting her arm around Virgo and winking at Elliot. 'But it can't hurt to get someone more . . . experienced on board, can it?'

'This is true.' Virgo nodded eventually.

'Hercules is indeed a mighty hero. I could learn a lot from him.'

'Babe – not being funny,' said Hermes. 'But you might not want to get career advice from my brother.'

'Why ever not?' said Virgo.

'You'll see,' replied Hermes as his iGod bleeped. 'Banging. Herc can see us tomorrow.'

'Kids – you've got a big day tomorrow,' said Aphrodite, sticking her tongue out at her sister as Athene landed a big book in her lap. 'You need to find us a hero. Go get a good night's sleep.'

'Father, Aphy – you keep researching how we can access the Vault at the Natural History Museum,' said Athene, pulling a huge legal book from her shelves. 'I'm going to find a way to protect Elliot from mortal law. There must be a loophole for someone trying to save the world ...'

Elliot felt the guilty twinge in his guts. He was trying do that too. Honest.

Of course you are, said his dark voice. *But is saving the world more important than saving your mum?*

13. Forgery

Unbeknownst to the other Gods, Hephaestus always spent the night just outside his forge. The cold didn't bother him – the heat of his furnace was never far away – and nor did the rain. These were strange times and someone needed to keep watch. And as far as Hephaestus was concerned, that someone might as well be him. Hera hadn't zapped his powers – she'd secretly been ordering his gadgets to spy on the immortal community for years, she needed him too much. So he was the only man for the job. And he was the only man who knew how to shut a ruddy gate.

Most nights in the sleepy Wiltshire countryside were much the same. As soon as the sun went down, the night-time creatures went about their business – badgers, foxes, hedgehogs . . .

But that night, there were other nocturnal visitors outside Home Farm. Years of working in a dark forge gave the immortal blacksmith exceptional night vision – and as the darkness conquered the day, he saw two new predators joining the nightly crew.

'Will you hurry up?' huffed a familiar voice.

Hephaestus frowned. Last time he'd heard that woman, she was shrieking her knickers off as he catapulted her out of Home Farm. What was that Patricia Porshley-Plum doing sniffing around here tonight?

An ugly-looking fella puffed up alongside her, carrying a large bag. Hephaestus picked up a scent in the air – vegetable broth . . . He retreated to the shadows and watched.

'I'm just saying that no restaurant should expect its customers to collect their own food,' whispered the Horse's Bum as she tottered over the field in the darkness. 'Trays should always be circular, always be silver and always be carried by someone else.'

'I don't see what you're moaning about,' said

the chubby bloke. 'You said you weren't prepared to walk to a restaurant. You wanted me to drive you. So I did.'

'To a motorway service station!' said Patricia. 'When I asked for a table with a view, I didn't mean the M27! So this is the fence, Mr Boil. You just need to climb it and put the camera on top.'

Boil. Darn silly name, Hephaestus thought.

'Why don't you do it?' demanded Boil.

'Because *I* am a lady,' said Patricia. 'So stop being such a lazy slob and get your great backside up that fence. Now.'

Hephaestus smiled as the bloke approached his fence. He'd just added a new layer of Disarming Varnish last week. Time to see how well it worked.

Boil put a hand tentatively on the fence.

'My glasses!' he shouted. 'They've disappeared!'

'They've probably just fallen off,' said Patricia, taking a step away from the enchanted fence. 'Keep going, Mr Boil.'

He placed a foot on the bottom of the fence.

'My shoe!' he said. 'Where's my shoe?'

'Go faster!' called Horse's-Bum from a fair distance away.

So he did. The next step took care of his other shoe, then his socks, his shirt and his trousers. By the time he reached the top, only his vest and pants remained.

'I am *not* taking another step,' he said. 'Get me down!'

'As you wish,' mumbled Hephaestus, pushing a button on a remote control in his robes.

Immediately, the wooden slats of the fence reconfigured into a giant slide, whooshing Boil, his camera and his pants down into the brown slush at the bottom of the fence.

'Well, that was traumatic,' said Patricia, looking in disgust at the muddy mess in underpants before her.

'*You* found it traumatic!' raged the lad. 'Look at me!'

'That's the trauma.'

'You're disgusting.'

'You're buying me dinner,' said Patricia as they made their way back over the field. 'This time I'm choosing the restaurant. We're going to Maison La Poche.'

'The fancy French place?' groaned Boil. 'If you want overpriced snails, I'll peel them off my shower curtain and charge you a tenner . . . What should I wear?'

'Some cleaner pants!' said Patricia. 'We'll have to come back here on Thursday. I'm covering for a colleague at Spendapenny until then. Pathetic little slacker.'

'Chucking a sickie?' asked Boil.

'Having a baby,' said Patricia. 'I loathe the work-shy. Come along, Mr Boil!'

The dopey pair made their way back across the dark Wiltshire countryside, and Hephaestus smiled into his cocoa. So they wanted a trap? Well they were gonna get one.

14. Non-Event

'So what does the Air Stone actually do?' Elliot asked Hermes on Monday morning, as Hades's chariot raced along the low-way, the immortal road system that ran directly beneath the Earth's own.

'Mate,' said Hermes. 'Not being funny, but you look rough as a satyr's stubble. Sleepless night?'

'Mum night,' said Elliot quietly. 'She wouldn't stay in bed unless I read to her. So I did. All night . . .'

Hermes nodded and gave him a gentle punch on the arm.

'According to *What's What*,' said Virgo officiously,

'the Air Stone controls the element of air.'

'Don't know how you'd manage without that,' said Elliot, to a cheeky wink from Hermes.

'Think about it,' said the Messenger God. 'If you control the air, you control the weather.'

'So you get nicer holidays?' said Elliot, thinking back to some of the soggier nights he and Mum had suffered on their camping trips.

'Bit more to it, mate,' said Hermes. 'The weather brings warmth, light, water. The basics of life on Earth. If you have power over those, you have some serious boom at your fingertips.'

Elliot tried not to think about what Thanatos would do with that power.

Not your problem, said his dark voice.

'And we're here,' said Hermes, pulling the horses to a halt beneath some roadworks in a suburb of Reading.

'What *is* this place?' asked Virgo.

'My bruv — Hercules,' said Hermes. 'He's organizing a party today — he runs an events business. Well. Kinda . . .'

'What do you mean?' asked Virgo, nose wrinkled.

'Let's go,' said Hermes as he flitted towards the building.

Virgo found herself experiencing a flutter of excitement at meeting the mighty Hercules. Her research had frequently named him as the greatest hero of all time. She hoped he wouldn't be too upset when she took that title from him. With him on her side, she was sure to win her quest. She'd be whizzing around in her star-ball – constellation – in no time.

Hermes knocked at the door, which was answered by a small golden penate, the knee-high household effigies reserved for manual work. Elliot's was the only mortal dwelling that Virgo had seen – but even so, No. 26 Elm Avenue seemed very strange. The hallway was almost completely dark, and sticky cobwebs hung from every surface.

'This place needs a visit from Hestia,' muttered Virgo, pulling some cobwebs out of her hair. 'It's most sub—'

'BOO!'

Virgo shrieked as a gigantic plastic skeleton swung down from the ceiling and cackled in her face.

'What was *that*?!' she cried, stepping backwards and immediately bouncing up into the air. She tried to get her footing, but the surface of the floor kept propelling her upwards. She was not enjoying this quest at all.

Suddenly, an almighty werewolf emerged from the darkness, brandishing a giant club through the cobwebs. Hermes stepped in front of Elliot and raised his fists.

'Hermes!' boomed an almighty voice from inside the werewolf, before giving Hermes a chest-bump that sent him flying across the hall-way. 'Good to see you!'

Virgo decided it was time to act. She used the bouncy surface to propel herself at the werewolf, landing squarely on its head. She was surprised, therefore, when that head came off in her hands. She decided that the optimal course of action was to scream extensively.

'Virgo – chill, babe,' said Hermes, helping her back to the ground as Elliot suffered some form of laughing seizure. 'Meet my bro – Virgo, this is Hercules.'

Virgo looked up at the werewolf. It now had a human head, surrounded by flowing grey hair.

'Sorry 'bout that – hidden trampoline,' grinned the gigantic man inside what was obviously a costume. Virgo had known this all along.

If the sheer size of the man didn't give away the man's identity, the bronze kardia around his neck did. The kardia of a Hero. So this was Hercules.

'You're here just in time,' said Hercules. 'The birthday girl is due back any minute. She's desperate for a scary party, so her parents are throwing one as a surprise – come on through.'

'Nice one, bruv,' said Hermes. A giant spider dropped down from the stairs and landed on his head.

'Great to see you all,' boomed Hercules amiably. They went through to the front room, which was covered in artefacts Virgo recognized from Hercules's adventures. There was a lion-skin rug on the floor, a boar's head on one wall, a deer's head on the other, a large club on the coffee table and a bow and arrow hanging from the TV. All were draped in blood-stained fake body parts. The effect was most unsettling.

'This must be Elliot and Virgo – good to meet you, kids.'

Elliot winced as Hercules squashed his hand in a friendly handshake. Virgo opted for a wave.

'It's an honour to meet you, Hercules,' she said, as Hercules piled her up with biscuits in the shape of dismembered fingers. 'Congratulations on the new business.'

'Well . . . keeps me out of trouble,' smiled Hercules, pointing Elliot towards a jug of human blood. 'Tomato juice,' he said with a wink. 'You just caught me, actually. Tomorrow I'm taking a group of workmates on an extreme wilderness experience in the Amazonian rainforest. We'll have no food, no water, no shelter – we'll be trekking day and night with no sleep, to fend for ourselves in one of the most hostile terrains on Earth.'

'Mate – sounds hardcore,' said Hermes.

'It's going to be the best retirement party ever,' grinned Hercules.

'This is cool,' said Elliot, picking up the bow and a quiver of arrows.

'Watch it, E!' said Hermes, wincing. 'That arrow is dipped in Hydra blood.'

'So?' said Elliot.

'Mate – it's one of the most dangerous substances in the world,' said Hermes. 'Hydra blood is so poisonous it can kill an immortal. Serious non-bosh.'

'Epic,' whispered Elliot.

Virgo had noticed that the risk of serious bodily harm seemed to excite mortal boys enormously.

'You can have it,' said Hercules. 'I'm trying to have a clear-out – you'd be amazed how much Hippolyte's Girdle fetched on gBay . . . Happy to see it go to a good home. Those arrows are

143

brilliant – they will always hit their mark. And you're never too young to learn how to handle a poisonous bow and arrow.'

Virgo took a deep breath. It was time for business. Her kardia depended on it.

'Hercules – we need to enlist your expertise,' she said. 'We're on a quest and . . .'

A wax penate rushed into the front room, pushing his spectacles nervously up his nose.

'Sorry to bother you, Mr Hercules,' he said. 'I'm afraid I have some bad news. Mr and Mrs Fontley are refusing to pay for their event.'

'You're kidding!' said Hercules. 'That romantic bungee-jump cost me a fortune! It was great!'

'It was their sixtieth wedding anniversary, sir,' said the penate. 'They never did find her teeth and his wig.'

'I don't understand!' said Hercules, throwing his hands up. 'People ask for the event of a lifetime, but when I deliver, they complain! Next you'll be telling me they didn't enjoy off-roading on their mobility scooters. So, how's Dad?'

'He's all right,' said Hermes. 'Getting a load of grief from Hera, but you know all about that.'

'Oh – she's not so bad,' said Hercules.

'You've got a short memory, mate,' said Hermes. 'She sent two snakes to poison you in your crib!'

'I know,' sighed Hercules. 'She really knew how to throw a christening. So what's this quest?'

'We need to obtain the Air Stone from the Natural History Museum,' said Virgo.

'Ah – the NHM – great venue,' said Hercules. 'I organized a brilliant event there just last month – we played laser tag all around the exhibits at night.'

'Sounds awesome, bruv,' said Hermes.

'I know, right?' said Hercules. 'No idea why Mother Superior didn't enjoy her eighty-seventh birthday ... Listen – I'm sorry, guys. The hero game isn't for me any more. I just want a quiet life.'

'But you're the greatest hero of them all!' said Virgo. 'You were adored by generations.'

'Until I wasn't!' snapped Hercules. 'One minute I'm slaying hydras, saving maidens and can't leave the house without someone wanting to carve my effigy in marble. The next – "Ooooh, he doesn't slay hydras as well as he used to," or, "He saves the wrong sort of maidens," or, "We need to airbrush his marble effigy – he's put on a few pounds ..."'

'People still talk about your adventures now, bruv,' said Hermes. 'You're a proper legend.'

'Exactly!' said Hercules. 'Everyone wants Hercules the hero. But do they want Hercules the clarinet player? Or Hercules the fan of foreign cinema? Or Hercules the performance poet? No. They just bang on about the old days. Fame is like dandruff. Once you've had it, it keeps coming back for no reason. No, I've moved on. You guys should try Theseus. He's still got plenty of fire in his belly.'

'If you're sure, bruv,' sighed Hermes.

'I am,' said Hercules. 'Good luck, though.'

Virgo was displeased. But if she couldn't harness Hercules's strength, at least she could benefit from his experience.

'Hercules, may I ask you a personal question?' she said.

'Please,' smiled Hercules. 'Unless it's about my scar. That's a private matter between me and that giant mutant tortoise.'

'What do you need to become a hero?'

Hercules paused to consider his answer. 'Courage, heart and wisdom,' he said finally.

'You're stuffed, then,' whispered Elliot. Virgo's elbow slipped into his ribcage.

'And easy access to a hospital,' added Hercules. 'You do not want to drive to a distant A&E with a giant-mutant-tortoise bite on your bum. Trust me . . .'

'Mr Hercules, Mr Hercules, they're here!' cried

a bronze penate.

'OK, everyone!' whispered Hercules. 'Places!'

The hero gestured to Elliot, Virgo and Hermes to hide behind the sofa while he tried – unsuccessfully – to conceal himself behind a pot plant in his werewolf costume.

The key turned in the lock.

'Hello?' cried a small voice.

'BOO!' yelled the skeleton, dropping from the ceiling as a terrified wail went up from the hallway.

'What the—?' shouted a man's voice as the lights went on in the front room.

'SURPRISE!' shouted Hercules, leaping out from behind the plant.

Virgo observed a small mortal girl in a pink dress – she estimated the child was about four years old – screaming at the sight of Hercules in his costume. An angry male mortal entered the room, followed by a stream of similar-sized little girls in party dresses, covered in cobwebs. They took one look at the werewolf and the blood-stained room and let out a cacophony of further screams.

Elliot and Virgo put their fingers in their ears.

'What do you call this?' roared the adult mortal as Hercules pulled off his head with a grin.

'Hi there, Mr Elsmore,' boomed Hercules. 'Here you go. One surprise scary party.'

'YOU IMBECILE!' roared Mr Elsmore as a small girl vomited on his feet. 'I ordered a surprise *fairy* party! Tilly is only four years old!'

'Don't worry, angel!' cried a woman's voice behind them. 'Mummy's got you a fairy cake! Everybody . . . Happy birthday to you . . . Happy birthday to you . . .'

A mortal female, whom Virgo presumed to be Tilly's mother, emerged with a huge cake in the shape of a giant fairy, with candles lighting up her wings. This appeared to calm Tilly and her friends, whose tears came to a halting stop as Tilly-Mum processed through the room, stepping carefully over dismembered limbs.

'Happy birthday, dear Tilly . . .' boomed Hercules. 'Oh – Mrs Elsmore – you might want to watch out for—'

As Mrs Elsmore went to put the cake down on the table her left foot hit another hidden trampoline.

'Look!' cried little Tilly, pointing. 'Fairy flying!'

And she was right. Her cake – and her mother – briefly took flight as the trampoline threw them into the air. Virgo watched the cake hurtle across the room, landing squarely on Mr Elsmore's head.

What a fascinating mortal birthday celebration!

'Wait until I get my hands on you!' cried Mr Elsmore, handing his screaming daughter to his wife and making for Hercules across the room.

'Er – right – we've gotta scoot, we need to get over to Theseus,' shouted Hermes as Hercules ran into the garden. 'Cheerio, bruv.'

'See you, guys,' cried Hercules over his shoulder. 'And remember, if anyone wants to base-jump from a skyscraper, I'm always happy to arrange baby showers …'

15. Labyrinth

Theseus's restaurant, Labyrinth, enjoyed a formidable reputation in fine-dining circles. The first restaurant to earn the World's Best Restaurant fifty times in succession, seven Michelin stars and an Oscar nomination, the waiting list for tables was so long that husbands made reservations to propose to their next wife. Labyrinth was particularly famous for its legendary twenty-four-course tasting menu, which included one course you had to digitally download, one that was an emotion served three ways and one that was presented through the medium of interpretive dance.

It was hard to say what was more famous about Labyrinth: the innovative food combinations or the stories of the chef who created them. Theseus was the bad-boy rock star of the cookery world. A rival chef allegedly said he'd eat his hat if the food was better than his own. Theseus promptly served his trilby with a béarnaise sauce so exquisite that the chef immediately retrained as a chartered surveyor. Even when Theseus deliberately gave three hundred diners food poisoning because his gas bill was too high, R. A. C. Bill from the *Sunday Times* described his resulting diarrhoea as 'edgy and bold' and gave it five stars.

Hermes filled Elliot and Virgo in on Labyrinth's illustrious history on the way to the Oxfordshire village of Whinney. As Elliot strolled past the endless queues of bejewelled and tuxedoed diners begging for a table, he had to admit he felt pretty cool.

'All right, mate!' chirped Hermes as they approached the maître d'. 'Table in the name of Fashion – party of three.'

'*Oui*, of course, Monsieur Hermes,' said the maître d'. 'Always a pleasure to see you. We 'ave ze best table in ze 'ouse for *vous*. Follow me.'

They were led to a round table right in the centre of the sumptuous restaurant. Elliot looked

around the room, which was filled with satisfied diners, moaning with delight at their delicious meals as a string quartet played elegantly in the background. He and Mum hardly ever ate out and certainly nowhere this posh. She always said that one day they'd have tea at the Ritz. Elliot felt his heart darken. There were a lot of things they'd never do 'one day'.

'Mate,' said Hermes, his belly gurgling as the waiter approached. 'What's cooking?'

'We have ze à la carte menu?' said the waiter.

'Boom,' said Hermes.

'Marvellous,' said the waiter. 'It is tattooed on the left knee of a wallaby. I shall send it over. We also have several specials this evening. As an appetizer, we have a Loch Ness monster cocktail, followed by Mignon of Minotaur with a pepper sauce.'

'Excuse me,' asked a diner on the next table. 'Would it be possible to have a little more pepper sauce?'

'Er . . .' said the waiter, all colour draining from his face. 'I'll just go and ask ze chef.'

The maître d' approached the swinging kitchen door, made the sign of the cross and walked inside.

'So what is Theseus like?' Virgo asked. 'Will

he be optimal for my quest?'

'Oh, he's a good bloke, really,' said Hermes. 'Bark is worse than his—'

'HE WANTS WHAT?!' a voice exploded from the kitchen. 'BRING ME TO THIS TASTELESS PHILISTINE RIGHT NOW!'

The whole restaurant fell silent and the string quartet took refuge inside their instrument cases.

The waiter appeared – was thrown, in fact – back into the room, as Theseus slammed back the double doors. Elliot could imagine how he looked in his youth, but now his chiselled face was hot and red from the heat of the kitchen and his muscular body was covered in stained chef's whites. Tucked beneath his arm was a gigantic pan of pepper sauce.

'WHO WAS IT?' he bellowed at the maître d'.

The miserable employee remained face down on the carpet and pointed a shaking arm at the nervous diner.

Theseus stomped to the table, making the man and his female companion shrink back into their seats.

'I hear you wanted some extra sauce!' Theseus yelled.

'Er . . . yes . . . please . . . if it's not too much trouble,' said the shaking man.

'I assume you spent the last four centuries at cookery school?' asked Theseus.

'Er, no . . . I did do an adult-learning course once, though . . .' he replied.

'But you must have studied under the best chefs in the universe?' shouted Theseus. 'Roux? Pierre-White? Swedish?'

'No . . . not really,' stammered his customer.

'Then tell me where your restaurant is, so that I can sample your award-winning cusine!' Theseus hollered in his face.

'I . . . I don't have one,' whimpered the man, practically under the table.

'THEN HOW DO YOU KNOW HOW MUCH SAUCE IS ENOUGH?!' screamed Theseus.

'I don't,' said the man in a tiny voice. 'I was wrong. I'm sorry.'

'No, sir, the customer is always right,' said Theseus, wielding a huge ladle from the pot. 'Here, have some more!'

Elliot tried not to catch Hermes's eye – he could hear the Messenger God sniggering behind his hand. With one of his muscular arms, Theseus ladled a huge dollop of sauce on to his customer's plate, covering his food, the table and most of his lap.

'Than-thank you, that's fine,' he said.

'No, it's not!' said a wild Theseus, slopping on ladle after ladle of sauce until it dripped over the edge of the table. 'Here – have some more!'

And with a great snort, he emptied the entire pot over the steak and the unfortunate diner's head.

'Now GET OUT!' he roared.

'O-OK, OK,' stammered the man. 'But please could I get my engagement ring back? I was going to propose to my girlfriend.'

'Oh, Wayne!' swooned his companion, wiping the sauce out of her eyes with a sauce-covered hanky from her sauce-filled handbag. 'That's dead romantic!'

'Sure!' shouted Theseus, grabbing a nearby giant meringue swan and punching it to retrieve the ring. 'Here's a proposal for you, sweetheart – don't marry this tasteless moron of a gerbil dropping!'

With an almighty grunt, Theseus kicked the pot across the floor, scattering waiters like skittles, and stormed back into his kitchen, smashing a massive tower of plates on his way. The maître d' crawled across the floor like a giant slug back towards Elliot's table as the string quartet resumed their minuet.

'Just to let you know,' he squeaked. 'We're out of pepper sauce.'

That was it. Elliot and Hermes collapsed with the giggles.

'I'm not sure how he's going to help on my quest,' said Virgo. 'I don't believe the Air Stone requires any condiments . . .'

'Now that's a chef's special,' said Hermes, wiping the tears from his eyes. 'Let's get Theseus over here. Mate – can we have a natter with the chef?'

'No, please . . .' said the waiter. 'I'm just out of hospital from the time someone said their steak was over-cooked.'

'No worries,' laughed Hermes, 'I'll go ask him myself.'

'No – please, sir, don't! cried the waiter as Hermes strode confidently into the kitchen with a whistle.

'NO CUSTOMERS IN THE KITCHEN!' screamed Theseus as the door swung to behind Hermes. 'GET OUT OR I'LL . . .'

The string quartet barricaded themselves in their instrument cases again, the maître d' hid the steak knives, and everyone waited nervously for another eruption.

But the only sound from the kitchen was a

gigantic belly laugh.

'I bet he never played piano again!' hooted Theseus as he came out of the kitchen with his arm around Hermes' shoulders. 'We were a right pair of terrors . . .'

'Those were the days,' laughed Hermes.

'Get on with it!' Theseus suddenly yelled at the string quartet. 'And play something up-tempo. You lot are as cheerful as a Fury's funeral.'

'Kids – this is Theseus,' said Hermes. 'Theseus – Elliot and Virgo.'

'Good to meet you,' said Theseus, nearly pulling Elliot's arm out of the socket. 'Always delighted to meet a mortal. Even if you do have ketchup with everything, you tasteless idiots. Won't hold it against you.'

Elliot smiled politely as he tried to get the feeling back in his fingers.

'So what can I get you tonight?' smiled Theseus. 'The tempura Titan buttock is excellent.'

'I'll have an extra-large one, thanks,' said Hermes.

'Theseus – we need to enlist your help on a mighty quest,' said Virgo. 'We need to access the Vault in the Natural History Museum. We feel this fits well with your skill set and you might relish the chance to relive your heroic glory days.'

'Glory days! Are you kidding me?!' said Theseus. 'They stank!'

'But . . . I don't understand. Your exploits are the stuff of legend,' said Virgo.

'Exactly – totally made up!' said Theseus. 'During my time as a hero, my stepmother tried to poison me, the Minotaur tried to kill me, I was chained to a rock in the Underworld for months, I lost my father, my son, two wives and my mojo! Being a hero is rubbish!'

'So you don't wish to return to your heroic past?' said Virgo.

'You catch on quick,' sighed Elliot. This was not going well.

'It's really important,' he added. 'We need to get the Chaos Stones to defeat Thanatos. We really need you . . .'

'No way!' said Theseus. 'It took me years of therapy to get over being a hero! I've had night terrors, anxiety attacks, abandonment issues – my therapist even suspects I have some unresolved anger, but I don't see it . . .'

'I don't understand,' said Virgo. 'You are considered one of the greatest heroes who ever lived . . .'

'Exactly!' said Theseus. 'I lived. And I want to keep it that way. But – I do want to help you guys. I hate Thanatos.'

'For the misery he heaped on the world?' said Virgo.

'For giving me a bad review on Odyssey-Advisor,' snorted Theseus. 'If I ever get my hands on him, I'll boil him for stock.'

'Boom!' said Hermes, offering a huge high five.

'Take this,' said Theseus, and he handed Elliot a ball of string.

'Er . . . thanks,' said Elliot, trying not to sound too disappointed. He needed to get the Air Stone, not wrap a parcel.

'I got it from Ariadne, my ex – nice girl, bad break-up,' Theseus explained.

'Mate – not being funny, but you, like, totally dumped her on an island and sailed away,' said Hermes.

'Yeah,' said Theseus. 'She was kinda clingy . . . Anyway, this twine will help you find anything. Majorly handy for impossible labyrinths. Like finding the loo in a shopping centre.'

'Thanks,' said Elliot, unconvinced, stuffing the string in his satchel. How was he supposed to save the world with string?

How are you going to save Mum? asked his dark voice.

'Tell me,' said Virgo. 'Do you have anything positive to recommend from your time as a hero?'

Theseus paused. 'Your quest may not lead where you expect,' he said. 'So make the most of the journey.'

'Sounds like good advice, mate,' said Hermes.

'Oh – and set reminders on your phone for anything important,' said Theseus. 'I forgot to put the right sail on my boat and my father jumped into the sea . . .'

'How tragic,' gasped Virgo.

'Not really,' said Theseus. 'Turned out the water only came up to his knees. But it made Christmas a bit awkward . . . Have you spoken to Jason?'

'The Golden Fleece guy?' said Elliot. Thank goodness – a lifeline.

'Yeah – he was always up for a good quest back in the day,' said Theseus. 'I bet he'd be game.'

'He sounds highly optimal,' said Virgo happily. 'We'll visit Jason after lunch. And make mine a Buchis Burger – with extra ketchup!'

16. Jason

'C an I ask you something?' Elliot said to Hermes as Virgo snoozed off her seventh dessert in the back of Hades's chariot.

'Mate – do it,' said Hermes, zooming through the Asphodel gloom.

'Do you ever wish your family could be . . . different?' Elliot said, looking at his feet.

'Every single minute of most days – boom!' laughed Hermes. 'Not being funny, but my lot make Shakespeare look like a soap opera . . .'

'If you don't mind me asking – is Zeus a good dad?'

'Well, he's a better dad than a husband, that's for

sure . . .' said Hermes. 'Nah – we've had our beef, like all dads and their lads. It was tough growing up – he always had somewhere else to be, something to save, someone to marry . . . He had a shocking temper back then. I once nicked a spear from a centaur. Most kids would get a clip round the ear. I got a thunderbolt. And it weren't in me ear.'

Elliot laughed. Hermes was so cool.

'But you've forgiven him?'

'Sure,' said Hermes. 'With an older bonce, I see how tough it was for him – all that pressure. So he made some mistakes. But he paid the price. I guess what I've learnt over the years is that he might be King of the Gods – but he's only ever trying to do his best. All parents are.'

Elliot thought of his dad, locked away for ten years for his mistake. Had he paid his price? Had Elliot's letter reached him? Would he write back?

'And I'll tell you another thing,' whispered the Messenger God. 'There's only one true test of whether a parent is any good.'

'What's that?' asked Elliot.

'Their kid,' said Hermes. 'So your olds did a banging job.'

Elliot smiled as Virgo awoke with an almighty snore.

'We're here,' said Hermes, pulling up outside a dilapidated building in the Asphodel Fields. Elliot looked around the shady realm. There was nothing to see but . . . murk.

'Where's here?' Virgo asked blearily, looking at her surroundings with distaste.

'Shabby Road,' Hermes announced. 'Recording studio to the former stars.'

'What's Jason doing here?' asked Virgo.

'Bit of a career change,' said Hermes. 'He'll tell you all about it.'

They saw that the peeling door was open, so they wandered straight into the rundown building. Virgo surveyed the mould-covered walls, hung with faded pictures of singers gone by, and the empty recording studios, filled with cobwebs and dusty equipment. This seemed a curious environment for a mighty hero.

'There he is,' said Hermes as they came to the end of the corridor. 'That's Jason.'

Virgo walked up to the window and peered at the lone figure behind the glass. Jason was hunched over a lyre and singing into a large microphone. He was a pale, slight man with lank, dark hair, most of which was swept over his face in a long fringe. His intense, scrunched-up face as

163

he strummed on his lyre suggested he either profoundly felt the music, or desperately required the lavatory.

Virgo took a deep breath. This was her last chance to bind a hero to her quest. She prepared her most optimal brilliance.

Jason looked up from his instrument and Hermes gave him a friendly wave. Jason gestured for them to come in.

The aroma of the recording studio reminded Virgo of Bessie's dungheap.

'Hey,' said Jason warmly, but without smiling through his pierced lip. 'How's it going?'

'Dude – great to see you,' said Hermes, proffering a friendly fist. 'These are my good friends, E and V.'

'Guys – peace,' said Jason mournfully.

'Mate – love what you're doing with your . . . everything,' gushed Hermes. 'Your debut album, *What's the Point?*, is still one of my most banging favourites.'

'Thanks, man,' said Jason. 'Always great to have a real fan. What's your favourite track?'

'Hard to say,' said Hermes. '*The Day I Lost All Hope* was kinda catchy, although *Death Do Me a Favour* is a classic.'

'That's so cool,' drawled Jason. 'Everyone

usually says *I Can't (Because a Chimera Ate My Heart)* but it just sounds so mainstream now.'

Virgo looked over at Elliot, who appeared to be struggling with a snorting attack.

'So what you working on?' asked Hermes.

'Something a bit different. I wanted my last album, *The World is Crueller Than You Think*, to bring people on a musical journey.'

'Where did it lead?' said Virgo.

'The job centre,' said Jason. 'Turns out no one wanted to come with me. So my label dropped me. Now I'm writing jingles for adverts. Tell me honestly, what do you think of this?'

He started to strum a haunting melody on his lyre:

> *Life is full of hurt and pain*
> *But DynoPlug can clear your drain.*

'Er . . . yeah, mate,' said Hermes. 'It's . . .'

'Deep . . .' Elliot grinned in a manner Virgo knew to be disrespectful. 'Like a blocked drain.'

'Exactly! I just want to write something real,' said Jason earnestly. 'I want to write the truth. I want people to feel something. I want them to know the anguish of having hair in your plughole.'

'That's cool,' said Elliot, pointing at a second lyre playing magically behind Jason.

'Thanks, man,' said Jason. 'It's played with all the greats. The Beatles. Clapton. Beethoven. Man, that cat could party. His "Moonlight Sonata" walk was, like, legendary.'

'Epic,' said Elliot. Virgo made a mental note to improve his vocabulary.

'You like it? Here,' said Jason, picking it up, 'have this one, little dude. I've got loads.'

'Wow – thanks,' said Elliot, plucking the strings. 'But I can't play.'

'You don't need to,' said Jason. 'It plays itself. Uses the power of music whenever it's needed. It's powerful stuff, man. And *Stairway to Heaven* sounds, like, mind-blowing on it.'

'So why aren't you a hero any more?' Elliot asked.

Virgo sighed. The child really did have the tact of a flatulent gorgon. This was not going to secure a hero. Nor her kardia.

'My soul was like, empty,' said Jason bleakly as Elliot's lyre started to strum a sad tune. 'Yeah, I was saving people, yeah, I was striking a blow for what is good and right, yeah, I had the love and adoration of the world. But – man. It was so creatively unfulfilling.'

'Well – anyway – I need to talk to you about something,' said Virgo, keen to return to her quest.

'Is it the ad for that new cat litter?' said Jason eagerly. 'I've been hoping to land that gig – I've been working on something . . .'

Jason scrunched his face into the lavatory expression again and strummed some funereal chords on his lyre:

Lost and don't know what to do?
Cat-Plop freshens kitty poo.

With Elliot and Hermes overcome with fits of snorting, Virgo decided it was time to take matters into her own hands.

'I am on a quest,' she said plainly.

'Sister, that's deep,' said Jason. 'I guess we're all on a quest. Towards death . . .'

'Well, I'm on a quest towards the Air Stone,' she retorted. 'I need you to—'

'Let me stop you there, friend,' said Jason. 'I can't go with you. I'm moving in a new direction now.'

'Grunge? Techno pop? Jazz?' asked Hermes.

'Torremolinos,' said Jason profoundly. 'A moist-toilet-tissue company there wants a jingle. I think this captures it:

Your heart is cold. Your senses numb
Arriba! Wipes will cleanse your bum.

'Respect, mate,' said Hermes, apparently supressing a belch. Virgo nudged Elliot to remind him of the gravity of their mission.

'Please will you come with us?' said Elliot. 'We really need some help.'

'There's more chance of my single *Everyone You Love Dies* being used for a Christmas ad,' said Jason. 'Being a hero just isn't my identity any more. I prefer to be known by this.'

He held up his hand to reveal a tattoo on his palm.

'What's that?' asked Virgo.

'It's an upside-down heart,' said Jason. 'It represents the turmoil in my soul.'

'It's a bum,' said Elliot. 'Is that in turmoil too?'

'This is deeply sub-optimal,' huffed Virgo. 'No one will assist us.'

'Hey, if being a hero taught me anything,' said Jason, 'it's that it's a lonely job. And that I'm majorly allergic to golden wool. Cruel, right?'

Virgo had heard enough. 'So be it,' she pronounced. 'If we are unable to seek heroic assistance, we'll just have to obtain the Air Stone on our own. Let's get back to Home Farm. We have plans to make.'

'Right on, sister,' said Jason. 'It's like I said in my Top 235 single – *Hold on to Your Friends (While You've Still Got Some)*.'

17. Mother Dearest

'**G**ive me one good reason why I shouldn't stuff you like a hunting trophy, you lying, cheating, treacherous scum!'

'Because you can't even kill a mortal child!' yelled Hypnos. '*And* you swore on the Styx you wouldn't kill me . . . so there!'

'Only if *you* killed the child!' shouted Thanatos. 'You failed. So now I'm going to . . .'

'You couldn't catch me if you tried!'

'I wouldn't have to try! It would be too easy!'

'Go on, then!'

'Don't tempt me!'

'ENOUGH!' roared Nyx, stunning both of her

sons into silence as they squared off in the Cave of Sleep and Death. 'Listen to you! You are Daemon royalty of the house of Erebus! Not a pair of screeching schoolgirls! Thanatos! Apologize for threatening to kill your brother!'

'I'd rather have my kidneys scooped out with a teaspoon,' said the Daemon of Death, eyeballing his twin.

'That can be arranged,' said Nyx. 'Apologize. Now.'

Thanatos's face twisted into a scowl as Hypnos smiled smugly.

'I apologize,' he muttered, then added, 'for not annihilating you while I had the chance.'

'Hypnos – say sorry for betraying your brother to Zeus!' barked Nyx.

'But, Mumsie – it's not fair! He gets all the best stuff and he's not even the eldest . . .'

'Don't make me ask again!' snapped his mother.

'Sorry, Thanatos,' sulked Hypnos, crossing his fingers behind his back.

'Now let that be an end to it,' warned Nyx. 'You are the sons of the greatest immortal who ever lived. What would your father think of you, brawling like a pair of common Harpies?'

'He started it,' muttered Hypnos.

'I'll finish it too,' snarled Thanatos.

'Not another word!' said Nyx. 'We have far more important problems. You've already let the Earth Stone slip through your fingers. We need to get it back and reunite it with the other Chaos Stones. Hypnos – where are they?'

'Not telling,' said Hypnos folding his arms.

'Tell us, or I'll pull it out of you!' said Thanatos taking a step towards his brother.

'You're not the boss of me! You see!' squealed Hypnos, appealing to his mother. 'He's going to kill me.'

'No, he won't,' said Nyx.

'Yes, I will,' smiled Thanatos.

'You will not!' shouted his mother. 'I forbid it.'

'Forgive me, Mother,' said Thanatos. 'But, to quote my pathetic excuse for a brother – you're not the boss of me. The moment I am able, I will tear him limb from limb.'

'So there,' huffed Hypnos. 'I'm not saying a word. Not to you, anyway . . .'

'What do you mean?' snapped Nyx.

Hypnos grinned at his brother.

'I just met your little mortal friend – nice kid – Elliot, is it?' smiled Hypnos. 'We had quite the chat . . . the weather, the latest bands, where I hid your Chaos Stones . . .'

'YOU DID WHAT?' Thanatos erupted, to his brother's obvious delight. 'That's it, I'm going to—'

'Thanatos – leave us,' said Nyx firmly.

'What?!' said Thanatos.

'Go – I need to speak to your brother privately,' his mother said.

'I will not!' said Thanatos.

'YOU WILL DO AS YOU ARE TOLD!' roared Nyx, spreading her wings and forcing her son to cower backwards. 'I am your mother and you will respect me! Wait outside.'

Thanatos looked hatefully at his smiling twin.

'Go,' ordered Nyx. 'Now.'

'Fine,' said Thanatos, storming towards the cave's entrance. 'But you can't watch him for ever. I'll get him in the end. I swear it.'

'See ya!' said Hypnos as Thanatos pushed past him out of the cave.

Nyx looked squarely at her eldest son, before sitting on Hypnos's sable-covered bed. She gestured for him to join her.

'Come to Mother, baby,' she cooed softly.

Hypnos grinned like a toddler and skipped to his mother. She encircled him with her winged talons.

'I missed you so much, Mumsie,' said Hypnos

with his head on her shoulder. 'Don't leave me again.'

'I'm not going anywhere,' lilted Nyx, stroking Hypnos's head. 'Mother's here now.'

They sat quietly for a moment, with only the sound of Nyx's claws scratching the cave floor to pierce the silence.

'It's not my fault – I didn't have a choice,' sulked Hypnos. 'I had to give Zeus the Chaos Stones, or I would have ended up in Tartarus like those other loser Daemons. You're not cross with me, Mumsie?'

'Of course not, my angel,' said Nyx. 'You were a very clever boy.'

'I was?' said Hypnos, snapping up like a happy meerkat.

'Yes, you were,' smiled Nyx, pinching his cheek. 'You always were the smart one. That's why Daddy gave you your trumpet. Let me see it again. It's been so long . . .'

Hypnos eagerly handed his weapon over.

'It's so beautiful,' she sighed, turning the curved ivory trumpet in her claws. 'When Zeus killed your father, he broke my soul in two. I will not rest until Zeus knows that pain.'

'I wish Daddy was here,' pouted Hypnos.

'I don't,' said Nyx.

'What do you mean?' gasped Hypnos. 'He was everything to you!'

'Which is why I'm glad he hasn't lived to see his son shaming his memory with secrets and lies.'

'But you don't understand!' squealed Hypnos. 'Everybody's threatening me and whatever I do, someone wants to kill me! I'm so scared, Mumsie!'

'Shhhhh, my baby,' soothed Nyx, wrapping her talons around Hypnos's hand. 'I understand why you didn't want to tell your brother.'

'Ahhhhh – thank you, Mumsie,' sighed Hypnos, putting his head back on her shoulder. 'I knew you'd understand.'

'I do,' said Nyx. 'But, Hypnos?'

'Yes?'

'You have to tell me.'

'But I—'

'Hypnos,' said Nyx firmly, stroking his face with a claw. 'You don't want to make Mother cross, do you?'

'No,' pouted the Daemon.

'So I'm going to ask you one more time. Where are the Chaos Stones?'

Hypnos shifted awkwardly on his seat and looked into his mother's green eyes.

'I can't tell you,' said the Daemon of Sleep.

'I swore not to on the Styx.'

Nyx's finger froze on Hypnos's throat. 'Why would you do that?' she said softly.

'They had my trumpet!' whined Hypnos. 'And Hades was keeping me prisoner just because I owed him some money and I just wanted to get out and they were going to hurt me and made me swear on the Styx not to say anything, so you see if I tell you then I'll die . . .'

'Shhh. Calm yourself, my child,' soothed Nyx. 'These things happen.'

'You . . . you're not angry?' said Hypnos cautiously.

'Anger is futile,' said Nyx. 'You were right to tell me the truth.'

'I was?'

'You were,' smiled Nyx. 'Besides, you won't go telling our family's secrets again, will you?'

'No, Mumsie, I promise,' said Hypnos. 'My lips are sealed.'

'I'm glad to hear you say that,' said Nyx. 'Because Mother's going to help you glue them shut.'

'What?' said Hypnos, sitting up in alarm.

'You lied, Hypnos,' said Nyx darkly. 'You betrayed our family and cost your brother his throne. And now you've betrayed us again. I can't risk that any more. Your brother is right. Your father was right. You're a liability. It's time for Mother to punish you.'

'No!' cried Hypnos, leaping away from her.

'Be a good boy now,' said Nyx, unfurling her wings. 'Mother knows best. Time for a little nap.'

'I'm sorry!' shrieked Hypnos, flying into the air. 'Don't do it!'

Hypnos darted towards the cave's mouth, but Nyx swooped ahead of him with a single flap of her black wings, blocking his escape. Thanatos appeared behind her with a twisted leer.

'Mumsie! Thanatos!' cried Hypnos, retreating towards his bed. 'Please . . .'

'Night night, baby,' said Nyx, raising Hypnos's trumpet to her lips. 'Sweet dreams.'

With a great breath, she blew a curl of thick black smoke at her son's head. Hypnos hung in the air for a moment as his own magic sucked every last atom of consciousness from his body. His head lolled to his chest and he dropped to the cave floor, landing in a crumpled heap.

Nyx stalked towards her son's comatose body and lifted a hand. He was out cold. She leant down and gave Hypnos a soft kiss on his feathered head.

'You've been a very, very naughty boy,' the

Goddess of the Night whispered in his ear. 'I hope you've learnt your lesson.'

'You always were the strict one,' said Thanatos, walking over and kicking his brother on to his back. 'What now? You can't kill the child. He's the only one who knows where to find the stones.'

'I need to get him here, to the Underworld,' said Nyx, crouching beside Hypnos. 'We need him to talk.'

'Like he's going to tell you,' scoffed Thanatos.

Nyx's green eyes flashed with malevolent delight.

'By the time I'm finished with him,' she leered, 'he's not going to have any choice.'

18. Unhappy Returns

Despite another bad night with Mum, Elliot had a spring in his step as he came down for breakfast on Tuesday morning. He paused on the bottom step, wondering what craziness his immortal housemates had cooked up for him on this special day. He strolled into the kitchen.

Josie was sitting alone at the table. Was everyone hiding?

'Hi, Mum,' said Elliot deliberately.

'Hello, Elly,' said Josie happily. 'What are you doing today?'

'Why?' asked Elliot with a sly grin.

'Because I'm your mum, silly!' laughed Josie,

ruffling his hair. 'Now, what are you doing today?'

'Nothing special,' said Elliot grumpily as he started to assemble her breakfast. He thought she would at least have remembered today.

At least she isn't raving about plants and keys, said his dark voice.

'So – what are you doing today?' asked Josie cheerily.

'Dunno,' said Elliot, pushing a bowl of corn-flakes in front of her.

'Have you locked the door?' Josie said, suddenly anxious.

Virgo skipped into the kitchen. 'Good news,' she said. 'Athene thinks she's found a way to shield you from mortal legal consequences – we've got to . . .'

'I'm going out,' said Elliot, suddenly desperate to be alone. 'I've got some . . . stuff to do.'

'That won't be possible,' said Virgo. 'I'm under strict instructions from the Gods to give you the illusion of freedom while in fact reporting back to them on everything you do. This is highly confidential, of course.'

'So were Zeus's custard creams,' said Elliot.

Elliot couldn't help but enjoy Virgo fumbling for an answer.

'So be it,' said Virgo. 'But ensure you are home shortly. I will go and write a report on the Sewage

Renovation of 1932 – you need to be back by the time I have finished.'

'Have you watered the plants?' Josie asked.

'No, I haven't,' snapped Elliot, slamming the front door behind him.

With no particular idea where he was going, Elliot had no particular idea why he ended up outside Kowalski Gems. He'd never been inside before – Mum always said that jewellery was for people who didn't have enough inner beauty – but now he realized that perhaps there was another reason why she had always rushed him past the twinkling window.

He hesitated outside. Walking through this door ten years ago had changed his dad's life for ever. Should Elliot go through it now?

He pushed the old wooden door open a crack. He couldn't see anyone inside, so he gave it another push.

DING-A-LING-A-LING!

The bell betraying his arrival made him jump. He considered turning and running, but before he could, a young man in a suit appeared.

'Can I help you?' he said, his voice tinged with suspicion.

'I'm doing a school project,' Elliot gabbled. He

quietly thanked his lying tongue for coming to his rescue again.

'About Kowalski Gems?' the man asked doubtfully.

'About local heroes,' said Elliot more calmly. 'I read there was a shooting here once and I just . . . wanted to talk to someone about it.'

'I see,' said the man with a warmer smile. 'Then you'd better come in.'

Inside the dimly lit shop, spotless glass cabinets displayed sparkling trinkets. Elliot's eyes lit on a picture hanging above the counter of three men, including the young assistant.

'I am Piotrek. That is my father and my grand-father,' Piotrek explained. 'Three generations of Kowalskis in this shop. My grandpa fled Poland during the war as a child. He worked his way up from nothing to buy this shop. He was a world authority on gemstones — he was obsessed. Even my name means "rock" in Polish. Kowalski Gems was his life — may he rest in peace.'

'Was he here when——?' Elliot asked nervously.

'No. Thank God,' said Piotrek. 'That was my father. It's a shame — you just missed him, he'd be able to tell you more than I can. He . . . saw it all.'

'That's fine,' said Elliot hastily. He didn't fancy meeting the man his father tried to rob.

'I was upstairs with my mother,' said Piotrek. 'We heard two men shouting, terrible shouting ... Then we heard the key turn in our apartment door – my father had locked it.'

Elliot swallowed down the sicky feeling in his throat. Someone else trying to lock his dad out.

'There was more shouting – so much noise. We heard Constable Simpson arrive and thought everything would be all right. And then ...'

'What?' said Elliot.

'We heard the gun,' said Piotrek. 'My mother screamed. I didn't know if my father was . . . We just waited. We didn't know what for.'

'Must have been awful,' said Elliot quietly.

'It was,' said Piotrek. 'It felt like we were in that room for hours. Eventually, a policeman opened the door. There were police cars, ambulances – people everywhere. My father wasn't there. Constable Simpson wasn't there. The men weren't there. But the blood – that was there. That might have been the worst moment of my life.'

'But your dad was OK?' Elliot whispered.

'He was,' smiled Piotrek. 'He had gone to get help for the wounded policeman – he came running back into the shop and we all hugged like we'd never see each other again. That might have been the best moment of my life.'

'I'm so sorry,' said Elliot, without thinking, his head drooping with shame.

'You're sorry?' said Piotrek, as the shop doorbell jangled. 'I didn't catch your name . . .'

'I don't believe it – I get to the car – no keys!' An older man with a heavy accent bustled in. 'One day, I will leave my head and . . . Get out!'

Elliot flinched as the man strode towards him.

'Papa?' said Piotrek.

'I said – GET OUT!' roared Piotrek's father, grabbing Elliot's coat and shoving him towards the door.

'Papa!' said Piotrek, grabbing his father's arm. 'What are you doing?'

'I know you,' shouted Mr Kowalski. 'I've seen you and your mother, walking past without a care . . .'

'No, you don't—' Elliot began.

'You can tell your father that he can rot in his jail! I will never forgive him for what he did! Never!'

'You're his son?' said Piotrek. 'You tricked me . . .'

'I'm sorry,' said Elliot. 'I shouldn't have come—'

'Next time, I call the police!' said Mr Kowalski, giving Elliot another shove. 'Now GET OUT!'

Elliot stumbled his way out of the door and ran down the street.

As soon as he was far enough away, Elliot stopped to catch his breath. With every pant, his shame turned to anger. He knew it wasn't the Kowalskis' fault, but if it weren't for that place, he might still have his dad. Rage boiled up from his stomach. He kicked a stone on the pavement with all his might, accidentally hitting a homeless man huddled in a doorway opposite.

'I am so sorry,' he said, rushing over to him.

'Nice shot,' said the homeless man in a familiar drawl. He raised his thin face and stared straight into Elliot's soul. Elliot's blood cooled.

It was Thanatos.

'What do you want?' growled Elliot, strangely pleased to have a new reason to be angry. He clutched the Earth Stone in his pocket watch. He was in the perfect mood to give the Daemon another kicking.

'Merely to wish you many happy returns,' said Thanatos. 'It is your birthday today, isn't it?'

Elliot's heart skipped a beat. How did he know that?

'It's in my best interests to know everything about you, Elliot,' smiled Thanatos, making Elliot wonder again if Thanatos could read his mind.

'Then you'll know I'm not in the mood for you right now.'

'I won't keep you,' said the Daemon. 'I'm sure your friends have all kinds of plans . . .'

Elliot said nothing. He wasn't prepared to admit to his enemy that this was the worst birthday ever.

'But perhaps you would accept a birthday outing from me?' said Thanatos. 'I thought we might take a pleasure cruise?'

'Why would I do that?' Elliot demanded.

'The last time we met, I said I could return your mother to you.'

Elliot felt his jaw clench at the reminder of Thanatos's promise. His mum cured in return for the Chaos Stones.

A mum who remembers your birthday, said his dark voice.

'I don't believe you,' said Elliot.

'I presumed so,' said Thanatos. 'So I thought you might like to see how I can deliver.'

'Like I'd go anywhere with you.'

'So much distrust. So young. So much potential,' sighed Thanatos. 'I swear on the Styx I won't harm you in any way. You will return to your home alive and well. For what it's worth, I'd like to help you.'

'Help me to die?' said Elliot. 'Thanks.'

'Why would I want you to die?' asked Thanatos. 'You're guarding the Earth Stone. You alone know where the other three are hidden. So if I lose you, I lose my Chaos Stones.'

'You're never getting them,' said Elliot.

'Well, that's entirely up to you,' shrugged Thanatos. 'One of these days, you might feel differently. So. How about our little trip?'

Elliot wavered. When he'd visited Thanatos in the Cave of Sleep and Death, he'd been lucky to escape with his life – and only because Virgo had saved him. Thanatos wanted him dead, and no one would know where he was.

But then again, the Daemon had sworn the sacred oath on the Styx – if he harmed Elliot, he would lose his kardia and become mortal. Thanatos would never risk that. And Elliot was curious – Zeus had said that the Gods couldn't heal Mum. So how could Thanatos?

'This isn't a trick?' he asked the smiling Daemon.

'Unusually, no,' said Thanatos. 'Come along. I'll summon Charon.'

Elliot paused for a moment. What harm could it do to see what Thanatos was offering? It wasn't like Elliot would ever take him up on it.

But good to keep your options open, said his dark voice.

With a quick look around him, Elliot followed Thanatos towards the River Avon to take a voyage with the Daemon of Death.

19. Devil in the Detail

Charon pulled up outside the imposing bronze wall of Tartarus in the Ship of Death. Elliot hesitated as Thanatos headed for the mighty gates. He knew that Tartarus was where the most evil souls spent eternity. It didn't look like a fun day out. He'd felt the same creepy sensation when Mum took him to Little Motbury's short-lived amusement park, Clownland.

'You're quite safe,' said Thanatos.

'Good to know,' said Elliot uncertainly. 'Charon, if I don't come back, get a message to the Gods.'

'Will do,' said Charon, producing a clipboard.

'If I could just take a few details . . .'

'Sorry?' said Elliot.

'Oh – new business venture,' he said. 'Courier service, DeadEx. What is the content of your package?'

'Er . . . "Thanatos is trying to kill me. Please save my life."'

'Righto,' said Charon. 'Would you like our premium same-day delivery or economy in three to four business days? It'll save you a fortune.'

'I'll pay the extra,' said Elliot.

'And would you like the item gift wrapped?'

'Why not,' said Elliot.

'Great,' chortled Charon, ticking his form. 'See you later. Or not!'

'Thanks,' said Elliot, following Thanatos to the security desk, where a ferocious dog was watching security screens with two of its heads and playing a computer game with the third.

'Hello again, Cerberus,' said Thanatos.

'Damn it!' yelled the dog. 'I'm all out of angry hamsters . . . All right, mate – how you travelling?'

'Well, thank you,' said Thanatos. 'I've brought young Elliot with me – this is Cerberus, the finest security guard any world has ever known.'

'Hiya, pal,' said Cerberus's left head. Elliot smiled weakly in response.

'How are you?' asked Thanatos.

'Totally skint, mate.' Cerberus shook his middle head. 'The wife's expecting again.'

'More pups?' asked Thanatos.

'More shoes,' groaned Cerberus. 'The woman must have more feet than a mutant millipede . . .'

Thanatos laughed cordially. 'Do you mind if we pop in?'

'No worries – help yourself,' said the hound, returning to his game. 'Ah – hamster-wheel power at last – result!'

The almighty gates to the fiery prison creaked open and the anguished screams of the inmates coloured the stagnant Underworld air. Elliot peered inside. On balance, he preferred Clownland.

'It's not so bad,' said Thanatos reassuringly. 'Quite toasty really. Come.'

Elliot stepped tentatively through the gates into the scorching wasteland. A tortured scream made him jump. Perhaps prison wasn't his worst possible future.

'So this is where you go if you're really bad?' he asked.

'Allegedly,' said Thanatos.

'What have they done wrong?'

'Ah – now that's a matter of perspective,' said Thanatos. '*Wrong* is a highly subjective construct.'

190

'You what?' asked Elliot.

Thanatos laughed.

'Let's say Man A kills Man B,' Thanatos began. 'You'd probably say Man A was wrong.'

'He is wrong.'

'OK. What if Man B had stolen from Man A?'

'Still wrong,' said Elliot.

'What if Man B was trying to set fire to Man A's house?'

'Man A and Man B are both wrong,' said Elliot.

Thanatos stopped and looked deep into Elliot's eyes.

'What if Man A's children were inside the house?' he asked. 'What if the only way Man A could protect them was to kill Man B? Still wrong?'

Elliot paused.

'Yes . . .' he said uncertainly.

'But it might be more complicated than that!' said Thanatos. 'What if Man A had hurt Man B's family? What if Man B was seeking justice? Who is wrong now?'

'Man . . . I . . . it's . . .' said Elliot.

'Ah — you see!' said Thanatos triumphantly. 'Now it's not so clear. Right or wrong? Good or evil? Hero or villain? It all depends what story you've been told.'

Elliot struggled to answer back. That was unusual. He thought of his dad's story. Was there a different one? A better one?

He stored 'wrong is a highly subjective construct' in his bank of excuses as they continued in silence through the wasteland of tortured souls.

'Oi!' shouted a passing woman as Thanatos knocked into her. 'You made me drop it!'

'Drop what?' scoffed Thanatos. 'You weren't holding anything.'

'Yes, I was!' said the woman, showing her damp hands. 'My sisters and I are trying to fill that over there.'

She pointed towards an immense bronze urn, the size of a large house, at the top of a steep cliff. A long chain of women were walking barefoot up the jagged rocks between the lake in the bottom of the valley to the urn hundreds of feet above.

'The jars they gave us to carry the water had holes in, but we can't leave until we've filled the urn,' she explained.

'I remember you – you're Asteria, one of Danaus's daughters,' said Thanatos. 'I came to your wedding. Fifty sisters marrying fifty brothers. Nice affair. Excellent buffet – the best-man speech was a riot. Just a shame that forty-nine of you murdered your husbands on your wedding night.'

'Don't I know it,' moped Asteria. 'And now we're stuck here. You try climbing up there with a handful of water. We're lucky to get two drops in the urn. Still – we're almost there. A few more runs and we've made it.'

'Well – you know what they say,' drawled Thanatos. 'Blood is thicker than water.'

'I'd slap you,' said Asteria. 'But there's a drop on my pinkie I don't want to waste.'

She trudged off up the cliff. Elliot and Thanatos came to a lone, scrawny figure pushing a vast boulder up the other side.

'Sisyphus!' cried Thanatos, throwing his arms open.

'You can keep your "Thithyphuth" to your-thelf,' he huffed. 'I am theriouthly not thpeaking to you! Latht time you thet my progreth back dayth and weekth and months. Thith ith impothible enough ath it ith!'

'I'm truly sorry,' said Thanatos, bowing in apology. 'I was only joshing. Here – let me help you.'

Sisyphus stood with his arms across his boulder. 'Not another thtep.'

'Please,' said Thanatos, bowing meekly. 'Let me make amends.'

Sisyphus looked to the top of his hill and back to the boulder. 'No funny buithneth?'

'None whatsoever,' said Thanatos. 'I'll have that up there in a jiffy.'

Thanatos rolled up the sleeves of his black robe and positioned himself beneath Sisyphus's boulder. Elliot watched as, with his Daemon strength, Thanatos rolled the boulder up the hill as if it were made of cotton wool.

'There!' he said at the brow of the hill, making sure that Sisyphus could bear the weight. 'I'll leave you the satisfaction of finishing the job.'

'Thith is thenthational!' cried Sisyphus. 'It'th the betht day ever! I will finally be releathed!'

'Well, I'll leave you to it,' said Thanatos, heading back down the hill. 'Enjoy your freedom.'

'I thertainly will!' strained Sisyphus, about to give the boulder one final push. 'You're a thuperthtar.'

Thanatos rejoined Elliot, then turned back to the hill.

'Oh, Sisyphus?' he yelled. 'One last thing . . .'

'Yeth!' groaned Sisyphus, milliseconds away from completing the task.

'Your flies are undone!'

'Oh, graciouth!' exclaimed Sisyphus, releasing the boulder and clamping his hands to his trousers. 'Thankth! That could have been thpectacularly embarrathing! Oh, no . . . ! No! NO!

You thly little thnake . . . !'

But it was too late. The boulder – and gravity – seized its moment. With a groan, the almighty rock began to plummet down the hill.

'I'll get you for thith!' yelled Sisyphus, as Elliot tried hard not to laugh.

But the boulder wasn't done yet. Such was the speed of its descent that after it reached the floor of the valley, it started to climb the other side – straight towards Asteria and her sisters.

'Look out!' Sisyphus cried.

'Don't you even—!' shouted Asteria, standing in front of the nearly full urn with her hands outstretched to protect it. 'No, you don't . . . no, you don't . . . OK, yes, you do . . . Aaaaaargh!'

She dived to avoid the approaching boulder, which crashed into the urn like a giant bowling ball, pouring centuries of water back down the hillside and into the valley below.

'YOU IDIOT!' shrieked the sisters as they raced down the cliff and up Sisyphus's hill, forcing him to flee ninety-eight angry fists.

'Now that was wrong,' laughed Elliot in spite of himself as they headed away from Sisyphus and the crowd of angry women baying for his blood.

'Fun, though,' smiled Thanatos as they continued through the firy wilderness. For an evil maniac, Elliot had to admit that Thanatos had a decent sense of humour. Although this place was no joke.

'Why have you brought me here?' he said, looking nervously back to the distant gates. He didn't ever want to be trapped in this place.

Don't get caught then, said his dark voice.

'I want to show you what I can offer you,' said Thanatos. 'Here we are.'

Elliot surveyed the stone prison built on a small island, surrounded by a river of fire.

'No offence,' he said, 'but it's not your best argument.'

'Comrades!' bellowed Thanatos. 'It is I, your leader – I have returned!'

Elliot could hear frenzied whispers within the prison.

'In order to verify your identity, we need to ask you a few security questions,' came a shrill voice.

'Epiphron, Daemon of Carefulness,' Thanatos whispered to Elliot. 'Stickler for procedure . . . Go on!'

'What is your date of birth?' asked Epiphron.

'I know! I know!' shouted a new voice enthusiastically. 'The second of June 1979 BC.'

'Shut up, Zelus!' Epiphron chided.

'Daemon of Competitiveness,' winked Thanatos. 'Proceed.'

'What was the name of your first pet?' asked Epiphron.

'Bubonic, my rat,' said Thanatos. 'He was wonderful.'

'Loyal?' said Epiphron.

'Tasty,' smiled Thanatos. Elliot stifled a laugh.

'And finally, please state the top-secret, randomly generated, highly secure unique password we sent you,' said Epiphron.

'"Password",' sighed Thanatos, raising an eyebrow.

'Correct,' said Epiphron. 'Now tell us, O great one . . . when the bloomin' heck are you busting us out of here?'

'Soon, my subjects, soon,' said Thanatos. 'But until then, might you give Elliot here an indication of your abilities? I'm trying to show how . . . pleasant we can make his life.'

'My name is Soteria – I am the Daemon of Safety,' a gentle voice began. 'I can take care of you, Elliot . . .'

'I am Eutykhia, Daemon of Luck,' came another voice. 'Every day is a lucky day when I'm on your side . . .'

'Let's be friends, Elliot – I'm Eudaemonia,'

laughed another. 'As Daemon of Happiness, you need never be sad again . . .'

'I'm Oizys, Daemon of Misery,' moaned another. 'I can make your life completely awful.'

'Bad example,' said Thanatos. 'You see, we Daemons each take care of a different aspect of mortal life. We understand mortals because we share your experiences. Can you say the same of the Gods?'

Elliot thought of Zeus trying to do the ironing and said nothing.

'But there's one Daemon I'm sure you'd like to know. Where are you, Hygeia?'

'I am here, Master,' said a soothing voice.

'Tell Elliot what you can do.'

'I am the Daemon of Health,' she lilted. 'There's no one I can't cure. You and your loved ones need never be ill again. I can give anyone perfect health.'

Perfect health? Elliot scanned Thanatos's face. Was he lying?

'It's true,' said Thanatos, reading his doubt. 'Isn't it Pistis, Daemon of Truth?'

'Yes,' came the reply. 'Although the chances of you staying alive long enough to take advantage of it are—'

'Fantastic,' said Thanatos. 'So you see – we have a lot to offer you.'

'But you want the Chaos Stones,' said Elliot.

'Not just want – need,' insisted Thanatos. 'Only they can free my Daemons from this place – it will take an earthquake, hurricane, flood and fire.'

'So why don't I just free them?' said Elliot. 'I don't need you at all.'

'I like your style,' nodded Thanatos. 'But I am their King. They only answer to me.'

'No, we don't,' squeaked a voice.

'Silence Dysnomia!' roared Thanatos. 'Daemon of Lawlessness,' he explained to Elliot. 'Total managerial headache . . . Think about it, Elliot. Don't you think the world could do with some more of these qualities – joy, happiness, good luck?'

'Misery, lawlessness . . .' said Elliot as they started back towards the gate.

'Every silver lining has a cloud,' said Thanatos. 'But these are not matters you need concern yourself with. You need only worry about your mother. And I think you worry about her a great deal . . .'

'Don't you talk about her,' snapped Elliot.

'Sorry,' smirked Thanatos. 'But as it's your birthday, I'm prepared to improve upon my initial offer. Give me the Earth Stone. Tell me where the others are. I will bring your mother to my

Daemons and heal her. You'll both be safe from my . . . plans, I swear it. I'll even throw in Plutus, Daemon of Wealth. Have a mansion on me.'

Elliot's brain worked overtime to remember what he'd be agreeing to if he handed Thanatos the Chaos Stones, the elemental gems so powerful even the King of the Gods feared them. Thanatos wanted to enslave enough mortals to serve him, then cull the rest with natural disasters. That meant innocent people, people he knew, people in Little Motbury indiscriminately wiped out with tsunamis or earthquakes. How could he live with that?

In a mansion, said his dark voice. *With Mum.*

'Think on it,' said Thanatos. 'You get your mother – I get the hassle of retrieving the stones. No rush.'

After a silent stroll back through the hellish wilderness, they arrived back at Charon's ship.

'Tell me,' Thanatos began. 'Why are you allowing the Gods to stay at your home?'

Elliot shrugged. 'They're my friends,' he said. 'They're protecting me.'

'Protecting you?' Thanatos asked. 'Or protecting the Earth Stone?'

He gestured towards the watch in Elliot's fist. Elliot hadn't realized he'd been holding it.

'Me,' said Elliot, less certainly than he'd intended.

'Just ask yourself, who is protecting what?' whispered Thanatos. 'Charon – you take Elliot home, I could use the leg-stretch.'

'Right you are, guv,' said the boatman. 'All aboard.'

Elliot stepped thoughtfully into the Ship of Death.

'Why can't you just release the good Daemons?' he said. 'Why not just leave the bad ones there?'

'Because I told you, Elliot – there's no such thing as good or bad. Only the story you've been told,' smiled the Daemon, removing a piece of parchment from his pocket. 'You must go. But if you ever need me, write me a note on this parchment and throw it into the night – it'll find me. I look forward to seeing you again. And, Elliot?'

'Yeah?'

'Happy Birthday,' said the Daemon of Death.

The ship pulled away from the bank, carrying Elliot and the weight of all his thoughts back towards the Earth. It might not have been the happiest birthday he'd ever had. But it certainly wasn't one he was likely to forget.

*

'WHERE HAVE YOU BEEN?' screamed Aphrodite, nearly knocking Elliot over with the force of her hug as he walked into Home Farm.

'Elliot, we've been worried sick,' said a harassed Athene. 'You've been gone all day. We thought . . .'

'Mate!' yelled Hermes, crashing into him with a mid-air hug. 'I've been flying around for, like, hours – where were you?'

'You said you'd be home soon!' said Virgo. 'Yet again, you said something that wasn't factually accurate! On a related note, I have conducted several controlled experiments and tomatoes do not blush when they see the salad dressing!'

'You could have let us know you were going to be late, old man,' said Zeus quietly. 'Anything could have happened to you.'

'Well, nothing did,' said Elliot grumpily, unable to meet Zeus's piercing stare. 'Except for my birthday.'

The Gods looked aghast.

'It's your birthday?' said Aphrodite. 'Elly – you didn't tell us.'

'I thought you'd know,' said Elliot, thinking that he hadn't had to tell Thanatos. He bit his tongue. He guessed that telling the Gods he'd spent the afternoon with their immortal enemy wouldn't calm them down.

'Happy Birthday, mate!' said Hermes, turning a nearby mug-tree into a huge bunch of balloons with Elliot's face on. 'Let's paaaarty!'

'No, thanks,' said Elliot. 'I'm not in the mood.'

A thought struck him that could save his rubbish day. If his dad received his letter yesterday and sent one straight back, it might have arrived today. That would be a birthday present worth waiting for.

'Has there been any post for me?' he asked hopefully.

'Nothing at all,' said Zeus quietly.

Great. His dad didn't give a stuff either. What a loser. All the feelings from a long day flooded through his mind – Mum forgetting his birthday, the Kowalskis, Thanatos's deal . . . Today was a punishment, not a birthday. He felt a cold rage build in the pit of his stomach.

'I'm going to feed Bessie.' He scowled and stormed outside into the cold night air, his head ringing with all the voices he'd heard that day.

But as he trudged across the paddock, one rang out louder than all the others.

Just ask yourself, it said. *Who is protecting what?*

20. A Different View

'Oi, oi, oi – not so fast, pal,' said Hermes, flying down in front of Elliot.

'Leave me alone,' growled Elliot, trying to swerve the floating Messenger God.

'Now listen, mate,' said Hermes, blocking his path at every turn. 'We can play dodge the God all night – I got the time. Or we can sit down and bash this out – bosh!'

Elliot tried every which way to get past Hermes, but the Messenger God was too quick. Every step he took to the left, Hermes darted right. Every step to the right, Hermes blocked to the left. Elliot yelled in exasperation. He plonked down on the grass and Hermes floated down next to him. They sat in silence beneath the stars. Elliot felt his anger start to cool.

'Listen, mate, no one's saying it's fair,' said Hermes gently. ''Cos it ain't.'

Elliot sulked into the grass.

'Your mum. Thanatos. Your ugly mug,' said Hermes. 'Life has not been kind, Elliot Hooper.'

Elliot had to work hard not to smile.

'You know what we're like – mad as a bag of spanners,' said Hermes. 'We can't agree on anything – Dad's shirts don't even agree with his shorts.'

The smile fought even harder.

'But the one thing that we are totes united on,' said Hermes, 'is you. We are card-carrying, paid-up, fully subscribed members of Team Elliot. We're behind you all the way, little dude. And if you think that having a toddler strop is gonna get shot of us, you're thicker than Athene's unplucked eyebrows. Now – are we in any danger of that mug cracking yet?'

Elliot tried to turn away.

'I can see you smiling!' sang Hermes, punching Elliot's arm gently.

'I can see you smiling!' he sang again, right in Elliot's ear, poking him in the ribs.

It was no use. Elliot burst out laughing as Hermes wrestled him to the floor and sat on his chest.

'We're bros, mate,' he said. 'You're my bruvva from anuvva muvva – boom!'

'All right, all right,' said Elliot, struggling for breath between laughs and Hermes's backside squashing his lungs.

'Now if you promise to keep it quiet, I've got a birthday present for you,' said Hermes, wiggling his eyebrows.

'I promise, just get off me!' laughed Elliot, pushing the God aside.

'Right – get off your bum and hold my wrists like this.' Hermes grabbed Elliot's wrists with his hands. 'Now shut your eyes and count to ten.'

'Why?' asked Elliot suspiciously.

'Because eleven is a stupid number, you turnip,' said Hermes. 'Just do it.'

Elliot closed his eyes with a sigh.

'One . . . two . . . three . . . four . . . five . . . six . . . seven . . . eight . . . nine . . . ten,' he counted, opening his eyes again. 'So what did you . . . AAAAAAAARRRRRRGGGGGHHHH!'

Elliot looked at his feet. They were several hundred feet above the ground. He clung to Hermes's wrists mid-air.

'I got ya, bruv,' said Hermes with a wink. 'Fancy a spin?'

Elliot nodded warily as Hermes started to float through the night sky. They drifted silently over the dark countryside beneath, the occasional lamp cutting a shard of light through the murky air.

'Right, when you're ready – let this one go,' said Hermes, waggling Elliot's left hand.

Elliot froze. 'I don't think I . . .'

'Like I said – I got ya,' smiled Hermes. 'On my count . . . One . . . two . . . three . . .'

Elliot cautiously let go of Hermes's wrist, just as the Messenger God started to take flight, holding Elliot by his right arm.

'Put your other arm out . . . boom!' said Hermes as they made their unsteady way across the darkness. Elliot looked down at the Earth. He was flying.

Shaking a little at the distance between him and solid ground, Elliot felt the cool breeze fly through his body. He closed his eyes and took a deep breath as he glided through the air. Everything was so clear up here.

'You ready to step it up a gear?' grinned Hermes.

Elliot smiled and nodded.

'Then let's do this!' yelled Hermes, kicking his winged trainers together.

'Woo-hoo!' Elliot shouted as the sudden burst of acceleration sent them soaring through the night, the rush of air blasting Elliot's face into a smile of pure adrenaline.

'Wicked, innit?' shouted Hermes as they raced over fields and rivers, houses and villages, their laughter carrying through the night air. Elliot watched the world whip beneath him. It all looked so small.

'Do you trust me?' Hermes shouted.

'What?' yelled Elliot, his ears blasted with air.

'Do. You. Trust. Me?'

Elliot looked into the smiling face of the winged God.

'Yeah,' he said. 'I do.'

'Then let go,' said Hermes with a mischievous grin.

Elliot looked at the dark, hard, distant Earth so far beneath his body.

'No, thanks,' he shouted firmly.

'Mate,' tutted Hermes with a disapproving shake of his head. 'Didn't have you down for a chicken. No bother . . .'

Elliot looked again at the ground whizzing beneath him. He'd have to be crazy to let go –

who knew what could happen? Terror? Injury? Death?

But it couldn't be worse than being called a chicken.

With a deep breath and a terrified cry, he released his grip on Hermes's arm. He plunged down through the night, free-falling through the darkness. His heart dropped into his stomach as he fell, his body turning end over end until he had no idea which way was up. The ground was getting closer . . . closer . . . too close . . .

'BOSH!'

He landed square in Hermes's arms just feet from the ground as the Messenger God swooped down and rocketed them back up into the night sky.

Elliot panted with fear. That was petrifying. That was dangerous.

That was EPIC.

'I'll always catch you, bruv,' winked Hermes, whooshing higher into the sky. 'Again?'

'Yeah!' shouted Elliot, punching the air.

'Hold tight!' shouted Hermes, propelling Elliot upwards and letting him tumble from even higher before catching him by his hands.

'THIS. IS. AWESOME!' shouted Elliot as the two friends flew around the night sky like wireless

trapeze artists, Hermes flinging Elliot around the darkness before catching him in ever more daring moves. Elliot front-flipped, back-flipped, every-thing-flipped, laughing breathlessly defying the dark gravity around him.

'Mate,' panted Hermes, catching him again after hours of aerobatics, 'I need a chill. You're heavier than you look . . .'

Elliot linked wrists with the Messenger God once more, and they flew towards a single cloud in the night sky. At Hermes's touch, the cloud transformed into a plush, nebulous sofa, and they plopped down on it in fits of exhausted laughter.

'Just look,' sighed Hermes when he'd caught his breath, gesturing to the Earth below. 'I'll never tire of that.'

Elliot took in the amazing vista from his cloud-top seat.

'It's really beautiful from up here,' he said.

'It's really beautiful from down there,' said Hermes. 'You just gotta know how to look at it.'

They sat silently for a few moments, drinking in the natural world laid out beneath them.

'This is what it's about, mate,' said Hermes quietly. 'The Chaos Stones, Thanatos, the Daemons . . . This is what we're fighting for. Not for our world. For yours. If Thanatos gets his hands on those stones, mate – millions will die. The rest will be his slaves. Not being funny, but we're talking apocalypse-level bosh-not.'

Elliot bowed his head. Hermes gave him a friendly punch.

'But this is what we really came up here for,' he said, looking at his iGod. 'Bang on schedule in three ... two ... one ...'

The opaque horizon was suddenly split by a ribbon of light, like a dark box being prised open from the inside. The golden band grew wider with every second as the sun lifted the night away from the ground, illuminating the black void with its warm glow. Elliot gasped involuntarily. It was the most beautiful sight he had ever witnessed. The dawn of a new day.

'You see, bruv?' whispered Hermes. 'Even the darkest night lights up again.'

Elliot watched in awe as the day conquered the night, dispelling the shadows to show the intricate detail of life on Earth. It was breathtaking.

'Blimey – I'd better get you home,' said Hermes, floating up from the cloud sofa. 'Mate, seriously – you are not to tell *anyone* that we did this. 'Theney would turn me into a throw cushion if she ever found I'd had you out all night. Not even joking.'

'At least you'd help her sore bum,' grinned Elliot as they linked arms across the sky.

Hermes laughed, guided Elliot back towards his home and flew him up to his open bedroom window. Elliot clambered in and returned Hermes's fist-bump.

'Now get some kip,' grinned Hermes. 'We've gotta spring the Air Stone later and boy do you need your beauty sleep . . .'

Elliot tried to punch his arm, but Hermes dodged out of reach.

'Too slow,' he grinned, waggling his fingers before running them through his hair. 'Happy birthday, bruv. Night night.'

'Night, Hermes,' said Elliot, with a calm, happy smile as the Messenger God turned a few flawless somersaults in the air before gliding away. 'See ya. Bruv.'

Elliot waited for the dark voice to poison his thoughts.

It had nothing to say.

21. Young Man

Several hours later, Elliot was woken by the acrid smell of burning coming from the kitchen. What was . . . ? Panic suddenly punched him into action. Was Mum trying to cook by herself? What if she'd left something on the stove? The farmhouse would burn down around him. He threw off his covers and sprinted down the stairs.

But he found Josie sitting calmly at the table, giggling with Hermes at the chaos unfolding around her. It took Elliot a moment to process the scene before him.

Hanging across the kitchen was a banner,

constructed from materials Elliot recognized from the recycling bin. Aphrodite was painting HAPY BIRTHDY ELLIT in dripping letters on cereal boxes, discarded magazines and empty toilet rolls. Athene was covering the kitchen table with a whole buffet of burnt offerings, from chargrilled jam sandwiches to a curiously singed trifle. Zeus was covering a cremated cake in bright green icing. It was how Elliot imagined a birthday party in Clownland.

'Morning, everyone,' he said cautiously.

'Oh, no!' pouted Aphrodite as the letter 'B' dripped on her head. 'We wanted to surprise you.'

'You've certainly done that,' said Elliot.

'We wanted to atone for missing your birthday, Elliot,' said Athene, extinguishing a small cocktail sausage.

'So we thought we'd throw you a little birthday brunch,' said Zeus, splatting another spoonful of bogie-coloured icing on the cake. 'Happy Birthday, old boy!'

'I tried to help them,' Hermes whispered with a wink. 'But they insisted on doing it themselves. Sorry.'

Elliot caught Josie's eye – she was trying desperately not to laugh, which set Elliot off as well. The two of them started snorting, then giggling, then guffawing, while the Gods stared in confusion.

'What's so amusing?' said Athene, waving the smoke off a bowl of cheesy puffs.

'Nothing,' said Elliot, wiping the tears from his eyes. 'This is really cool. Thank you.'

'Hope you don't mind – I crashed here last night,' said Hermes, filling his coffee cup with brown sludge from the kettle. 'Hung out with J-Hoops for a bit. She's wicked, your mum. Tells the dirtiest jokes ...'

Elliot smiled gratefully at Hermes. He'd given him some sleep. That was the best present of all.

'What are you all doing?!' screeched Virgo, storming into the kitchen with bundles of paper. 'Today's the day! The day of my quest! The day I regain my kardia! We need to get to the Natural History Museum at once! I've constructed a brilliant, flawless plan!'

'Hide in the bogs until the museum closes?' said Elliot. 'Not exactly *Mission Impossible*, is it?

'It's perfect,' Virgo pronounced. 'So hurry up! What could be more important!'

'Lots of things,' smiled Zeus at Elliot.

'Anyhow – we gotta make a stop on the way,' grinned Hermes. 'We're off to see an old mate of yours.'

215

'Who?' said Elliot.

'I've had a breakthrough in my research,' said Athene excitedly. 'There is a way you can take the Air Stone with no fear of punishment!'

'Brilliant!' said Elliot. 'What is it?'

'A royal pardon,' said Athene proudly.

'What is that?' asked Virgo, serving herself a bowl of steaming jelly. 'Something a monarch needs if they break wind?'

'It's a bally get-out-of-jail-free card,' said Zeus. 'Quite literally.'

'Brainy Bum was boring on about it all yesterday,' moaned Aphrodite. 'If you have a royal pardon, you can't get in trouble. You just have to go and get it from . . .'

'The Queen!' Elliot grinned. It would be fun to see her again.

'So we need to get a shift on – today's the last day before the Vault closes,' said Hermes. 'I'll go saddle up Uncle H's chariot – that Bessie's been giving the stallions the eye in the shed for days, she's a right flirty cow . . . So we'll drop in on the Queen, get your royal pardon, bosh, bang and a double portion of boom.'

'Top hole,' said Zeus. 'But be on your guard at all times.'

'I'm so jealous,' pouted Aphrodite. 'I'd love to

meet the Queen. She's such an inspiring figure of female leadership. And her bling is off the scale . . .'

'We're going to be busy,' said Athene, handing Zeus and Aphrodite pieces of parchment. 'These arrived from Hera this morning. They're our assessments. We must complete all these tasks before the end of the day.'

'Why the bally heck would I need to cartwheel backwards while reciting Hamlet!' roared Zeus reading his sheet. 'This is outrageous!'

'Let's just get it done and get these zappers off,' said Athene. 'Children – good luck today. We'll be thinking of you.'

'All will be perfect,' said Virgo. 'We will return with the Air Stone tonight.'

Elliot's hand went to the Earth Stone in his father's watch. By the end of the day, he could have another Chaos Stone. Zeus was right. With Thanatos in his head, and the power to control the element of Earth in his pocket, one was a heavy burden. Could he handle two? But that was a problem for later. First, he had to get his hands on the Air Stone.

'Let's bounce,' said Hermes, throwing Elliot his satchel. 'London's calling! Bosh!'

*

Having found some convenient roadworks near Green Park, Hermes parked the chariot on the low-way and led Elliot and Virgo through a nearby manhole up into the park itself. Virgo reflected on their last visit to Buckingham Palace, when they had been surprised to discover that in addition to being Head of State and wearing charming hats, Her Majesty Queen Elizabeth II in fact possessed impressive secret ninja skills.

'. . . and then she kicked Hypnos's butt into the middle of next week,' said Elliot as he recounted their last meeting to Hermes. 'She's awesome.'

Virgo had endured a bad night – she'd had barely nine hours sleep. Thoughts of her quest and her kardia ran through her mind. If she was successful, she could return to her perfect life back in Elysium. She waited for this prospect to make her very happy but nothing happened. Perhaps her emotions were still asleep?

The trio headed across Green Park towards the majestic sight of Buckingham Palace. Virgo had observed on her previous visit to London that there was always something happening in every corner of the city. Even on this crisp February afternoon, there was a man juggling beer bottles, a woman dressed as a gold statue and a production of something entitled *Peter Pan* taking place in the wide green spaces of the Mall.

'This is quite lovely,' said Virgo, taking in the scenery. 'I had been led to believe that London was filled with rude, impatient mortals.'

'You'll fit right in,' said Elliot, putting out his arm to prevent her from walking in front of a black London taxi-automobile.

'Oi – are you blind?' yelled the driver.

'Not at all – I can see your second chin from here,' snapped Virgo after him.

'See – you're a natural,' smiled Elliot, and Hermes snorted behind them.

They crossed the road, passing a large memorial topped with a bronze winged statue. This impressive centrepiece was covered in scaffolding and builders, with signs dotted around the outside saying RESTORATION IN PROCESS. Virgo was impressed by the mortal regard for history, although as she choked on the traffic fumes thickening the air, she felt they should pay more attention to their future.

They arrived at the palace gates, which were heavily guarded by soldiers and policemen.

'Hermes – the invisibility helmet, please?' asked Elliot.

Hermes began rummaging through his infinite

bag. Out came a frog, a tagine, an ornate lamp-stand and a mouthguard for a riding camel. But despite his frantic grabs, Hermes couldn't find the helmet.

'Mate,' he whined. 'I must have left it in my other bag. I am such a turnip. Major misbosh . . .'

This was most sub-optimal. The royal pardon was vital to the success of the quest. Virgo decided she wasn't going to panic.

'How are we going to get in?' she panicked.

'Not sure,' said Elliot, looking around for inspiration.

An American mortal in a large hat approached a policeman as the gates opened to let a car into the palace courtyard.

'Excuse me, officer,' he said loudly, 'is this Bucking Ham Palace?'

'Yes, sir,' said the policeman with a shudder. 'How may I help you?'

'Can I get a selfie with the Queen?' said the tourist. 'My mama's just crazy 'bout her.'

Virgo looked towards the open gate. If they were quick, perhaps they could just . . .

'Can I help you?' said the policeman suddenly, as if he'd read Virgo's mind.

'Er . . . um . . . yes, pleeeeeze,' said Elliot, putting on a ridiculous accent for reasons that weren't entirely clear. 'Is theeez my hotel? I just arrive in Londooon and I looking for somewhere to stay. I very tired and want to sleeeeep.'

Virgo had recently learnt the word 'muppet'. Elliot was an excellent example of one.

'I'm sorry, sir,' said the policeman in a slow, loud voice. 'You'll have to find somewhere else. This building is fully booked.'

Suddenly, from deep inside Elliot's satchel, Virgo heard a series of musical chords. This was no time for a performance from Jason's lyre.

'OK, zank you, Mr Policeman, sir,' said Elliot, in an entirely different accent to the first one as the lyre started to play more loudly. At the sound of the tune, the policeman involuntarily began to tap his feet. 'I'll just keep looking for . . .'

'Young man!' said the policeman suddenly, in time with the lyre. 'There's no need to feel down!'

'Er . . . thanks,' said Elliot. 'I'm feeling fine, actually . . .'

'I said – young man!' said the policeman again, doing a neat spin on the spot. 'Pick yourself off the ground!'

'Really, I'm all good,' said Elliot as the policeman stepped, tapped and clicked his fingers. 'I'm sure there's a Budget Inn down the road . . .'

221

'I said – YOUNG MAN!' bellowed the policeman, gyrating to the lyre. "'cos you're in a new town, there's no need – to – be – unhappy!'

A nearby builder front-flipped off the Victoria memorial and knelt at Elliot's feet.

'What is this curious mortal ritual?' Virgo whispered. 'Are Londoners quite optimal?'

'Young man,' sang the construction worker, 'there's a place you can go!'

'I said – young man,' sang the American mortal, 'when you're short on your dough.'

'You can stay there,' boomed a deep voice as one of the *Peter Pan* actors wearing some kind of ceremonial outfit joined them, 'and I'm sure you will find many ways – to – have – a – good time.'

'What's that one?' asked Virgo.

'A Native American chief,' smiled Elliot.

The lyre plucked a series of five identical chords. The policeman, the builder, the American mortal, the chief and everyone nearby burst into a chorus:

'It's fun to stay at the Y-M-C-A!' they sang in perfect harmony. 'It's fun to stay at the Y-M-C-A!'

Virgo looked around her. London had come to a total standstill as everyone joined in with Jason's lyre. As far as the eye could see, tourists, businessmen and a particularly enthusiastic traffic warden were singing and dancing to the lyre. It was the most bizarre, if beautifully choreographed, spectacle Virgo had witnessed.

'Come on – quick!' Virgo gestured to Elliot and Hermes, who were arguing over the correct way to make an 'M' with their arms.

They darted inside the gates, careful to avoid the two secret service officers, who were busy assuring each other they could get themselves clean and have a good meal.

'Well,' said Virgo with an approving nod, 'I'll give London this much. Its tourist information is most illuminating.'

22. A Right Royal Barbeque

lliot, Virgo and Hermes snuck around the outside of the palace until they were in the gardens. Immaculate flowerbeds punctuated the beautifully manicured lawns, which spread out like a velvet green carpet as the sun started to descend from the sky.

'This is optimal,' nodded Virgo approvingly.

'Shhhh!' scolded Elliot. 'We don't want to draw attention to our—'

The sound of a dozen triggers being cocked told Elliot that it was a little too late.

'Who are you?' shouted a secret service officer. 'And how did you get in here?'

'I'm . . . I'm . . .' spluttered Elliot, thinking how many bullets were aimed at his skull.

'Mr Hooper,' said an elegant voice. 'Terrence, instruct your men to stand down. Mr Hooper is an old friend.'

'Yes, Ma'am!' yelled the head of the secret service, whipping his hand to his head in a salute. 'Lower your weapons! Sorry, sir.'

Elliot felt the blood return to his veins as the guns sank to the ground.

The guards parted, revealing Her Majesty the Queen. She exuded her natural regal grace – which was particularly impressive given that she was wearing a Wonder Woman apron over her immaculate twin-set and holding a large sausage on a fork. She extended her hand. Elliot wasn't sure whether to shake or kiss it, so he did a little bit of both, essentially wiping his nose over the Queen's knuckles.

'And Miss Virgo, how lovely to see you again,' said the Queen politely. 'Is Pegasus not with you today?'

'No, Ma'am,' said Elliot quickly. 'But this is Hermes – he's the Messenger God.'

'Your Maj,' said Hermes with a grin, fluttering up and bowing mid-air. 'It's an honour to meet you, your Royal Babeness.'

'Enchanted,' said the Queen with a warm smile. 'We're just having a barbeque supper. Would you care to join us?'

'Cor – yeah!' said Elliot, who had nothing in his stomach but toasted jammie dodgers.

'Marvellous,' said the Queen. 'Come and meet the family.'

She led the way to a sheltered patio area, where the other members of the royal family were enjoying their barbeque beneath a row of heat-lamps.

'Everybody – this is Mr Elliot Hooper, about whom you've heard so much,' said the Queen.

'Hello there!' Prince Harry and Prince Philip waved their cheeseburgers. 'Good to meet you.'

'Care for a banger?' said the Prince of Wales as the Duchess of Cornwall tended the barbecue.

'Did you bring any Daemons with you this time?' joked Prince William as he and the Duchess of Cambridge encouraged Prince George and Princess Charlotte to eat their vegetables.

'Not today,' grinned Elliot.

'I'm glad you found us all right,' said the Queen, putting another slice of processed cheese on her burger. 'It can be frightfully tricky to get in and out. It's a nightmare when one wishes to nip out for a kebab.'

'Tell me, Liz – one icon to another – how do you stay in such banging shape?' asked Hermes.

'Well, the corgis do keep me on my toes . . .' said the Queen, patting her neat hair.

'Do you have a martial arts sensei who trains you for hours every day?' asked Virgo.

'Not at all!' laughed the Queen. 'But it's amazing what one can pick up from celebrity fitness DVDs . . . Now, who wants a hot dog? Oh, what a shame. It's clouding over. Looks like it might rain.'

Elliot looked up into the early evening sky, where a large black cloud now hovered over the palace.

'Your British weather is even less reliable than your buses,' sighed Virgo.

They watched the cloud begin to descend, blackening the air. Elliot suddenly had a very, very bad feeling.

'Children,' said the Queen slowly while the cloud unfurled long, black wings. 'Go behind that wall. I think we have an uninvited guest.'

'Nyx!' said Hermes as the black cloud transformed into a ferocious winged monster swooping down towards them. 'What the—?'

'So you're having a party?' screeched Nyx, revealing the rocks that were clutched in her talons. 'Mind if I join you? Here's my contribution . . .'

The party scattered like drops on a window pane as Nyx pelted them with the huge rocks, which shattered into a million pieces, sending shards of shrapnel flying across the garden. She raised one high in the air and aimed it straight at Elliot.

'Elliot – no!' cried Hermes, diving in front of him and taking a hit to the head.

'Hermes!' cried Virgo as the Messenger God fell dazed to the ground.

'Is everyone all right?' asked the Queen from behind the barbecue lid she had used as a shield.

'I'm fine,' shouted Prince Philip, wearing a silver salad bowl on his head like a helmet. 'But that wretched creature spilt my drink!'

'Look out – she's coming around again!' yelled the Prince of Wales, diving into a nearby fountain.

Nyx swooped back up into the sky as a plume of black smoke, spinning around to throw her next batch of missiles.

'Who's Nyx?' Elliot shouted.

'Goddess of the Night,' Hermes mumbled groggily. 'Aka – Thanatos's Mum. Like, literally, the mother of all unbosh . . .'

Elliot's heart raced. Given how her sons had

turned out, he didn't have high hopes for Thanatos and Hypnos's mother.

The Messenger God slumped to the ground unconscious.

'Elliot!' shouted Virgo. 'Jump!'

The pair leapt from their hiding place just as a huge boulder landed where their broken bodies would have been had they remained there a split second longer.

Another giant rock smashed a nearby crystal bowl, splattering the Queen with potato salad.

'How dare you!' shouted Her Majesty, wiping mayonnaise out of her eyes with a lace hankie. With a terrifying, disapproving glare, the Queen retied her scarf around her forehead like a commando and pulled a machine gun out of her apron pocket. 'Right! That's it! One is frightfully sorry, Nyx, but you have not been granted an audience! Family – let's kick some bottom!'

The Queen grabbed some corn on the cob and loaded it into her gun as ammunition. She fired. Pieces of corn whistled through the air, pelting Nyx with a relentless barrage of tiny bullets but doing nothing to stop her swooping down on the gathering again.

'One needs something bigger, harder, more deadly,' said the Queen. 'Camilla – where are those rolls you baked?'

'Already on it,' shouted the Duchess of Cornwall, yanking a statue out of the ground by its personals, revealing that the garden ornament was in fact a huge bazooka. Kicking off the statue's head, she loaded her baking into the weapon.

'Nyx!' she screamed, pushing her Chanel scarf aside so she could hoist the bazooka up to her shoulder. 'Your bread is buttered!'

A shower of bread rolls exploded at Nyx, sending her spinning off course.

'Yesssss!' said Camilla, dropping to her knees with a fist-pump. 'Catherine – you're up!'

'I know,' said the Duchess of Cambridge, rummaging through an elegant salmon-pink handbag, pulling out wet wipes, a tiara and the perfect shade of nail polish for her outfit. 'It's in here somewhere . . .'

'Come along, darling,' smiled Prince William, loading halloumi kebabs into a small cannon while wiping ketchup from Princess Charlotte's face.

But the pause was enough for Nyx to recover. Her green eyes sought out her prey and homed in on Elliot. With an awful smile, she stretched out her wings and leant forward into a dive, her talons outstretched.

'You're coming with me!' she screeched at Elliot, who stumbled backwards across the lawn. He picked up some flowerpots and threw them at the approaching Goddess. He wasn't going anywhere without a fight.

'Catherine, dear,' said the Queen calmly as Prince Charles emerged from the fountain with his tie around his head and a flame-thrower in his arms. 'Could you move it along a little, please?'

'You is a stinky poo-poo head!' shouted Prince George at Nyx as Prince Harry manoeuvred a small tank across the lawn.

'George – we don't speak like that,' chided Prince William. 'What we say is: *One* is a stinky poo-poo head.'

'Found it!' said Catherine, flicking her perfect hair out of her eyes as she pulled a hand grenade out of her bag. She pulled the pin out delicately with her teeth, reapplying her lipstick with her free hand. She grabbed a nearby lacrosse stick and lobbed the grenade into the air. 'Nyx – catch!'

'Quick – duck!' said the Queen, grabbing Elliot and Virgo and diving behind an upturned picnic table.

The explosion ripped through the sky and sent a stunned Nyx spiralling through the air. She turned and tumbled and, for a moment, looked as if she might drop from the sky altogether. But after a few disorientated seconds, she once again spread her dark wings to steady herself.

'So you don't like my presents?' she screeched manically down at everyone. 'Well, let's see how you like my fireworks!'

Nyx jetted upwards, closing her eyes and muttering sinister incantations as the sky darkened at her command. Flashes started to illuminate the darkness, wiry fingers lacing together to form an almighty red bolt of lightning.

'She's going to strike the palace!' said Elliot. 'It'll burn it to the ground – quick, we have to warn everybody!'

But there was no time. As Nyx commanded the darkness, peals of thunder rumbled and the lightning filled the sky.

'Hermes! Hermes, wake up!' shouted Virgo at the motionless God as Elliot ran towards the palace.

'Here you go!' cackled Nyx as she summoned the lightning to her hands to aim it at the palace. 'A party fit for a queen!'

But just as she brought her arm back to hurl the thunderbolt, a huge searchlight flicked on with a clunk. The Goddess of the Night instinctively shielded her face with her wings, casting the lightning aimlessly into the evening sky. Another searchlight followed. And then a third. Nyx started weaving around in mid-air as she tried to get her balance. This split-second delay was all the security guards needed to regroup.

'Take aim!' shouted Terrence.

'I will hunt you down, Elliot Hooper!' cackled Nyx, wincing at the light. 'It's only a matter of time!'

'Fire,' ordered the guard as a hundred bullets were launched at Nyx, who simply clicked her fingers and disappeared in a wisp of black smoke.

'Is everyone all right?' asked the Queen as the security guards surrounded her family. 'We haven't had a scrap like that since we played charades last Christmas.'

'Er – mates, babes – I'm fine, in case you were wondering,' said a dazed Hermes, picking himself up and pulling a chicken drumstick out of his winged hat.

'What a nasty piece of work,' said the Queen, straightening her apron. 'Calm down, everybody. I'm fine. Just the British weather playing its tricks. Who'd like a nice cup of tea?'

'We'd better motor, mate,' said Hermes. 'Looks like Thanatos has good old Mum to do his dirty work. That is a chronic bosh-not for you. Your

Babeness – we have something to ask you.'

'Of course,' said the Queen. 'How might I help?'

Elliot explained about the Air Stone, the Natural History Museum and the need for a royal pardon. Virgo talked about her kardia and why mortal digestive systems were sub-optimal.

'I see,' said the Queen, pulling a scroll out of her apron and handing it to Elliot. 'Well, as our friend has just reminded us, you are acting in the interest of world safety. Here, take this. One always keeps a royal pardon to hand in case one breaks wind.'

'Epic,' said Elliot. 'Er . . . it doesn't work anywhere else, does it? Like school . . . ?'

'I'm afraid not,' smiled the Queen.

Shame. Elliot liked the idea of shoving a royal pardon in Boil's face every time he threatened detention.

'Before we go, I've brought you something,' he said, rummaging around in his bag. 'Sorry it's a bit late.'

He produced the Imperial Crown from his satchel and presented it to the Queen.

'How kind, Mr Hooper,' she said. 'People are always borrowing things and not returning them. One has been waiting for ever for the Sultan of Brunei to return one's boxed set of *Harry Potter*.'

'Kids – we gotta split,' said Hermes. 'The museum shuts in twenty minutes!'

'Terrence – take our friends to the Natural History Museum,' said the Queen. 'They're in a rush.'

'Thanks,' said Elliot. 'Sorry I got you attacked. Again.'

'No bother,' said the Queen. 'There's always some menace. If it's not mythological monsters, it's those frightful prime ministers.'

'Thank you, Your Majesty,' said Virgo with a curtsey. 'It's been very optimal to see you again.'

'Nice to see you, everyone,' said Elliot, running across the lawn.

'You too, Mr Hooper,' winked the Queen. 'You know where I am if you need me.'

'I do,' shouted Elliot with a smile, looking back at the sea of elegant, one-handed waves.

23. The Vault

Despite Terrence's best efforts in the Queen's limo, Elliot, Virgo and Hermes arrived at the Natural History Museum just as the security guards were closing the mighty front doors.

'Er – sorry – I left my . . . umbrella in there,' said Elliot, racing up the steps. 'Can I just run in and grab it?'

'Sorry,' said the guard, blocking his way. 'You'll have to come back tomorrow. The museum is closed.'

'But, please! It's my mother's favourite umbrella!' Elliot lied desperately. 'Her mother gave it to her and her mother gave it to her . . .

It's a family heirloom! It's been passed down through five generations of my family!'

The guard paused and stared at him. Had it worked?

'About time you bought a new one, then,' he said. 'The. Museum. Is. Closed.'

And the massive doors slammed in Elliot's face.

'What do we do now?!' hissed Virgo, consulting her notes for the heist as they retreated around a corner. 'My meticulous plan relied on us being inside the museum before it closed! I have to win the quest ... What are we going to do?'

'Not sure,' said Elliot, looking around for another way inside. He was going to get that Air Stone. 'How do you break into a museum?'

'*Take the first left, then continue for twenty metres,*' said a muffled female voice from inside his satchel.

Elliot pulled the bag off his shoulder. There was a faint glow at the top, which brightened as he opened the flap. He rummaged around the depths of the bag until he pulled out Theseus's ball of string. It was shining bright gold.

'*Take the first left, then continue for twenty metres,*' chimed the voice again.

'That's Ariadne's voice,' said Hermes. 'She must have pre-programmed it. Nice one, babe.'

'*Beware speed cameras, roadworks and heartless*

237

heroes who ditch you on an island,' the voice continued. *'Proceed to the route.'*

The golden twine glowed and twitched in
Elliot's hands. A single golden thread poked out
from the tightly rolled ball, appeared to look
around and then dropped to the ground. It started
to wind along in the grass, signalling a thin golden
path around the side of the museum.

'Look – it's showing us the way!' said Virgo as
the thread disappeared around a corner. 'It's going
to help me conquer the maze! My quest is on!
Let's go!'

Elliot, Virgo and Hermes crept as quickly as
they could behind the twine, which led them
towards the rear of the great building.

'Caution: security guard at next junction,' whispered the voice. The group dived into a dark
recess just as a security guard rounded the corner.
As soon as his torchlight disappeared, they continued carefully along the golden path.

In a dark corner, the twine suddenly disappeared underground. Elliot let out a frustrated
groan.

'Mate!' Hermes shook his head. 'You have got
to be kidding me.'

'Where is it leading us?' asked Virgo. 'It appears
to be some manner of subterranean cave.'

'It's a drain,' said Elliot. 'We're going in through the sewer.'

'That doesn't sound so bad,' shrugged Virgo.

'It's not the sound that's the problem,' said Elliot.

'*Proceed through the poop for 150 metres,*' the twine instructed. '*Your destination is through the lavatory.*'

'Here you go, kids,' said Hermes, pulling three sets of plastic overalls and welly boots out of his bag. 'Epic boggy bosh-not.'

With his magical touch, Hermes tapped the drain, which immediately transformed into a small door. He pulled it open and he and Elliot were knocked backwards by the stench that assaulted their nostrils. Virgo remained untroubled.

'Can't you smell that?' Elliot retched.

'My sense of smell is perfectly optimal, thank you,' said Virgo, pulling on her overalls.

'Then why doesn't it bother you?' said Hermes. 'Not being funny, but this stinks worse than your jokes.'

'A true hero doesn't balk at the first sign of difficulty,' said Virgo grandly as she headed undaunted into the sewer. 'Besides, you forget, I have experience in these matters. I share a bathroom with Elliot. Hurry up!'

After possibly the most disgusting ten minutes of his life, Elliot emerged behind Hermes, Virgo and the golden twine into a dark bathroom inside the Natural History Museum. He yanked off his stinking overalls and heaved violently into the toilet Hermes had moved to allow them to climb out from the sewer.

'*You have reached your destination,*' said the twine. '*Have a safe onward journey. Unless you're Theseus, in which case I hope you die slowly. Happy travels.*'

'That was gross,' said Elliot as the string wound itself back into a ball and ceased to glow.

'Welcome to my world,' said Virgo. 'Come on – we're not there yet. We need to find the Vault.'

They crept out of the bathroom and into a huge, dark hall. Virgo picked up a map.

'This is Hintze Hall,' said Virgo. 'The Vault is therefore . . .'

'That way, you idiot,' whispered Elliot, pointing to a huge sign directing them upstairs. 'Why do you need that?'

'There is no such thing as too much information,' said Virgo.

'I'll remember that next time you want to show me what you found in your belly button,' said Elliot.

He glanced up and saw a giant blue-whale skeleton hanging overhead, looking as if it were ready to dive from the ceiling.

'Cool,' he said as they ran up the staircase to the balcony up above. 'This place is—'

'Stop right there!' yelled an angry voice. Elliot nearly jumped out of his skin to join the nearby skeletons. He was blinded by a torch shining in his face.

'What do you think you're doing?' It was the security guard from the front door.

'Uh – looking for my umbrella?' said Elliot hopefully.

'Do me a favour, sunshine,' said the security guard. 'The moths in the education centre were born yesterday. I wasn't. You three, come with me. I'm calling the police.'

Elliot panicked. A royal pardon was all well and good, but he hadn't managed to commit the crime yet. He needed that Air Stone.

While ideas pinged around his brain, he heard Jason's lyre strike up a mellow tune from within his bag.

'Not now!' he whispered.

'What's that?' said the security guard, flashing his light in Elliot's eyes again.

'Er . . . just my – ringtone,' said Elliot.

241

'Well, switch it off,' said the guard, stifling a small yawn. 'We need to . . . excuse me.'

He let out a big yawn.

'Right – let's get on with . . . Blimey,' he said, stretching his arms and giving a second huge yawn. 'Long day.'

Elliot pulled the lyre out of his bag. It was playing a soothing lullaby.

'Cor – dunno what's come over me,' said the security guard, his eyes lolling. He plopped down on a bench. 'I'll just . . . er . . . rest me . . . y'know.'

'Shhhh – there you go,' said Hermes, pulling a pillow and a teddy bear out of his bag. 'You have a lovely kip, mate. Don't worry about us.'

'Maybe just for five . . .' said the security guard, before an enormous snore erupted from his lips. He was sound asleep.

Elliot, Hermes and Virgo scampered quietly along the balcony. Every time they passed a member of the security team, they found that the magic lyre had cast its spell – they too were fast asleep, snoring, sleep-talking or sucking their thumbs. A signpost directed them left into a long side gallery.

'Wow,' Elliot gasped. Between the square pillars lining the room, large oak cases housed thousands of geological specimens, gemstones and minerals. There were enormous lumps of rock, sparkling with mineral deposits, huge nuggets of gold, meteorites, and loads of . . . Elliot didn't know what they were. But they were awesome.

'What is this place?' asked Virgo, gazing at the rows of colourful specimens.

'The Mineral Gallery,' Elliot read.

'These were all made by the Earth?' exclaimed Virgo. 'Extraordinary! How can a realm capable of such exquisite natural beauty also produce Brussels sprouts?'

'Mate, not being funny – but there it is!' Hermes whispered, pointing to the far end of the gallery.

There on the back wall were thick metal double doors, with THE VAULT written in big black lettering above them.

With a quick backwards glance, Elliot, Virgo and Hermes ran the length of the Mineral Gallery until they reached the massive doors. Hermes tried to transform them. They were locked tight.

'Not gonna happen,' he said. 'Mortals aren't daft – something's stopping my powers.'

'According to my research,' said Virgo, consulting her notes, 'the Vault is protected by an advanced hi-tech security system.'

'You're not wrong,' said Hermes. 'They've made these immune to magic. They're locked tighter than my dad's underpants.'

'Noooo!' squealed Virgo. 'We have to get in! I have to fulfil the quest! I have to get my kardia back … Oh, and keep the mortals safe, etcetera …'

Elliot sighed. Being a jewel thief was rubbish. His mind flickered to his dad. Had Dave Hooper got a thrill from his robbery? Elliot couldn't see the fun in it. His hand clasped the watch in his pocket.

The watch.

A thought flashed into Elliot's head. Wasn't one of Hephaestus's modifications …?

He pulled the watch from his pocket and held it to the security doors with trembling fingers. He turned the winder until it reached 'safe-cracking', then pressed the button down. He closed his eyes. He really needed this to work, it was their only …

As soon as the watch touched the metal, a series of clicks and clunks started up inside the doors. The three friends looked at each other with bated breath. Could the watch really unlock the Vault?

Their question was answered as the doors

quietly slid open. The flashing alarm lights around the room froze. The Vault was theirs.

'Woah,' whispered Elliot as the white room revealed its treasures to the intruders. There were precious gemstones, a priceless snuff box, even a piece of rock from Mars.

But there, straight in front of them, was the Air Stone.

It hit Elliot like a slap. It was huge, a massive hexagonal lump – an emerald the size of a teapot. The display cabinet lit it up from the inside, but the Air Stone didn't need any illumination. It glowed with its own magical splendour. Elliot had never wanted to possess something so much in his life.

They approached the glass case that displayed the mighty gem.

'So how do we get it out?' Virgo asked. She began pacing the floor as she considered the options. 'Perhaps we could wish the glass away with the wishing pearl. Or did Aphrodite give you a potion that could prove helpful? Or perhaps—'

SMASH!

Elliot and Virgo snapped their heads around to see Hermes standing in front of the broken display case with a hammer and a big grin.

'This method is also effective,' said Virgo.

Elliot crunched over the broken glass and stood before the Air Stone. He reached out. Like a magnet, it was drawing his hand towards it, glowing brighter as his fingers came closer, as if willing him to possess it. With the lightest of touches, Elliot made contact with the Air Stone. He immediately felt the same sensation he'd experienced with the Earth Stone. He could do anything. He could beat a Daemon. He could save the world.

Or you could cure Mum, said his dark voice triumphantly.

'Come on, mate,' said Hermes, looking back at the doors. 'We need to make like my leather trousers after Christmas dinner – and split.'

Elliot opened his father's watch to reveal the Earth Stone. The magical diamond was still beautiful. But the Air Stone would make it look even better. He slowly brought the watch to the emerald.

The moment the Air Stone made contact, it started to tremble, shrinking in a green glow until it magically filled a quarter of the watch cover. Elliot looked at his two Chaos Stones. They were stunning. And he could only imagine the power they had together.

'Banging,' said Hermes, snapping the watch closed. 'Let's motor.'

They darted through the Mineral Gallery and back towards Hintze Hall.

'I've done it!' squealed Virgo. 'I've won my quest! I will have my kardia! I will have my immortality! I will have my beautiful silver hair!'

'Shhhhh!' said Elliot. 'We're not safe yet.'

'Of course we are. My plan was flawless . . .'

'*Your* plan?' hissed Elliot.

'And I must say,' Virgo replied, 'winning my quest wasn't nearly as challenging as I expected. Perhaps being a hero isn't so . . .'

A nearby light suddenly extinguished. And then the one next to it. And the next . . . The hall grew as dark as a shadow as every light around the room flicked off.

'Who's doing that?' asked Virgo, looking around the empty museum.

'Dunno, babe,' said Hermes cautiously, instinctively grabbing both children. 'But let's be on the safe side . . .'

He fluttered up, holding Elliot and Virgo, and flew them quickly down the stairs.

'OK,' said Hermes, flying inches over the ground towards the doors. 'Time to—'

'Leaving so soon?' said a lone figure, emerging

from the darkness and blocking their escape. Elliot drew an unsteady breath as a single moonbeam illuminated the intruder.

'Hello, Elliot,' said Thanatos with a smile. 'Good to see you again.'

24. Fight at the Museum

'Thanatos!' said Hermes, moving in front of Elliot. 'Not being funny – but what the daemonic unbosh are you doing here?'

'Oh – just a spot of sightseeing,' said Thanatos. 'You were in my sights and I wanted to see what you were doing. Besides – Elliot and I had such a lovely time yesterday . . .'

'You spent time with Elliot yesterday?' scoffed Virgo. 'That is highly illogical. Elliot would be insane to . . .'

Elliot could feel her gaze on his downturned head. 'It's . . .' he started.

'It's all right, mate,' said Hermes. 'No biggie.'

'So, got any good souvenirs?' said Thanatos. 'Fossil fridge magnet? Fluffy dinosaur? Given the hour, I'm guessing that either there's a sleepover I wasn't aware of ... or you've just found one of my Chaos Stones.'

'Yeah. Banging as it is to chat with you, mate – time for us to rock,' said Hermes, taking a mighty leap into the air with Elliot and Virgo.

'I really wouldn't do that if I were you,' warned Thanatos.

'Yeah, well – with all respect and everything,' said Hermes, whizzing towards the museum doors, 'I don't give a—'

The doors suddenly blasted open in a plume of black smoke, the explosion sending Hermes into a spin and tossing Elliot and Virgo across the floor of Hintze Hall.

'Don't worry,' whispered Hermes, flying down beside them and taking up his position in front of them. 'I got this ... What do you want, Thanatos?'

'Oh, I think you know perfectly well what I want,' smiled the Daemon. 'I want my Chaos Stones back.'

'Well, Armani want me to model next season's underwear,' said Hermes. 'Looks like you're both gonna be disappointed.'

'Elliot?' said Thanatos, taking a menacing step

towards him. 'Have you had a moment to consider my deal?'

'Nice try,' said Hermes, putting his arms in front of Elliot. 'But you can't touch him.'

'This is true,' said Thanatos. He gestured behind them. 'So I've brought a little assistance. I've believe you've met . . .'

Elliot turned around as the plume of smoke funnelled to the ground. It cleared from the floor up, forming a pair of talons, a pair of jet-black wings . . . and the smiling face of . . .

' . . . my mother,' drawled Thanatos.

'Hello, Elliot,' said Nyx, stalking towards him with Hypnos's sleep trumpet, the tips of her wings reaching towards him like long, dark fingers. 'It's not nice to take things from other people. Those stones belong to my son. Give. Them. Back.'

Elliot took a step backwards – but Virgo's firm hand on his arm reminded him that Thanatos was approaching from the opposite direction. They were trapped.

With a terrifying grin, Nyx unfurled her wings and leapt up. She hovered in the air front of them, her black wings outstretched, like a scorched angel.

'Well, if you won't give them to me,' she said, raising her talons to snatch her prey, 'I'll just have to—

A deafening groan rang out through the hall. Elliot clasped his hands over his ears and looked up at the ceiling to find the source of the air-shattering noise. He couldn't believe his eyes . . .

Swimming elegantly through the air was the enormous blue-whale skeleton. Following his gaze, Nyx also looked up, just in time to see the almighty skeleton dive down from the ceiling with its jaws gaping . . .

'Mate!' said Hermes, riding on the back of the whale, his magical touch bringing it to life. 'Seriously! Run!'

'Come on!' Elliot shouted to Virgo, grabbing her arm just as the whale plunged at Nyx. The Goddess of the Night tried to fly out of its path, but the skeleton was too quick. With one almighty gulp of its vast jawbone, it swallowed her, before crashing to the floor with an almighty crack, knocking Thanatos sideways and trapping Nyx in a bone prison.

'Elliot!' shouted Thanatos. 'Stop, I just want to talk to you—'

Elliot raced towards two archways at the far end of the hall. He turned to check on Hermes – the Messenger God was whizzing around the room, dodging blasts from Hypnos's trumpet as Nyx tried to wrestle her way free from the whale's skeleton. But Thanatos was already on his feet.

'Go left!' cried Virgo, shaking her hand free of Elliot's.

'How do you know?' said Elliot, heading that way.

'Because some of us picked up a map,' said Virgo smugly, pulling the piece of paper from her pocket.

'There's nowhere to run, Elliot!' cried Thanatos behind them. 'I will catch you.'

'Down there!' shouted Virgo. They ran through a cafe, towards a corridor where a large turtle was hanging from the ceiling and reptilian exhibits stared at them from the glass cases on either side. They reached a turning to the left and to the right.

'Which way?' said Elliot desperately.

'One moment . . .' said Virgo, turning the map around. 'I'm just working out the optimal escape route . . .'

'Well, hurry up,' said Elliot, snatching the map from her. 'Thanatos will be here any—'

'There you are,' said Thanatos, slamming a hand down on Virgo's shoulder. 'Now let's all just calm down and have a little chat . . .'

At the Daemon's touch, Virgo suddenly took a

gasping breath.

'Virgo?' said Elliot. 'Are you . . . ?'

But Virgo couldn't speak. Elliot watched her grow sickeningly pale as the life force was sucked from her mortal body by the touch of the Daemon of Death. He faltered and panic rose in his chest. Last time Thanatos touched the immortal Virgo, he could only hurt her. This time, Elliot knew he could kill her.

'Let her go,' he said shakily.

'First,' said Thanatos, not moving, 'we have a few things to discuss . . .'

'Not until you let her go,' said Elliot more forcefully. He could hear Hermes and Nyx shouting in the hall.

'She's free to go anytime she likes,' said Thanatos. 'I am not restraining her in any way.'

Elliot looked at Virgo's gasping body as she collapsed to her knees.

'So I have all the time in the world for our little chit-chat,' said Thanatos, looking down at her. 'But I think our friend here would appreciate us hurrying it along a bit. Now, about my Chaos Stones . . .'

'E – move it!' shouted a voice behind it. 'She's coming . . .'

With a rush of air, Hermes swooped through

the corridor. But as he flew along, he touched each glass case, muttering mystical words. At the sound of his voice, the exhibits slowly creaked to life.

'What are you—?' Thanatos began, releasing his deathly grip on Virgo as the corridor started to fill with turtles, lizards and a particularly excitable crocodile.

'Thanatos!' shouted Hermes, picking up a huge snake. 'Catch!'

He threw the massive serpent and it coiled instinctively around the Daemon's body.

'Child!' screeched Nyx from the hallway. 'I'm coming for you . . .'

'I'll try to hold her!' yelled Hermes. 'Shift it!'

'Come on!' said Elliot, gathering Virgo up from the floor, as Thanatos wrestled with the enormous snake. The lyre started to play some thumping drum and bass music.

'Go left!' Virgo groaned as the life-blood returned to her face.

They ran down a long, empty corridor, the sounds of the battle between Hermes and Nyx ringing through the museum.

'Where now?' shouted Elliot as they reached a turning.

'Straight ahead,' panted Virgo, pointing to a set

of white double doors.

'That's a dead end!' said Elliot.

'That's the lavatory,' said Virgo, consulting her map. 'It's been hours, I'm absolutely bursting ...'

'Elliot!' Thanatos boomed down the corridor behind them. 'Elliot — I'm starting to lose patience ...'

'Over here!' said Elliot, dragging Virgo into a big hall marked 'Mammals'.

'Elliot — look out!' exclaimed Virgo, pushing them behind a door as Hermes hurtled past them, hotly pursued by Nyx. The Messenger God flew low around the hall, animating the huge mammal exhibits. Nyx, hot on his feathered heels, was about to catch him when a herd of stampeding rhinos knocked her to the ground and trampled her.

'We need to move faster,' Elliot hissed. He saw a brown horse in a nearby display case and had an idea.

'Hermes!' he yelled. 'Over here!'

The Messenger God zoomed over and touched the display case.

'Gotcha, mate!' said Hermes as the glass magically vanished. The horse stepped out into the hallway. Elliot quickly patted his nose, before clinging on to his mane and swinging up on to the horse's back. He used to ride bareback with his mum on the farm and his body slipped quickly into the happy memory of riding these beautiful creatures.

Nyx was still struggling to get to her feet beneath the rhinos. She spied Elliot across the hall.

'There you are!' she screeched. 'I'm coming for—'

She was silenced by a stampede of the giraffe family.

'Hermes!' shouted Virgo, narrowly avoiding an antelope. 'I'll need a steed too!'

'Totes, babe!' said Hermes, doing a second circuit of the hall and bringing the next exhibit to life. 'Bosh!'

'Eey-ore,' brayed the furry donkey. Virgo looked aghast, but got on.

'Let's go,' said Elliot, spurring his horse on and riding bravely through zebra, buffalo, wildebeest and an enormous warthog in the Mammal Hall.

'Stop!' shouted Virgo suddenly.

Elliot turned, expecting Virgo to be in Thanatos's fatal grip once again.

She was pressing the buttons on the Massive Mammal exhibit.

'Apparently, a blue whale is 175 times my

weight! Isn't that fascinating?'

'Elliot!' shouted Thanatos, appearing from behind a school of flying dolphins. 'Come back here!'

'This way!' shouted Virgo, leading the way into a darkened room.

'Is this a good hiding place?' whispered Elliot.

'No idea,' said Virgo, flicking on the lights. 'But it sounded like a marvellous gift shop . . . Perhaps a rubber lizard would show my gratitude to the Council for giving my kardia back . . .'

Elliot heard Hermes and Nyx and a cacophony of animal noises behind them. They exited the gift shop and charged on, dodging armadillos, lions, tigers and a friendly chimpanzee that jumped on to Virgo's back. They emerged into a big hallway, just as the chimp stole Virgo's map and scampered away.

'I don't know where to go!' said Virgo, looking down the long corridor.

'Let's try in here,' said Elliot, dismounting from his horse and creeping into a dark side room.

'Right,' whispered Elliot. 'Let's hide. He'll never find us h—'

'RRRRROOOOOAAAAAARRRRR!'

Elliot turned to see an almighty T-Rex rearing up behind them.

'I thought dinosaurs were extinct!' cried Virgo.

'Well, we're gonna join them if we don't get out of here – run!' shouted Elliot.

They bolted in different directions through the dinosaur exhibit.

'Virgo!' shouted Elliot, as a velociraptor nipped at his toes. 'Where are you?'

'Over here!' cried Virgo from somewhere.

Elliot jumped over barriers and dived under displays as the T-Rex crashed through the hall behind him, destroying everything in its path.

Elliot saw a light up ahead shining through a glass door.

'Virgo!' he yelled again, but this time received no answer. With a frustrated shout, Elliot burst through the door and found himself back in Hintze Hall. He spun around to see the T-Rex lumbering closer, closer, closer . . .

With an almighty roar, the dinosaur charged at the door – and promptly knocked itself out on the stone wall above it.

'No wonder you lot died out,' said Elliot, shaking his head.

He looked around the hall. It was completely empty.

'Virgo?' he whispered into the echoing space. 'Hermes? Are you guys—'

Without warning, he was suddenly snatched up into the air. He looked up, expecting to see the kindly face of Hermes. Instead, the green eyes of Nyx were glaring down at him.

'Gotcha,' she hissed, soaring up to the high roof of Hintze Hall. 'Let's see how well your friends can protect you now!'

Nyx dangled Elliot precariously from a single talon and extracted the watch from his pocket with another.

'Give that back!' said Elliot, swiping for his watch and nearly losing his grip.

'Now,' her discordant voice sang out. 'You need to tell me where my idiot son hid the other Chaos Stones . . .'

'Get stuffed,' yelled Elliot, desperately clinging on to her talon.

'All right,' she said. 'Let's try this another way. The drop from here might not kill you. But it will break most of the bones in your body. Up to you, of course. I'll give you to the count of one . . .'

'Bruv?' a voice whispered through the hall. 'Do you trust me?'

Nyx whipped her head around, but Hermes was nowhere to be seen.

'Two . . .'

'You know what to do,' said Hermes. 'I've got ya, bruv.'

Elliot looked down at the tiled floor. This was gonna hurt. He took a deep breath.

'Thr—'

Before Nyx could finish, Elliot lunged for the watch, yanked his arm free of her talon and hurtled towards the floor. What had seemed such a vast distance from up high felt a lot shorter as he plunged headlong. He braced himself. Where was Her—?

'BOOOOOOM!'

A familiar pair of arms caught Elliot in their strong embrace and flew him safely to the floor. The Messenger God winked at his friend.

'I'll always catch you, bruv,' he smiled, before shouting up at Nyx, 'Oh, babe. You couldn't catch a cold!'

Hermes whizzed a few victory laps around the hall, waggling his bottom at Nyx.

'Or a fish in a barrel!'

Elliot watched Nyx hover behind Hermes, her face distorted by a twisted grin. What was she . . . ?

Hermes continued his taunts with a small airborne victory dance.

'I'm not being funny, babe. But Nyx – you

couldn't catch . . .'

Doof!

Hermes went totally silent, his face frozen in an empty grin as a small curl of black smoke wafted up behind him.

'Hermes!' Elliot cried as the Messenger God fell to the floor and crumpled into his arms. 'What's—'

Standing triumphantly behind him, brandishing Hypnos's sleep trumpet, was Thanatos.

'No!' Elliot shouted, shaking his friend. It was no use. Hermes was out cold.

Nyx cackled with glee as Elliot dragged him behind a pillar.

'Hermes!' he cried. 'Hermes – wake up!'

'Oh, he won't wake up for days,' said Thanatos as Nyx landed beside him and took the trumpet. 'And by the time he does, it will be far too late. Or will it? I'll give you one more chance. Where are my stones?'

'Tell him,' said Nyx, holding up the trumpet.

'Not a chance,' said Elliot.

'I don't know how you've been brought up,' said Nyx, 'but in my household, when Mother asks you to do something, you do it.'

'If I'm asleep, I can't tell you where the stones are,' said Elliot.

'True,' said Nyx. 'But I have a feeling after I've taken you to the Underworld and tortured you for a while, you might wake up a bit chattier. Tell him.'

'Don't make this so hard for everyone, Elliot,' urged Thanatos. 'My deal still stands. Just tell me where they are. I can help you. You and your mother. Let me give you what you really want.'

Elliot tried to silence the dark voice screaming in his consciousness.

Do it, it said. *Get the life you deserve. Get Mum back.*

Elliot stared at the Daemon. He couldn't tell him. Could he?

'No,' said Elliot weakly.

'Suit yourself,' sighed Nyx, bringing the trumpet to her lips. 'Boys always do things the hard way. Goodnight, Elliot.'

She took a giant breath. Elliot winced as he awaited the blow.

Before Nyx could take her shot, the silence in the hall was shattered by an almighty rumble, shaking the floor and bringing exhibits crashing to the ground.

'What the—?' snapped Nyx as the rumble grew louder.

'Troops!' cried a familiar voice. 'Attack!'

In a heartbeat, the hall was filled with all the animated exhibits of the Natural History Museum, led by Virgo astride her donkey. A flock of angry birds attacked Nyx with beak and claw, while Thanatos was beset by swarm after swarm of insects.

Dinosaurs, mammals, reptiles and a vicious armadillo charged at the Daemons. Nyx turned her trumpet on the animals, but no matter how hard she blasted them, they kept up their relentless march.

'They're dead! The trumpet doesn't work on them!' said Thanatos, kicking away a battalion of dung beetles. 'Do something!'

'Halt!' a voice shouted as a piercing light flooded the hall. 'Police!'

Blinded by the floodlight and deafened by Nyx's screeching, all Elliot could make out were the tiny red lasers of dozens of guns trained on Nyx and Thanatos.

'Stay right where you are!' shouted the policeman. 'There's no way out.'

'There's always a way out!' screeched Nyx, taking Thanatos into her arms and blasting up through the ceiling of the Natural History Museum. 'Until next time, Elliot . . .'

Elliot covered Hermes's body as the bullets

whizzed up through the brick dust and rubble towards Nyx. But it was no use. She was gone.

Elliot shook the comatose Hermes. He couldn't wake him up . . . *Wake up!* He grabbed his bag and quickly found Aphrodite's potions. He held Hermes's lips open and administered a huge dose of Aphrodite's Wake-Up Juice.

'Hermes! Hermes!' he whispered.

The Messenger God's eyes flickered open.

'Mate,' he groaned, rubbing his head. 'Epic anti-bosh.'

'You're under arrest,' shouted a policeman. Elliot threw his hands in the air. 'You have the right to remain silent.'

'Can I just say—' Virgo began.

'Shut up,' hissed Elliot.

Their friend the security guard wandered sleepily into the wrecked museum. He turned his head slowly around the hall, before snapping awake.

'All this!' he cried, pointing at Elliot. 'All this for a poxy umbrella!'

Two armed officers approached Elliot and Virgo. 'They're just kids,' said one to the other. 'Children – we're going to need to contact a responsible adult. Who should we call?'

'Um,' said Elliot, pulling the royal pardon out of

265

his bag and looking at the crowds of police now swarming all over the Natural History Museum. 'Does anyone have the number for Buckingham Palace?'

25. Busted

After a few hours persuading the Metropolitan Police that Elliot hadn't downloaded his royal pardon from the internet, followed by a timely phone call from Her Majesty, Elliot, Virgo and Hermes arrived back at Home Farm late on Wednesday night. They headed straight for the shed, where Zeus was pacing anxiously around the floor.

'You're home!' he boomed gratefully. 'So . . .'

'So . . .' grinned Elliot, pulling out his watch to reveal the two stones. 'We did it!'

He was nearly suffocated by a giant bear hug from the King of the Gods.

'My quest is won,' said Virgo quietly. 'That's it. I expect I'll be recalled to the Council any second.'

In this moment of triumph, Elliot was surprised that he didn't feel all that happy about the thought of life at Home Farm without Virgo. She was annoying. She was a pain in the butt. She was ... a girl. But he'd got kind of ... used to her. A quick look at her confused face made him wonder if she felt the same.

'Hermes – may I use your iGod?' she asked. 'I must inform them of this development at once.'

'Help yourself, babe.' Hermes yawned. 'I need to sleep this off – night, all.'

'Who's with Mum?' asked Elliot.

'She's with Athene,' said Zeus.

'No, she's not,' said Athene, coming into the barn. 'I had to prove I could juggle seven aubergines while counting to one thousand in Swedish for my assessment. Aphy took over ...'

'Until I had to unicycle across a tightrope while singing the Italian national anthem,' scowled the Love Goddess, stomping into the shed. 'But don't worry, I left a note for Heffer – he'll be with her. I expect they're in the front room watching that London property show she likes – *Overpriced, Over-budget, Over-a-kebab-shop.*'

'I'll go and say hi,' said Elliot, heading for the door.

'Oh, Elliot – before I forget,' said Athene, grabbing an envelope from her desk. 'This letter arrived for you this morning. I must say, your postman is most indiscreet. I think I know more about Mr Durrant's constipation than he does ...'

Elliot's whole body tingled. He recognized that writing.

'Thanks,' he said, practically snatching the letter and running outside into the paddock.

There was barely enough moonlight to read by, but Elliot tore open the envelope with quaking fingers and tried to concentrate on the trembling words.

My Beloved Boy,

Wow. Words can't describe how I felt receiving your letter today. I have read it so many times I worry I'll wear the words out – but just touching something that has come from you, knowing that you were thinking of me, makes this the most precious thing I have held since I last held you.

You say you have many questions – this must be a very confusing time. I supported Mum and Dad's wish that you weren't to know where I was, but please know that it has been torture not being able to talk to you, to see you, to help you these

past ten years. I haven't been there for you, Elliot, and you deserve to understand why.

Elliot steadied his nerves. He wasn't sure how much more truth he could handle. But there was no going back now.

My parents were wonderful people – I know they will have raised you to be a fine young man. But, of course, I didn't appreciate them, growing up. I was always something of a tearaway – living on a remote farm seemed so boring to me in my youth, so I went looking for my own entertainment. I'm not going to lie, Elliot. As a kid, I was a pain in the bum.

Elliot smiled. That sounded familiar.

But then your mother came along. From the moment I laid eyes on Josie, I'd found the rest of my life. When we were blessed with you, all I wanted to do was to make the best life for you both at Home Farm.

Dad was a great farmer and happy with his lot – too much so, I thought. I wanted to grow the farm and buy the surrounding fields. But your grandad was having none of it. He said the land was bad and would never grow crops. I was convinced I was right and went to the bank for a loan. But no bank in the world was going to lend money to a Hooper.

Thinking I knew better, I did something incredibly stupid. I borrowed money from Stanley Johnson, a local scumbag who gave big loans with no questions asked. What he asked instead was enormous interest — so huge, you never had a hope of meeting your payments. Dad was right. The land was bad. The money was wasted. Stanley's loan got bigger and bigger until there was no way I could ever pay it back.

Elliot sighed. Another massive loan causing problems for his parents. Financial planning was clearly not his family's strong point.

And that's when Johnson offered alternative means of repayment. At first it was small things — running errands, passing on messages. Then he wanted me to hide things for him — I guessed they were stolen, but I didn't want to know. Your grandad had plenty to say about that. And then . . . well, you can guess what he asked in the end. He wanted me to go with him to rob the lovely Kowalski family. You must think I should have told him to take a running jump. But let's just say that Stanley could be very persuasive.

You've no doubt heard what happened that night and must think me a terrible person. But you have to believe me, Elliot — I never meant to hurt anyone. Least of all poor Felix Simpson.

Felix — the librarian? Constable Simpson? Were they the same person? Was Felix the policeman his dad had shot? Why hadn't he told him?

There is so much more to tell you, Elliot, but I must go if this letter is to reach you for your birthday. I so hope it does — and that it is such a happy thirteenth birthday for you. Every year I go to

the prison chapel, light a candle for your special day and wish that one year I will be able to celebrate it with you.

I won't contact you again unless I hear from you. This is a huge amount to take in, and I understand if you and your mum want nothing to do with me. But Dad always said that the pen writes on. And while it does, I'll keep wishing on that candle.

With all my love – and please tell your mother how much I love her too,

Dad

Xxx

PS – I like eating too and always hated school. Ties are a bad idea, as is prison food.

Elliot folded the letter and released a slow breath. His dad wasn't a ruthless crook. He was a desperate man.

A desperate man who shot someone in cold blood, said his dark voice.

Elliot had a sudden urge to talk to Mum – perhaps if she read the letter, it might jog some memory, perhaps she could tell him some more?

As he walked towards the front door, he noticed smoke curling out from under the door. He smiled – Hephaestus must be cooking.

He pulled his keys out of his satchel and tried to push his doorkey into the lock. It wouldn't fit.

'Mum?' he called softly, struggling with his key. 'Mum?'

He choked slightly on the smoke. Mum must have locked the door from the inside. Her keys would be in the lock.

'Mum!' he shouted, knocking at the door. 'Mum! Hephaestus!'

'Elliot? How do?' said a familiar voice behind him.

Elliot spun around in horror. Standing next to him was Hephaestus. If he was out here – then who was . . . He started to hammer at the door.

'MUM!' he yelled, throwing his body at the door. 'MUM! She's stuck inside – I think there's a fire!'

'Stand back!' roared Zeus, unsheathing a thunderbolt as Athene and Aphrodite came running from the barn behind him.

Receiving an almighty zap for his efforts, Zeus hurled the thunderbolt at the oak door, blasting it apart.

'Elliot – wait,' said Athene. 'You don't know—'

But Elliot wasn't waiting for anything. He charged into the smoke-filled hallway, the Gods hard on his heels.

'Mum? Mum – where are you?!' cried Elliot as Athene raced to extinguish the pan that was on

fire in the kitchen.

'E – look!' cried Hermes. Water was cascading down the stairs. The pair of them ran up to the bathroom, where the overflowing bathtub was sloshing water all over the floor.

Elliot pushed back the tears as he choked on the smoke still filling the house. He burst through his mum's bedroom door. There was Mum, lying totally still on the bed. Was she ... ?

'Please,' he whispered tearfully. 'Please ...'

'Elly?' she said sleepily, wincing at the light invading the dark room. 'Is it time for breakfast?'

A tsunami of relief overwhelmed Elliot as he hugged his mum.

The Gods came bundling into her bedroom behind him.

'Where the blazes were you, Heffer?' shouted Zeus.

'I left you a note in the forge!' shrieked Aphrodite.

'Haven't been there all day,' said Hephaestus. 'I had a ... building project to work on.'

'Josie!' sighed Athene, running in and taking her in her arms. 'Thank heavens! I'll get the kettle on ...'

'Leave her alone!' hissed Elliot, pushing the Goddess away. He was beyond anger.

'I made you some supper and ran you a bath,' said Josie, sitting up with a smile. 'Did you enjoy them?'

'They were great, Mum,' said Elliot, scowling at the ashen-faced Gods. '*I'll* get you that cup of tea.'

Ten minutes later, Elliot returned to the black-ened kitchen, where the Gods were assessing the damage from the fire. He was trembling with rage. As soon as they saw him, the Goddesses ran over and embraced him.

'Elly – we are so, so sorry,' pleaded Aphrodite with tears in her eyes. 'We had no idea she was on her own.'

'It's completely unacceptable,' said Athene. 'We should be with her at all times, please accept our sincerest apologies, we are mortified.'

'I'm so sorry, young Elliot,' mumbled the blacksmith. 'I'll make this right, I swear it . . .'

Zeus looked mournfully at Elliot with his lined face. Elliot silently refused the apology.

'I just don't understand how you can—' Elliot began.

'Elliot?' said Josie angrily, running into the kitchen. 'Where are the keys? I need to find my keys . . .'

'It's OK, Mum,' sighed Elliot impatiently.

'We've got the keys.'

'The keys – we must stop the bad man,' muttered Josie, hurrying into the hallway.

'Please, Elly,' begged Aphrodite. 'You have to trust us. We can keep you safe . . .'

'Like you kept Mum safe!' Elliot shouted.

The Gods looked shamefully at each other.

'The truth is that you're living in *my* house while I'm out there trying to find *your* Chaos Stones and you can't even be bothered to do the *one* thing I ask of you!'

'Elliot, that's not true,' said Zeus. 'We'd do anything for you and Josie . . .'

'Except the one thing I really need you to do!' shouted Elliot. 'You won't cure her!'

'Elliot, we can't cure her – no one can . . .' said Athene, reaching for him.

'You don't know that!' yelled Elliot, knocking her arm away. 'You don't know anything about her! You don't know anything about me! You don't—'

'Elly . . . we must find the keys!' shouted Josie, running back into the kitchen. 'Where have you put—'

A volcano of anger, pain and frustration erupted inside Elliot. He spun around to his mother.

276

'NO ONE HAS TAKEN YOUR STUPID KEYS, OK!' he shouted in Josie's face. 'SO JUST SHUT UP ABOUT THEM!'

The kitchen fell silent. Elliot's mother looked as though her son had punched her in the stomach. Tears welled up in her eyes and she started shaking uncontrollably.

'I . . . I . . . I'm sorry,' Josie sobbed, 'I just want to find my keys. We need to lock the door. We need to stay safe.'

'Elliot!' cried Athene, running to Josie's side.

'Everyone just . . . just . . . LEAVE ME ALONE!' shouted Elliot, snatching his satchel from the table and storming up to his bedroom.

26. Fallen Heroes

'**Y**ou should have told me, Felix!' Elliot raged in the Little Motbury library the next morning. 'You should have told me it was you!'

Virgo puffed up the stairs behind him. Running across a wet field chasing an angry mortal child was highly sub-optimal compared to constellation travel. If only the Council would send her kardia back – she must have left a dozen messages . . . Besides, it was all very well for the Gods to say that Elliot might listen to her, but she would've liked to have seen Zeus try to keep up.

'Hello, Elliot,' the librarian said calmly. 'Would

you like a cup of tea?'

'Hello, Felix,' said Virgo, rushing in. 'I'm afraid—'

'I don't want a cup of tea!' shouted Elliot. 'I want some answers!'

'Then perhaps you should ask some questions,' said Felix. 'Please. Take a seat.'

Virgo happily collapsed into the chair he placed before her.

Felix pulled up another chair and waited for Elliot to sit down. He stood defiantly. That boy was as stubborn as a middle-class mule. But eventually he slid into it.

'Thank you,' said Felix. 'Now, what would you like to know?'

'You were there!' said Elliot. 'You were there at the robbery! My dad shot you! Why didn't you say anything?'

'You had just discovered one difficult truth,' said Felix. 'I feared another one would distress you further. It appears I was correct.'

'What . . . when . . . how . . . ?' Elliot burbled.

Virgo had only gleaned snippets of information from a breathless Elliot as they ran towards the library, but the situation could be summarized roughly thus: Elliot's father was a butt-head, this gentleman Felix was a butt-head, all the Gods were particular butt-heads, should Virgo venture an opinion, she too would be a butt-head and Elliot was generally displeased with the universe and everyone in it, who were, broadly speaking, all butt-heads.

Virgo observed Elliot more closely. It appeared his eyes were starting to leak.

'You've had a big shock,' said Felix. 'Please let me make you that tea.'

Elliot wiped his face with his sleeve and nodded weakly. Felix poured two cups of tea from the pot on his desk.

'Thanks,' said Elliot sheepishly.

Virgo accepted hers politely. She had noted that tea was the standard mortal response to a crisis. Further investigation was needed to fully understand this beverage's powers.

'Perhaps it would help if I told you about that night from my perspective?' said Felix.

'OK,' said Elliot, taking a sip of his tea.

'Ten years ago, I was Little Motbury's policeman,' Felix began. 'I confess I found the life of a village bobby rather dull – so when a call came in about an armed robbery at Kowalski Gems, I was quite excited. Too excited, in fact – I charged in without back-up.'

Felix offered Elliot and Virgo a custard cream.

Biscuits also seemed to solve a great deal of mortal problems, Virgo reflected, but this she understood better.

'I was a younger man then and rather more brave – foolish, some might say,' Felix continued. 'I burst into the shop and wrestled Stanley Johnson to the floor, kicking his gun away. In my haste, I hadn't realized that your father was also there and armed with a shotgun.'

'So he shot you,' whispered Elliot, looking at the floor.

'Johnson screamed at him to shoot me, but your father hesitated,' Felix explained. 'Stanley wriggled out of my grasp and went for his gun – it was clear to us both that once he got his hands on a weapon, *he* would not hesitate to use it. I could see your father struggling as Stanley reached for his gun, so he did the only thing he could.'

'By shooting you?'

'I'd known your father since we were boys,' smiled Felix. 'He was quite the local Jack the Lad, but his heart was in the right place. Dave Hooper was a famous crack shot. If he'd wanted to kill me, he could have done so easily. The shot he took at my leg was enough to make Johnson believe he'd taken me out. Johnson saw his chance and ran away.'

'But the police caught my dad,' mumbled Elliot.

'When they arrived – fifteen minutes later,' said Felix.

Elliot stared at him. Virgo shared his confusion – that was highly illogical.

'Elliot, your father stayed with me,' said Felix. 'He bandaged me up, stopped the bleeding, remained by my side until help arrived. The same help that arrested him. He could have run and saved himself. But he chose to save me instead.'

'Why didn't you say something?' asked Elliot. 'Maybe he wouldn't have gone to prison.'

'Let's just say I was a little less . . . philosophical at the time,' said Felix. 'That night cost me my police career. For a long while I was in a lot of pain, physically and mentally. In time, I did what I could to help him. But, ultimately, your father shot a policeman. That's a serious crime.'

'I don't understand,' said Virgo through a mouthful of biscuit. 'Elliot's father caused you enormous pain and distress. The logical response would be considerable anger and possibly some swears. I have compiled a list if you require some . . .'

'I was angry for a while,' said Felix. 'But time

calms the heart. I have a son who, back then, was not much older than you two. The greatest joy of my life has been watching him grow. Your father has been denied your childhood. I can't imagine a worse punishment.'

Elliot sat in silence. Felix rose from his chair and opened a small drawer in his desk. He produced a letter.

'I received this from the parole board last week, informing me of your father's possible release,' Felix continued. 'They say he's been a model prisoner. Did you know he's taken a law degree during his time there?'

'Really?' said Elliot.

'Really,' said Felix. 'He tutors other inmates who didn't have the benefit of an education. He's really turned his life around. As have I. In a funny way, that night set us both on a different course. One that I hope will lead us both to happiness.'

'You wish him to be happy?' said Virgo. 'After what he did to you?'

'Elliot's father has paid his dues,' said Felix. 'He wrote to me from prison to apologize for what he did. It took me a while, but eventually I wrote back. We've been pen-pals ever since. I wrote to him only this week, in fact, to tell him I'd met his son – and what a fine young lad he was.'

'I don't understand,' said Elliot.

'Anger is a heavy burden, Elliot,' said Felix. 'It's exhausting to carry around. Forgiveness lets us put it down.'

'Forgiveness?' said Virgo. 'This is what Hercules sought. So this "forgiveness" allows you to cease being angry and return to a state of calm?'

'It does,' smiled Felix.

Virgo was impressed. Forgiveness was even more powerful than custard creams.

'Do you think I should let him come home?' Elliot asked.

'Only one person can answer that, Elliot,' said Felix. 'You need to talk to your mother.'

'I wish I could,' Elliot said quietly. He suddenly twitched strangely in his chair. Virgo pondered whether it was the arrival of inspiration, or merely lice.

'Thank you,' said Elliot, rising to leave. 'I'm sorry for what my dad did.'

'There's no apology needed from you – your father has done that many times over. You shouldn't regret a past you can't change,' said Felix. 'Focus on the future that you can. I found my peace a long time ago. I hope your father finds his. And most importantly, Elliot Hooper – I hope you can find yours.'

Felix opened his arms and embraced Elliot.

'Gracious,' said Virgo. 'This forgiveness is extraordinary. I will try to remember it next time you forget to flush.'

27. Caught in a Trap

Hephaestus had kept his eyes peeled for any sign of Mrs Horse's-Bum or Boil all morning. Whenever those dozy blighters dared to show their faces, he was ready for them – he'd spent all day yesterday building them a little surprise. Everyone was in a right mood with him – who reads a stupid note anyway? – but once they saw what he'd been doing, he'd be the hero of the hour.

But by lunchtime, there was still nothing. Perhaps the national idiot convention was in town and they'd got held up?

The Gods had told him not to take his eyes

off Josie while they cleaned up the damage to the farmhouse, so he peered in on the dear girl, who had been napping quietly in her chair the whole morning. Fast asleep. The blacksmith didn't know what all the fuss was about. This was a piece of cake.

Something twitching beyond the fence caught his eye. Checking Josie was still asleep, he crept outside with a smile. Show time.

With all the palaver of the last few days, Hephaestus hadn't mentioned his plan to Zeus. He couldn't wait to see the look on his boss's face when he got home and found Horse's-Bum and Boil suspended in a giant iron net. Zeus would have a thunderbolt with their names on it. That'd learn 'em.

The blacksmith listened at the gate, where he could hear his prey scuttling around.

'Right, you pair!' he said as he laid his hand on a nearby lever. 'Film this, you nosy beggars!'

With a great wrench he pulled the lever and stood back to admire his handiwork. A giant stone ball rolled down a slide, hitting a button at the bottom that sent a hammer shooting up to ring a bell. The swaying bell knocked over a weight, which flew through the air, hit a target dead centre and released the iron net over the bushes.

Hephaestus allowed himself a satisfied chortle as he opened the gate to catch his game. This was going to be—

'Elly!' Josie suddenly shouted from the door, her hair wild and her face frantic with worry. 'Where are you?'

'Don't worry, pet,' said Hephaestus, hobbling over to her. 'The boy's fine, gone off gallivanting with his pal.'

'The keys!' screamed Josie, coming out into the yard. 'You didn't lock the door!'

'I was just getting some fresh air, m'love,' soothed Hephaestus. 'We'll have everything ship-shape in one minute. Don't you fret, now.'

'Elly?' cried Josie, going back indoors. 'Where is my son!'

Hephaestus dithered – he should go after her – but unless he tied up his net, those two dingbats would get away. The Gods were in the house and he'd only be a moment. He was still pretty nippy for an old-timer. Whatever anyone else said.

He lurched as quickly as he could over to the net and pulled a second lever.

'Gotcha!' he cried as the net shot up into the tree above with a whistle. 'What the . . . ?'

Hephaestus looked at his catch. Where the two despicable dunderheads should have been was an angry badger and a rather confused rabbit.

'Snordlesnot!' yelled the blacksmith, lowering the net back to the ground. He was about to reset his trap when something else caught his eye. A tiny red light, shining over on the other side of the field. It was Horse's-Bum and Boil. And they were aiming their camera straight at him.

'Come over 'ere, you two!' yelled Hephaestus, watching the pair of them scamper off into the woods. 'I'll give you some footage all right . . .'

He looked back to the farmhouse. He'd only be a minute – once he'd caught up with Stupid and Stupider, he'd be straight back to Josie.

Hephaestus ran through the open gate, thinking of his boss's face when Zeus discovered he'd let those two dunderheads get their footage. If anyone was getting a thunderbolt, it was going to be him.

Especially as he forgot to shut the ruddy gate.

28. The Whole Truth

After a silent walk back across the fields, Elliot and Virgo arrived at Home Farm to find the Gods arguing around the kitchen table. At the sight of Elliot, they sprang apart.

'You're home,' said Athene. 'Thank goodness.'

'Please will you talk to us, Elliot?' said Zeus. 'There's nothing we can't straighten out with a natter.'

'Come and sit with us, Elly,' said Aphrodite. 'We only want to help.'

'I need to talk to Mum,' said Elliot.

The Gods looked at each other, but no one moved.

'Alone,' said Elliot firmly.

Zeus sighed and nodded to his children.

'We'll be in the shed, mate,' said Hermes, putting his hand on Elliot's shoulder as he led Virgo and his family out of the kitchen.

Elliot went to the front room, where Josie was watching the TV. He switched it off and sat next to her on the sofa.

'What are you doing?' she started, getting up from the sofa and pacing around the room. 'Have you watered the plants? You know what Grandad will say . . .'

Elliot calmly pulled his dad's watch out of his pocket and laid it on the table, setting the stop-watch to seven minutes. He rummaged in his satchel and pulled out the wishing pearl. He'd thought of doing this so many times. But he knew that he could only do it once, and that seven minutes would never be long enough. Today, it would just have to be.

Clasping it in his fist, Elliot whispered softly to the pearl.

'I wish,' he said slowly, 'to have my mum back.'

The pearl jingled in his hand. He turned to look at Josie, who suddenly stopped in the middle of the room. She slowly lifted her head and took a deep breath, looking around her as if for the first time.

'Mum?' said Elliot. 'Are you OK?'

Josie turned to her son and smiled. 'Never better,' she sighed happily. 'Hi, baby.'

'Hi, Mum,' he said tearfully. She was back.

Josie rushed over to the sofa, sat beside her son and held out her arms. Elliot collapsed into them, clinging to her as his body shuddered with sobs.

'Don't worry, my darling,' whispered Josie. 'Everything's going to be fine. There's nothing that love can't cure ...'

He sat up and looked into his mum's clear, untroubled face. He went to wipe his nose on his shirt, but found a tissue pressed gently into his hand.

'No snotty sleeves, thank you,' smiled Josie.

Elliot glanced over at the watch. Six minutes left.

'Mum, I need to talk to you,' he started slowly. 'About Dad.'

'Of course you do,' she said softly, stroking his cheek. 'You must be so confused.'

Elliot felt his heart surge as he looked into his mum's smiling eyes. 'I know what he did,' he said.

'There so much you don't know, Elly, so much I haven't told you ...'

'I still don't understand,' said Elliot. 'Why did he do it?'

'The same reason anyone does something wrong,' said Josie. 'Because they can't see another way.'

She wiped Elliot's tears and held his hands in hers.

'The night of the robbery, we were all having supper in the kitchen. Well, you were throwing yours on the floor – you were only two. Your dad was trying to get you to eat your carrots by distracting you with his watch – it worked every time.'

Elliot smiled. So he'd always loved that watch.

'Suddenly, Stanley Johnson bursts through the back door with one of his thugs – like all bullies, he never did anything alone,' scowled Josie. 'He says that he needs your dad to do a job for him, that it's time to repay his debts.'

Elliot glanced at the watch. Five minutes.

'What did Dad say?' he said.

'I can't tell you that,' smiled Josie. 'Let's just say it was a firm no.'

Elliot felt a surge of pride. If only he didn't know how this story ended.

'Stanley just stood there, smiling,' said Josie angrily. 'But next thing we know, the thug has grabbed you out of your high chair and is flying you around the room. I'm not going to lie, Elly. I launched myself at him like a mother tiger. I hope he still has the scratch marks.'

Elliot couldn't help but smile. His mum was so awesome.

'Stanley told your dad to reconsider, just as this idiot starts throwing you up and catching you,' said Josie, angry tears coming to her eyes. 'Says that he wouldn't want his friend to drop you. Says that he's a very bad man . . .'

Her voice trailed off as she let out a shaky breath.

'So your dad went with Stanley,' said Josie tearfully. 'That was the last time he was in this house. He made a terrible mistake and we all paid a terrible price. He never meant to hurt Felix . . . Your father's a wonderful man, Elliot. You have to believe that.'

Elliot looked at the watch again. Four minutes. Not enough . . . Josie followed his gaze.

'Before he went, he pressed that watch into my hand,' she said. 'He told me to give it to you when you were old enough. It was as if he knew he wasn't coming back. Then he kissed me, told me he loved us and was gone. And the worst part? It was all my fault . . .'

'What?! Your fault?' Elliot cried. 'Why would you think—'

'Stanley Johnson could never have got to you,' said Josie, 'if I'd only remembered . . .'

'Remembered what?' Elliot whispered.

Josie took a deep breath. 'If only I'd remembered to lock the door.'

Elliot's heart thundered in his chest. The keys. The door. She'd been trying to keep him safe. She always had.

'Dad wants to come home,' said Elliot slowly. 'Should I let him?'

Josie's eyes spilt over with fresh tears. 'I've wanted nothing else for ten years,' she cried. 'It's been so hard . . .'

Elliot fell into his mother's arms and the sadness poured out of their souls. His body heaved with heavy sobs as he felt Josie's tears run into his hair. Wordlessly, they cried. They cried for a lost past, they cried for a difficult present and they cried for an unknown future. After months of living their lives in different keys, Elliot and his mother were finally in perfect harmony.

The watch signalled three minutes. Josie started to sing softly into Elliot's hair.

'*Hush, little baby, don't say a word. Mama's gonna buy you a mockingbird.*'

A distant memory stirred from his younger years. She used to sing this to him when he was sad. She had such a beautiful voice.

'*And if that mockingbird don't sing, Mama's gonna buy you a diamond ring.*'

She sang until the tears dried and his body stopped shaking. She sang until the world turned the right way up. She sang until he was just a boy who needed his mum.

'Elly?' said Josie softly. 'I need to ask you something.'

Elliot checked the watch. Two minutes.

'Yes?'

Josie pulled him up and took Elliot's face in her hands. 'Elly – I need to know.'

'Know what?' asked Elliot, wiping his face.

'What's wrong with me, Elliot?'

Elliot's whole body clenched. 'Nothing, Mum – you're fine ...'

Josie smiled. 'We don't lie to each other, Elly,' she said. 'I'm not fine. I know it. Everything is so ... wrong. My head is full of something ... Life feels ... strange. Blurred. Scary. Like someone else has moved into my body. I don't feel like me.'

'You're going to be OK,' said Elliot. 'I'm going to take care of you.'

'I know you will, sweetheart,' said Josie. 'But

that's not your job. That should never be my son's job.'

He had less than a minute left with his mum. He was going to hold on to her for every second.

'Elliot,' whispered Josie.

'Yes, Mum,' said Elliot, holding her tighter.

'I need you to do something for me. Something important.'

'You should have told us about Elliot's father,' Athene said to Virgo as the Gods hurried back to the farmhouse.

'With respect, if I always told you every irregular thing Elliot did, we'd speak of nothing else,' said Virgo. 'And you'd certainly never use the lavatory after him. How can deploying the flushing mechanism be *that* hard?'

'We shouldn't have left them,' said Aphrodite. 'Josie has been so confused lately . . .'

'Yes, we should,' said Zeus. 'He needs her. More than he needs us right now.'

They arrived at the back door and walked quietly through the house to the front room. Elliot was lying on Josie-Mum's shoulder.

'When the time comes,' she said to her son. 'I really need you to . . .'

Zeus cleared his throat. 'Everything all right in

here?' he said. 'We were just—'

'Not now,' said Elliot, holding his hand up to Zeus – most impolitely, Virgo thought. 'Yes, Mum – what?'

'Who are these people?' said Josie.

'Don't worry about them, Mum, just talk to me,' said Elliot urgently, looking at the watch on the table. 'We don't have long . . .'

Josie-Mum rose from the sofa and confronted the Gods. She looked different, Virgo realized. Younger. Stronger. Scarier.

'You need to get out of here right now!' said Josie. 'This is my home and my son and you have no right—'

'It's OK, J-Hoops, it's us,' grinned Hermes. 'Your mates.'

'I'm not your mate! Get out of my house!' yelled Josie.

'Mum, please,' said Elliot, appearing highly distressed. 'They're fine. What did you want to tell me? We only have a few seconds . . .'

'It's OK, baby,' said Josie-Mum kindly, returning to Elliot on the sofa. 'I just need you to—'

A small bell rang on Elliot's watch. Josie-Mum immediately sprang up from the sofa and started running her hands through her hair as she paced around the room. Now Virgo recognized her.

'Where are the keys?' she cried, pushing Elliot away. 'We can't just let anyone in — where are the keys?'

Virgo watched Elliot's head drop into his hands. He looked as if the air had been sucked from his body. Josie-Mum was frantically pacing the room, turning over ornaments and throwing magazines off the table. Virgo felt an unpleasant sensation seep around her heart.

'Mum — it's OK,' Elliot said flatly. 'We've got the keys.'

'No, we haven't!' she shouted. 'Anyone can get in here — who are all these people? What are you doing in my house? Get out!'

'What did you do that for?' Elliot hissed at the Gods. 'I had her . . . I had her back . . .'

'We were worried,' said Athene. 'We just wanted to help . . .'

'You call this helping?' whispered Elliot, trying to take Josie-Mum's arm as she started throwing cushions from the chairs. 'Mum! Mum — you need to calm down. Everything's OK . . .'

'EVERYTHING IS NOT OK!' screamed Josie-Mum.

'It is, Mum,' said Elliot, trying to hold her hand. 'We're safe and well and everything is going to be—'

'LET GO OF ME!'

Josie-Mum yanked her arm away with huge force, striking Elliot hard around the face. He fell to the floor, holding his cheek.

'Wha—?' said Josie-Mum, running her hands through her hair.

'Elliot!' shouted Athene, diving towards him. 'Are you OK?'

'STAY AWAY FROM MY SON!' shouted Josie, pushing Athene aside to kneel beside Elliot.

Virgo looked to the other Gods for guidance on how to proceed, but they were apparently as paralysed as she.

Josie-Mum cradled Elliot in her arms and started rocking frantically. 'Elly? Who did this to you? Who hurt you? Shhhh, my darling, shhhh. Mummy's here now . . . *Hush, little baby . . . hush, baby . . . Mama's gonna buy . . . mocking rings . . .*'

Virgo tried to smile at her friend. But Elliot merely lay blankly in Josie-Mum's arms as she rocked him back and forth, the tears already drying on his dark red cheek.

Virgo quietly took out her *What's What*.

'How can I help?' she whispered into the parchment. But if an answer did appear, she couldn't read it. Her vision was too obscured by the multiple droplets of water gathering in her eyes.

Indeed, her eyesight was so sub-optimal at that moment that Virgo also couldn't see the small red recording light of a video camera shining through the window. Nor the triumphant smiles of Patricia Porshley-Plum and Boil as they shook hands on a job well done.

'Elly,' said Aphrodite, knocking on his door that evening. 'Elly, can I come in?'

Elliot lay on his bed, staring at the ceiling, as he had been doing for hours.

'Elly?' Aphrodite's pleading voice came again. 'Please?'

Elliot pulled himself slowly off the bed and walked towards the door. He caught his reflection in the mirror as he passed. His fingers ran over the red mark on his cheek. He opened the door to the Goddess of Love.

'Hi.' She smiled sympathetically. 'Some day, huh?'

'Some day,' said Elliot.

'Everyone's downstairs,' said Aphrodite. 'Come and sit with us.'

'How's Mum?' asked Elliot.

'She's fine – fast asleep now, everything's calm,' said Aphrodite. 'Please come down.'

'I don't really ...'

'Please,' pleaded Aphrodite, taking his hand. 'Athene's filled her cauldron with hot chocolate. It's not even that burnt.'

Elliot shrugged and followed the Goddess down to the kitchen, where all the Gods were assembled around the table.

'Where's Virgo?' he asked.

'Asleep,' said Athene. 'Since becoming an adolescent mortal, she constantly eats and sleeps.'

'And is always right,' said Elliot with a weak smile.

'Of course,' winked Zeus. 'Always. Can we get you anything?'

'No, thank you,' said Elliot. 'I shouldn't have shouted. I know it wasn't your fault. It was just . . .'

'We completely understand,' said Zeus. 'You have absolutely nothing to apologize for. But we do.'

'It's fine,' said Elliot.

Zeus looked nervously around his family. 'The thing is, old bean, we've been talking and we all feel—'

'*Some* of you feel,' said Hermes, unusually stiffly. 'I am totes not on board.'

'*Most* of us feel,' said Zeus, 'that we need to do a bit more to help your mum.'

Elliot's heart swelled up. 'You're going to cure her!' he said. 'I knew you could do it, I knew it! Let's go now, she won't mind if we wake her up ...'

Aphrodite's hand reached for Elliot's over the table. 'No,' she said gently. 'We can't do that.'

Elliot slowly withdrew his hand. 'You can't?' he said. 'Or you won't?'

'Mate!' shouted Hermes. 'No way!'

'If any of us had the power, don't you think we would have done it the moment we walked through your door?' gasped Aphrodite. 'We love you. We love Josie. We would never let you both suffer. Is that what you think?'

'I don't know what to think,' said Elliot quietly, sitting down.

Athene came and crouched down next to him, taking his hand in hers. 'This is an incredibly confusing time for you,' she said. 'You've been dealing with things that people four times your age would struggle with. You've done an incredible job looking after your mother. You're a wonderful, wonderful boy.'

'Thanks,' said Elliot weakly as Aphrodite took his other hand.

'And we will do anything we can to support you,' said the Goddess of Love. 'Absolutely anything.'

303

'All we're trying to say,' said Zeus, 'is that perhaps it's time your mum had some . . . other help. To make life easier for you both.'

'OK,' said Elliot eagerly. 'Who do you know? Do immortals have a medicine or something?'

'We don't,' said Zeus quietly. 'But mortal doctors might.'

The sentence hung in the air like a smouldering gunshot.

'Mortal doctors?' said Elliot finally. 'You want me to take her to the doctor?'

'We're just asking you to think about it, that's all,' said Aphrodite. 'They might be able to help you.'

'Help us?' said Elliot, standing up and shaking his hands free of the Goddesses. 'By taking her away? By taking me away? You think that's going to help us?'

'Boom! My point entirely,' huffed Hermes. 'J-Hoops belongs here with us. We can care for her better than total strangers.'

'That's not the only alternative,' snapped Athene.

'And we would never let that happen,' said Aphrodite. 'We're your family . . .'

'YOU AREN'T ANYTHING TO ME!' shouted Elliot. 'I DON'T HAVE A FAMILY. I

DON'T HAVE ANYONE!'

'That's just not true, Elliot,' said Zeus, coming over to him. 'You have us. You'll always have us.'

'Until you get your hands on the Chaos Stones!' said Elliot, yanking open his father's watch, revealing the Earth and Air Stones inside. 'You're just using me to get to these! Well, go on then! Take them! I don't even care any more!'

'Listen, mate,' said Hermes, flying over to him, 'you are way off-base. That's not it at all. Seriously.'

'It's *you* we want to help,' said Athene. 'We swear it.'

'You're so angry, Elly,' said Aphrodite. 'Please tell us what's wrong.'

'Everything!' shouted Elliot. 'Everything is wrong! I just want it to stop!'

'No one can do that,' said Zeus. 'The best we can do is help you to make the right choices for you. And for your mother.'

'So that's it, is it?' said Elliot. 'That's your "help"?'

'It's all we have,' said Zeus softly.

'Fine,' said Elliot, storming up the stairs. It was crystal clear to him now. If the Gods couldn't help him, he needed the one person who could.

In his room he rummaged through his satchel

until he found the piece of parchment Thanatos had given him in Tartarus. He grabbed a pen and scrawled all over it. He folded the parchment and threw his words out of the window. Elliot watched with ragged breaths as they twisted and turned up into the night sky.

Meet me at 4 am. at Stonehenge.
We have a deal.

29. The Mother of All Dilemmas

It had become normal for Virgo to get hungry in the middle of the night. This made perfect sense to her – in order for her to sleep for as long as she required, she needed fuel. Her research had told her that many of Earth's animals and all of its teenagers behaved in a similar fashion.

So in the depths of the night she was in the kitchen preparing a light snack of ham, cheese, lettuce, pickles and mayonnaise between two slices of bread – twice – when something caught her eye out of the window.

It was Elliot, fully dressed, heading out of the farm. Where was he going at this hour?

The Gods had stressed the importance of Elliot having time to himself to process a difficult few days. So she pulled on a coat and wellies and decided to follow him, in order to ensure he was quite alone.

With nothing to guide her but the light from Elliot's torch, Virgo struggled to keep sufficient distance to avoid discovery, while keeping close enough to see where he was going. At one point, Elliot appeared to sense he was being followed and turned around. Virgo ducked into the long grass to avoid detection. For the first time, she was grateful that her silver hair hadn't yet returned.

They came to the river and progressed silently along its bank. After a short distance, a familiar set of shapes loomed out of the gloom. They were at the stone circle – Stonehenge, the mortals called it. *Why on Earth—?*

'What are you doing here?' hissed Elliot, turning suddenly and shining the torch straight in her face. 'It's nearly four in the morning – go back to the farm!'

'Where are you going?'

'Nowhere – it's none of your business.'

Ah. The code.

'I will not,' huffed Virgo. 'And unless you tell

me where you're going, I'll go and inform the Gods that you—'

'Don't you dare,' seethed Elliot, lifting his fist sharply behind him.

Virgo felt a most unpleasant sensation, as if her heart were about to explode. She shielded her face with her arms as a strange squeal escaped her throat.

For a moment, nothing happened. She dared to peek out from her hands. Elliot had apparently seen a ghost.

'Virgo,' said Elliot shakily. 'I'm sorry – I would never . . .'

'Now, now, children – play nicely,' said a horribly familiar voice.

The Daemon of Death emerged from the shadows.

'Thanatos!' cried Virgo, grabbing Elliot's arm. 'Come on, Elliot – run!'

But Elliot stayed rooted to the spot.

'I told you,' he said quietly. 'Go home, this isn't your problem.'

'You heard the gentleman,' said Thanatos. 'Go.'

Virgo considered her options. If she remained, she would almost certainly be eliminated. She was unarmed, mortal and wearing pink pyjamas.

'Discretion is the better part of valour,'

Sagittarius had once told her. Broadly, she understood this to mean, 'Think before you do something sub-optimal'. She couldn't assist Elliot here. But she could help in another way.

'All right,' she said, withdrawing slowly from the stone circle. 'As you wish.'

She walked slowly across the field until she was out of sight, then ran as fast as she could back towards Home Farm.

'So here we are again,' said Thanatos. 'I can't say I care for your choice of venue.'

Elliot pulled his coat closer against the cold, dark air. He couldn't stop shivering. And not just because of the cold.

'Last time I came to your place, you tried to kill me with Lethe water,' he said. 'It didn't work out so well for me.'

'Fair point. But you trapped me beneath several tonnes of stalactites,' sighed Thanatos. 'So me neither.' The Daemon began to walk slowly around the stone circle.

'So you've decided to accept my offer?' he said. 'I'm delighted, of course.'

'First you heal Mum,' said Elliot. 'I want to see her, healthy and well. Then you get your stones.'

'I like to think I'm an efficient man,' said

Thanatos, continuing his slow circuit. 'So I predicted you would say that. In order to hasten our arrangement, I took the liberty of delivering my side of the bargain.'

'What do you mean?' said Elliot. 'How could you—?'

'Elliot?'

Elliot's breath caught in his throat. That sounded exactly like . . .

Josie stepped into the circle. She was smiling, alert, wearing fresh clothes . . . she looked as good as new.

'Mum?' gasped Elliot. 'How did you get here?'

'He did it, Elliot,' said Josie, smiling at Thanatos. 'He did it. He cured me.'

'What?' said Elliot, looking at his mother's untroubled face.

'I thought we had an arrangement,' said Thanatos. 'So when I found your mother wandering out of the gate – some care your friends take of her – I took her to my Daemons. She's as good as new.'

'It's done. Give him what he wants, Elliot,' beamed Josie, beckoning to him. 'Give him the stones, tell him where the others are and let's go home.'

Elliot ran towards his mother's outstretched

arms. It was true. Thanatos had given her back. She was—

'Stay right where you are, E,' said a voice above his head.

Elliot looked up into the dark night sky. Floating down to Earth was Hermes, with Elliot's satchel slung over his shoulder. And he was pointing Hercules's Hydra bow straight at Josie.

'I knew it!' Elliot shouted at Hermes. 'I knew I couldn't trust you!'

'Come, Elliot,' urged Josie. 'Please?'

'I'm telling you, E, stay put,' said Hermes, his eyes not moving from Josie's. 'That ain't your mum.'

A breathless Virgo panted up the hill.

'I might have known you'd betray me,' Elliot spat at her.

'You're not optimal, Elliot,' said Virgo quietly. 'You need help.'

Help. He hated that word.

'Come over here, Elliot,' said Josie. 'I can keep you safe.'

Elliot took a faltering step towards his mother.

'Just a few steps,' said Josie. 'Just a few steps and we'll have you safe.'

Elliot took another trance-like step. It was Mum. She was well again. They could have their

312

life back. They could have each other back. They'd finally have all those 'one days' . . .

'I'm sorry, mate,' said Hermes, drawing the bow. 'But I can't let you do this.'

'Elliot?' pleaded Virgo, running to his side. 'Come away. We're trying to help you.'

'I said LEAVE ME ALONE!' shouted Elliot, giving Virgo an almighty shove. The force of his anger sent her flying across the grass, straight into a nearby stone.

'Ow!' Virgo put a hand to her head. When she brought it back down, Elliot saw it was covered in blood.

'What . . . ?' she whispered.

'Virgo – I . . .' Elliot stammered.

'Who are you?' said Hermes to Josie. 'Babe. Tell me now, or – not being funny – I'm gonna fill your veins with Hydra blood.'

'What . . . I don't . . . Elliot?' said Josie.

'Drop the act,' said Hermes coldly.

'Stop it,' said Elliot. 'You're scaring her.'

'You can trust me, bruv,' said Hermes. 'I promise.'

'How touching,' said Thanatos. 'So you've told him about the prophecy? *The Daemon you place in the shackles of iron needs a young mortal child with the heart of a lion . . .*'

'What's he talking about?' said Elliot.

'*The child can't die from a terrible deed by the hands of the Daemon he generously freed . . .*'

'Oh, shuuut up,' scowled Hermes.

'*But now he could claim the power Death owns and conquer the world with the help of four stones . . .*'

'Conquer the world? What?' Elliot demanded.

'Nothing,' said Hermes, not taking his hate-filled eyes off Thanatos. 'Ignore him, mate.'

'Then ignore the truth!' said Thanatos. 'Ignore your destiny! They know, Elliot – they know how powerful you are! They know that with the stones you will be more powerful than them!'

'Elliot, he's trying to corrupt you – this is what Daemons do,' said Virgo groggily. 'Don't listen to him . . .'

'Corrupt him!' laughed Thanatos. 'I'm trying to enlighten him. After all, if it were my destiny to rule the world, I think I'd want to know.'

'Hermes?!' Elliot cried.

'It's complicated, mate . . .' said Hermes.

'Is it true?' Elliot asked the Messenger God. 'About the prophecy?'

Hermes looked desperately at his friend. 'Yeah,' he said. 'I'm sorry, mate. It is.'

'Why does everybody keep LYING TO ME!' raged Elliot, pulling out his watch and holding it over his head. The Earth and Air Stones stored in the watch started to glow, before shooting out their incandescent beams, twisting together to form a ray of sparkling green light.

'Yes, Elliot – yes!' said Thanatos. 'Use your powers! Use them to free yourself!'

'Elliot,' said Virgo nervously. 'You need to proceed with extreme caution . . .'

Elliot looked from Thanatos to his friends. Even he didn't know what he was going to do. This was an impossible choice. Just like his dad's.

No one moved an inch.

'Elliot. Mate. Listen to me,' said Hermes quietly. 'I get it, truly I do. You have every right to be mad. But this is not the way—'

'More lies!' roared Thanatos. 'Listen to me, Elliot. I speak the truth!'

'Here is the truth,' said Hermes. 'You belong at home with us and your mum. We'll take care of you, Elliot. I swear it on the Styx.'

'How can I trust you?' said Elliot. 'How can I trust a word anyone says?'

'Because we love you, mate,' said Hermes. 'We can protect you. You and J-Hoops. You need us.'

'You won't need them,' laughed Thanatos. 'You'll rule the world! You'll have power! You'll have control! You'll have . . .'

'You'll have me, Elliot,' said Josie.

'You'll have to the count of three,' said Hermes, turning his bow back on Josie. 'One . . .'

'No, please!' screamed Josie, running towards the Heel Stone. Hermes advanced with the weapon. 'Elliot!'

'Hermes!' shouted Elliot. 'You can't do this—'

'Two . . .' said Hermes, squinting down the arrow to take aim.

'Please, help me!' shouted Josie as Hermes drew back the bow.

'Three.'

Hermes loosed the arrow from the bow.

'NOOOOOOOO!' shouted Elliot, pointing the beam of light at the arrow. The Air Stone filled the night with a green blaze. 'BLOW!'

From nowhere, an almighty gust of wind blew through Stonehenge, nearly knocking everyone off their feet. Elliot watched the magical arrow slice through the air towards his mother, determined to find its mark despite the gale.

'BLOW!' he commanded, struggling to stand against the wind as the empowering force of the Chaos Stone surged through his body from the soles of his feet to the tips of his fingers. 'BLOW!'

The arrow started to slow and waver.

'BLOW!' said Elliot maniacally.

Inches from Josie's heart, the arrow stopped in

mid-air. The enchanted wind was too strong for it. At the last instant, it was blown off course, flying straight up into the air before looping back and seeking out a new target.

Hermes.

Overcome with rage, Elliot pointed the Air Stone at Hermes, directing the deadly arrow towards the Messenger God, who dropped the bow and held his hands up in surrender.

'You could have killed her!' shouted Elliot.

'Mate – if I'm wrong, you have every right,' yelled Hermes quickly, watching the arrow quiver at his chest. 'But before you do, ask her something. Something that no one else could possibly know.'

Elliot stared into Hermes's sincere face. He felt his anger begin to subside.

'Please, bruv,' said Hermes. 'Just ask.'

Elliot looked from Hermes to his mother. He needed to prove him wrong.

'Sing them our song,' he said at last.

'Which song, baby?' smiled Josie.

'You know the one,' he said.

'Elliot – I'm so confused,' said Josie pulling her hair. 'Who are these people?'

'You just said you were cured,' said Elliot, turning to face her. 'Mum? Just sing the song.'

'It's all such a blur, Elliot,' said Josie. 'I just don't . . .'

'Why do you keep calling me Elliot? You call me Elly . . . Mum?' said Elliot, staring more intently at the figure shuddering against the Heel Stone. He lowered the Air Stone. The Hydra arrow dropped to the grass. Hermes breathed a slow sigh of relief.

'Busted,' said Thanatos, and Josie's face immediately darkened with an evil grimace. She stood upright and stared defiantly at Elliot.

'You're not my mum,' he said.

'True,' said Thanatos as a dark cloud encircled Josie's body. 'But she is mine.'

When the dark cloud cleared, it revealed the fearsome figure of Nyx.

'Hello again,' she smiled. 'Elly.'

'You disgusting, filthy—' Elliot charged at Thanatos, but was repelled by the force that always prevented their touch. He scrambled to his feet, ready for another attack, but was quickly scooped up by Hermes.

'Don't play into their hands, mate,' said the Messenger God, grabbing Virgo and taking flight. 'Let's just get you home. They'll keep.'

'Put them down,' said Nyx behind them.

'Yeah, babe, whatevs,' said Hermes. 'See ya.'

'Hermes,' said Virgo, tugging on his sleeve. 'You might want to pay attention . . .'

'Elly?'

The cry fast-tracked to the part of Elliot's brain that told him his mum needed help. He turned back. There, shivering in the stone circle, was Mum. This time his heart knew it was her. His whole body froze.

'Given the nature of our negotiations thus far, you'll forgive me for taking out a small insurance policy this time,' said Thanatos.

'Elly?' said Josie. 'Elly, what's going on?'

'How did you . . . It's OK, Mum, everything's OK,' Elliot said as Hermes touched lightly back down.

'Your mother really will do anything for you,' said Thanatos, as a new plume of smoke surrounded Nyx. When it cleared, she was the exact replica of Elliot.

'Elly!' said Josie with a smile.

'Let's go to Stonehenge, Mum!' said Nyx with Elliot's voice. 'Let's go on a night-time adventure! Just come with me, Mum!'

Elliot felt as if he were going to faint. They'd got Mum. They'd won.

'Now,' said Nyx, reforming as herself and looking up into the sky as the darkness started to lift.

'I'm tired of this. Let's move it along.'

She picked up the bow and Hydra arrow and aimed it at Josie.

'You will hand over the stones. You will tell us where the other two are. Or you can kiss your mummy goodbye.'

Elliot held out the watch. 'Take them,' he said 'I'll tell you anything you want. Just, please, don't hurt her . . .'

He tried to remember where Hypnos said he'd hidden the Water Stone. It was a name he'd never heard . . .

Elliot looked desperately at Nyx and threw the watch towards her. It sailed through the cold night. Until Hermes caught it mid-air.

'Mate, you don't want to do that,' he said. 'Trust me. Even the darkest night – remember?'

'Oh, dear. You missed your chance,' said Nyx. 'As my sons will tell you – I don't make idle threats. Kiss Mummy goodbye!'

And she loosed the arrow from the bow.

'No!' cried Elliot as the enchanted arrow flew towards his trembling mother. He didn't have his Chaos Stones. There was nothing he could do. Time slowed and he could barely look. He waited for the arrow to strike . . .

'Remember the light!' cried Hermes as he

suddenly darted forward, throwing the watch back to Elliot.

Doof.

The Hydra arrow stopped. Right in the middle of Hermes's chest.

'Elly!' screamed Josie as Elliot ran to his friend.

'Hermes!' Elliot yelled, dropping to his knees and cradling Hermes. 'I'm so . . .'

'Oh, dear,' said Thanatos. 'It appears you're quite alone.'

'If you kill me,' said Elliot, standing in front of his mother, 'you'll never find out where the other stones are hidden.'

'Good point,' said Thanatos, signalling to Nyx.

The Goddess of the Night yanked the arrow out of Hermes and put it back in the bow, aiming it this time at Virgo.

'Let's try this one,' she cackled. 'There's no one to save her. Where are they?'

'Er . . . Elliot,' said Virgo shakily. 'I require some urgent assistance . . .'

Elliot's mind was spinning. The light? The light? What did Hermes mean, *Remember the light* . . . ?

Even the darkest night lights up, he heard Hermes say.

'I need light!' he suddenly shouted.

321

'No, Elliot,' said Virgo nervously as Nyx drew back the string. 'This is a parlous time to start smoking. The proven effects of nicotine are horrendously sub-optimal for mortal bodies ...'

'Not *a* light – light!' exclaimed Elliot. 'That's what stopped her at Buckingham Palace – and at the museum. She's the Goddess of the Night – she's allergic to light!'

Elliot closed his eyes and raised the emerald to the sky.

'Don't you dare ....!' shouted Thanatos.

'SHINE!' he yelled into the darkness.

At once, a fluorescent beam radiated from the Air Stone. A sword of light pierced the night and illuminated the stone circle with sunshine.

'Nooooo!' Nyx screamed, her feathers starting to singe. 'Desist!'

Elliot raised his other arm to shield his eyes. The light was so bright ... too bright. He lowered the stone slightly for fear of blinding himself. The light instantly grew dimmer.

The moment's respite was all Nyx needed. Between two heartbeats, the Goddess of the Night swooped over, snatched Thanatos and Hermes and soared high into the sky.

'Give him back!' Elliot commanded.

'You want him?' shrieked the Goddess of the Night as her feathers began to smoke. She ripped Elliot's satchel from the Messenger God and, with a yell, she released him from her grasp.

'Catch!'

Hermes's limp body hurtled towards the floor. Immortal or not, if he hit the ground, Elliot knew he would shatter into a million pieces. He dropped the Air Stone, immediately extinguishing the sunlight.

'Until next time,' screamed Nyx, blasting away with Thanatos in her talons. 'Good night!'

Elliot watched helplessly as Hermes dropped like a ragdoll.

'Quick!' said Virgo. 'Do something.'

But Elliot was powerless. Again.

Without warning, a great blast swooped through Stonehenge, knocking Elliot and Virgo off their feet.

'What was that?' Virgo groaned as she picked herself up.

Elliot scrambled to his knees with a sickening panic. Hermes must have hit the ground by now. Where was he?

But there was nothing there.

Another giant gust of air blasted overhead as a familiar voice boomed around the stone circle.

'I'll have to recommend that time-management course,' said Pegasus, who came to an elegant halt on the grass, the prostrate Hermes draped across his back. 'Looks like I got here in the nick of time.'

30. Council of War

'THIS. ENDS. NOW!'

Elliot winced as Zeus ripped the Zapper from his leg with sheer brute strength and slammed the remains down on the Zodiac Council's golden table, sending a booming echo around the glass chamber.

The King of the Gods was flanked by Athene and Aphrodite, their expressions as dark as their father's. Elliot and Virgo exchanged glances. This was going to get ugly.

'Your Highness,' Aquarius stammered, 'thank you for responding to our invitation at this difficult time. I appreciate you are upset . . .'

'Upset?!' roared Zeus. 'UPSET?! We warned you Thanatos was on the loose and you did NOTHING. He and Nyx launched an attack in plain mortal view, nearly killed Josie and Virgo, and my son ...'

Zeus's voice broke as he took a series of faltering breaths.

'Yes. How is Hermes?' asked Libra gently.

Zeus tried to answer, but the words wouldn't come.

'He's stable,' said Athene, shooting a worried look at her sister, whose eyes were brimming with tears.

'Has he regained consciousness?' asked Scorpio.

Athene took Aphrodite's hand. 'No,' she said solemnly. 'But it's only been two days. We're remaining hopeful.'

'Well, please let us know of anything we can do assist you,' said Pisces. 'And tell him that, given the circumstances, we are prepared to overlook his road traffic infringements. All 4,568 of them ...'

'Assist us?' cried Zeus. 'It's thanks to you that he's in this state!'

'Father,' said Athene, putting a soothing hand on her father's shoulder. 'That's not entirely fair ...'

'I'll tell you what's not fair!' roared Zeus.

'Because of your blind stupidity, we were sitting around picking our navels while my boy was risking his life for . . .'

Elliot bowed his head and swallowed down the lump in his throat. The Gods hadn't said as much. But he knew that secretly they must blame him.

Because it was all your fault, his dark voice whispered.

'Well, you'll be pleased to know that we have evaluated Lady Hera's report and have decided not to proceed with her recommendation that you are "locked away for the rest of your miserable existence with only your own bodily odour for company",' smiled Aquarius. 'Your powers are of course fully restored and all restrictions on your movement entirely lifted.'

'About time,' growled Aphrodite.

'The Council thanks you for your co-operation.'

Aquarius put down his clipboard and smiled contentedly.

'So that's it, is it?' said Zeus, quietly. Elliot instinctively looked for cover. He could feel a thunderbolt coming.

'Unless you have anything to add?' said Aquarius.

'Oh, I have something to add all right,' said

Zeus. 'But if this Council spent less time shuffling bally paperwork and more time actually doing something, I wouldn't have to! War is coming. We need heroes, not half-wits! We need courage, not clipboards! We need spears, not spreadsheets!'

A gasp went up around the room.

'How dare you!' bumbled Aquarius, shuffling papers frantically. 'This Council is a progressive organization that believes in dynamic action over corporate time-wasting! We learnt that at our Wilderness Circus Skills away-day!'

'Well, said!' said Sagittarius. 'I've a good mind to fill out form R67*(4-Aardvark), *Recording Displeasure on a Sunday*. Scorpio – make a note of that on my spreadsheet. There's a print-out on my clipboard.'

'Your Highness, are you actually suggesting,' said Libra, aghast, 'that this noble Council, which has successfully supported the immortal community for thousands of years in the wake of *your* retirement, isn't doing its job competently?'

'There's no suggesting about it,' boomed Zeus. 'When I handed my responsibilities over to you, it was in the hope that you would do anything to protect the mortal and immortal realms that we so loved. But it's abundantly clear that you're not fit for the task. So let me be very plain: Thanatos is back. But so are we. We're taking the fight to him. And I pity anyone who tries to stop us.'

Elliot barely dared breathe as the tension festered in the chamber, the Zodiac Council locked in a staring match with Zeus and his daughters.

Virgo gently cleared her throat. 'Er . . . sorry to interrupt,' she chimed, 'but seeing as I'm here anyway, I thought you may as well return my kardia to me now . . .'

'I'm sorry?' said Aquarius, breaking his death stare with Zeus.

'My kardia,' said Virgo, pointing to where the crystal necklace glistened in her former place at the table. 'Don't get up – I'll get it myself . . .'

'You'll do no such thing,' said Aquarius. 'You haven't earned it.'

'What?!' cried Virgo.

'Give it back to her. Now,' growled Zeus.

'I'm sorry, Your Highness,' said Cancer, consulting one of her leather books, 'but whatever powers you believe yourself to have, you have no jurisdiction here. Virgo is still an employee of this Council. Decisions regarding her future lie exclusively with us.'

'But – but – but . . . I did the quest!' burbled Virgo. 'I did an impossible task. I solved the maze.

I won the priceless artefact.'

'The Council feels that you did not fulfil the terms of our agreement to our satisfaction,' said Aquarius. 'Thanatos is still at large.'

'Not that we know anything about that,' added Pisces.

'Quite,' said Aquarius. 'But if we did, then the threat to the mortals remains. This hardly makes you a hero.'

'So you're asking me to be the other kind of hero ... but that's impossible ...' said Virgo.

'No hero ever became one easily,' said Sagittarius.

'It would be awful, terrible, risky . . .' said Virgo.

'Then that is what you must do,' said Taurus.

'So let me get this straight,' said Virgo. 'If I'm to be a true hero, I'm going to have to ...'

'Go on, child,' said Aquarius. 'Face your fears ...'

'I'm going to have to ... go on a reality-television contest!' said Virgo. 'But that's unthinkable!'

The Council stared blankly at their former colleague.

'I suggest you return to Earth and redouble your efforts,' said Aquarius, bringing his golden gavel down to declare the meeting over. 'Until you prove yourself a true hero, your kardia will remain here with us. Although if you did want to participate in *Immortals' Got Talent*, I'll happily lend you my Swiss cow bells and lederhosen.'

31. Candid Camera

Just over a week later, Elliot was back at Brysmore, trying to summon the will to live in Mr Boil's Monday morning double history lesson. Elliot had to give Boil one thing – he was certainly consistent. He was now halfway through his second year at Brysmore and every history lesson was just as boring as the last. Athene said that great historians could bring the past to life. Boil somehow killed it for the second time.

But Elliot had something else on his mind.

'What do you think this meeting with Call Me Graham is about?' he whispered to Virgo.

'Your woeful disregard for authority, education

and personal hygiene?' Virgo suggested.

'Nah,' said Elliot, shaking his head. 'It sounded like it was something new.'

'Hoopers!' shouted Boil as he wobbled into the classroom. 'Silence in my class!'

The headmaster's secretary, Maud, appeared at the door. There was a rumour that Maud used to play for the England women's rugby team, but Elliot didn't believe it. It was more likely she played for the men's.

'Excuse me, Mr Boil,' she boomed. 'The head-master is ready for you.'

'Excellent,' leered Boil. 'Hoopers! Follow me!'

'Er . . . sir?' said Elliot. 'You're coming too?'

Boil's face jiggled like stale custard. 'Yes,' he grinned. 'Proceed to the headmaster's office at once.'

Virgo and Elliot snatched worried glances at one another.

'Now!' snapped Boil.

'Did you put chilli powder in his coffee again?' whispered Virgo as they walked down the corridor.

'No,' said Elliot, making a note to do so soon.

'Silence!' roared Boil, pounding his fist on the door to the head's office.

'Aaaargh! Come in,' came Graham's weak reply.

Elliot could hear voices – one of them sounded exactly like . . . *No. It couldn't be. Why on Earth would*—?

'DUMPLING!' screeched Patricia Porshley-Plum as the door swung open. She gathered Elliot into her tweed-clad arms. He nearly choked on her perfume. It smelt like flower vomit.

'Ah, Elliot, Anna . . . Mr Boil – take a seat. This is Ms Givings. She's our school welfare officer.'

Elliot's heart froze.

'Who?' whispered Virgo out of the corner of her mouth.

'The person I've spent the last year trying to avoid,' Elliot whispered back.

A young, smiling, red-haired lady rose from her seat and gave Elliot and Virgo warm handshakes.

'Hi,' said Ms Givings. 'Great to meet you both.'

'You too,' said Elliot unconvincingly as he and Virgo took their seats.

'Now, Elliot,' said Call Me Graham, 'as you know, at Brysmore Grammar School staff take the welfare of our students extremely seriously.'

'Unless they dislike a child,' said Virgo. 'I've observed that they seem rather less concerned about those ones. Take Mr Boil, for example . . .'

'Be quiet, Girl Hooper!' roared Boil. 'Before I put you in detention until your funeral!'

'Ha-ha-ha-ha-ha-ha-ha!' stammered Graham, grinning nervously at Ms Givings. 'Little Anna Hooper and Mr Boil. Such jokers . . .'

'If I were joking,' Virgo continued, 'I'd be trying to persuade you that Napoleon kept his armies in his panties . . .'

'It's his armies in his sleevies, you freak . . .' Elliot whispered.

'Anyway, you two,' said Graham hastily. 'You know that we are here to help in any way we can. And we were wondering if you might need a little more help?'

Help. Elliot truly hated that word now.

'We're fine − thank you,' said Elliot, with the most convincing smile he could manage.

'Are you, though?' said Graham, his wet eyes full of concern. 'Really?'

'Really,' said Elliot. 'So if that's everything, sir . . .'

'Now come along, pigeon,' pouted Patricia with her monkey-bum mouth. 'You know how much I adore you and your family . . .'

'You tried to throw us out of our home,' glowered Elliot.

'The Hoopers were interested in developing their property portfolio,' Patricia whispered at a ridiculous volume. 'This little . . . lad struggled to adjust.'

The other adults nodded understandingly. Elliot resisted the urge to punch them all.

'As an old family friend, pumpkin,' Patricia continued, 'I just wanted to make sure you were getting the help you need. You know. With Josiekins . . .'

'Don't you dare say her name,' spat Elliot.

'Mrs Porshley-Plum has come to see me with some . . . concerns about your home life,' said Graham. 'And you can tell me anything. I won't say a word. You ask the school bursar. I've turned a blind eye to him using the petty cash to finance his Bentley for ages . . .'

'What Mr Sopweed is trying to say—' said Ms Givings.

'You can call me Graham,' whispered Graham.

'Er . . . thanks,' said Ms Givings. 'We want you to know this is a totally safe place. You're not in any trouble. Nothing you say here is going to cause problems for you. We're here to support you.'

'Thanks,' said Elliot. 'But we're fine. Really.'

Ms Givings and Graham exchanged a look that Elliot didn't quite understand but knew he didn't like.

'Elliot, Anna – if a member of the community has come forward with concerns about your welfare,' said Ms Givings, 'we have to take that very seriously. If you just answer our questions, I'm sure we can sort everything out.'

Elliot nodded reluctantly. Questions were the very last thing he needed.

'Could you explain to me how you two are related?' smiled Ms Givings.

'We. Are. Cousins,' said Virgo in her terrible lying voice.

'On whose side?' asked Ms Givings.

'My mother's,' said Elliot.

'His father's,' said Virgo simultaneously.

'I see,' said the welfare officer, making a note on her pad.

'It's complicated,' said Elliot, frantically faking his family tree. 'Our mothers are ... sisters and our fathers are ... brothers.'

He paused for a moment. Did that work?

'Right . . .' said Ms Givings, figuring it out herself. 'So two sisters married two brothers? How unusual!'

'Not in the country,' smiled Elliot with relief. 'Everyone marries everyone in Little Motbury.'

'But your uncle is American?' said Graham with a wrinkled nose.

'I thought he was Greek?' said Patricia with a joyless grin.

'Yes – yes, he is,' stumbled Elliot. 'He and my dad . . . moved around a lot. During the war.'

'Which war was that?' asked Ms Givings.

'Second World War?' said Elliot uncertainly, naming the only one he'd heard of. Had there been a third one yet?

'Gracious,' said Graham. 'That would make your uncle . . .'

'He's older than he looks,' said Virgo, obviously happy she could say something that was true.

'What about your mother?' Ms Givings asked Elliot with a piercing stare. 'I understand she is a . . . photographer?'

'Yes,' said Elliot. 'She's away a lot. That's why her family has moved in to help. So everything is under control.'

Patricia nodded to Boil, who produced the video camera and began connecting it to the television in the corner of the office.

'Now Mr Boil and I share a keen interest in . . . bird-watching,' said Patricia. 'Why – we were out twitching just the other day when we caught a glimpse of something deeply distressing . . . Mr Boil?'

'Absolutely,' leered Boil. 'Feast your eyes on this horrifying situation!'

He pressed Play on the camera and turned

towards Elliot to enjoy every moment of his torture.

Elliot's pulse quickened. What had they seen? He braced himself as the TV flickered to life. A truly awful image filled the screen. Everyone gasped. Boil grinned.

'Er – Mr B-boil?' stammered Call Me Graham. 'This appears to be a film of you in the shower . . .'

'You idiot!' hissed Patricia. 'You didn't press Record! This isn't a film of the Hoopers' house – it's yours.'

'What?' said Boil, spinning around to face the screen. 'But – but that's not possible . . .'

'Eurgh,' said Virgo, peering at the screen. 'Is shaving one's nose standard showering behaviour?'

'Nice pink shower cap, sir,' smirked Elliot.

'How do you switch this thing off?' said Boil quickly, turning the camera around.

'Is that music in the background?' laughed Elliot. 'Didn't have you down as a Beyoncé fan, sir.'

'She's a very versatile artist,' spat Boil, wrestling with the camera. 'Why won't this stop?!'

'How intriguing,' said Virgo, turning her head sideways. 'You're attempting one of her dances. Respectfully, Mr Boil – I don't think anyone's going to put a ring on that . . .'

'And you need to be careful with that towel,' said Elliot, wincing. 'If you're not careful it's going to—'

Silence fell. So did Mr Boil's towel.

'Enough!' said Boil, throwing the camera on the floor, smashing it to pieces. A few shards flew against the window, where Elliot was sure he could make out the figure of a certain immortal blacksmith lumbering off into the distance. He smiled. The Gods really did have his back.

'Well – fun as this has been,' said Elliot, rising to leave, 'I'd love to get back to double history.'

He strolled towards the door with a satisfied grin.

'Oh, Ellykins,' cooed Patricia in a tone that could freeze lava. 'Why don't you tell these lovely people about your daddy?'

Elliot's soul shook. He turned to look into Patricia's cold, unsmiling eyes.

'Yes, Elliot,' said Ms Givings. 'There's no mention of your father on your record. Do you have contact with him?'

'He's in prison!' shouted Boil triumphantly.

'He is?' exclaimed Graham. 'Elliot – you never said.'

'It's not what it sounds like . . .' said Elliot desperately. 'He's not a bad man, honest. He just made a mistake . . . He's been really good in prison . . . He might be coming home soon . . .'

Elliot wished he could suck the words back into his mouth. An ex-convict father. The welfare officer was bound to be interested in that.

'Will he be coming to live with you?' asked Ms Givings with a smile, writing on her notepad.

'I don't know . . . I mean, his parole could take ages . . . It's . . .'

'And how do you feel about that?'

'I – we – he . . .' Elliot babbled. This was a disaster.

Ms Givings nodded at Call Me Graham. 'It sounds like you're very well cared for by your family,' she said. 'And you're both doing very well at school.'

Elliot let out his tense breath. He'd got away with it. He gave Virgo a relieved smile. Boil and Patricia scowled.

'But we'd still like to pop round and talk to your mother.'

His blood seized in his veins as Patricia and Boil exchanged a sickening smile.

'No need,' said Elliot. 'Don't worry – I can call my aunt and uncle, they're always happy to come in . . .'

'No,' said Ms Givings firmly. 'We find it better

to talk to families in the home setting. That way we can get to know you properly. Away from school. Is that OK?'

Elliot tried to summon his heart back from his shoes. What else could he do?

'Sure,' he said with a weak smile.

'Great,' said Ms Givings. 'We'll schedule a visit as soon as possible. Absolutely nothing to worry about. We're just here to help.'

There it was again. Elliot vowed that if the Chaos Stones did allow him to rule the world, he'd banish the word 'help' from the face of the planet.

Later that day in Spendapenny, Patricia and Boil toasted their success with a can of Spendapenny Pop.

'Phase one complete,' belched Boil. 'The authorities will be all over Hooper like the warts between my toes. It's only a matter of time before he's taken into care.'

'They'll throw Josie into the loony bin and then Home Farm will be up for sale,' said Patricia. 'Not that it's any use to me without all my lovely money. Oh, how I miss being rich. I don't suppose you . . .?'

'On a teacher's salary?' said Boil. 'I can barely afford my special garden fence to electrocute the baby robins.'

'I'm so close,' whined Patricia. 'There must be a way to get my hands on some money quickly . . .'

'You could always try the lottery, dearie,' said Betty, tottering up to the counter. 'Maybe your luck's in?'

Patricia gulped down her disdain. She couldn't abide the lottery. Giving free money to people who'd done nothing to earn it – it was disgraceful. That reminded her – she needed to update her fake passport if she was to claim her second unemployment benefit this week.

'Could you check me numbers?' said Betty, producing a handful of lottery tickets. 'It was a triple mega-rollover at the weekend – £87.5 million! Just imagine all the dog food you could buy with that!'

'You'd spend all that money on your dog?' sneered Boil.

'Who said anything about a dog?' said Betty.

'Give them here,' said Patricia with a sigh. She scanned the first ticket into the machine and checked her screen.

No Match.

'How much do you spend on this rubbish every week?' asked Boil with distaste.

'Three pounds,' said Betty.

Patricia scanned the second ticket.

No Match.

'That's £156 a year!' said Boil. 'Imagine what you could do with that money!'

'Good point,' gasped Betty. 'I could buy a hundred and fifty-six lottery tickets.'

Patricia scanned the third ticket. Her machine started bleeping and her screen flashed frantically.

Jackpot winner! Call Lottery HQ immediately!

She gasped.

'What is it, dearie?' asked Betty.

'You've . . . you've won!' said Patricia.

'Oooooooooh!' squealed Betty. 'You see! I told you! Worth every penny!'

Patricia's heart leapt with icy delight. Betty had bought the winning lottery ticket. The piece of paper in her hand was worth £87.5 million. One phone call and Little Motbury would have its first millionaire.

'How much have I won?' asked Betty.

'Brace yourself . . .' said Patricia dramatically. 'You've won . . .'

'Yesssss?' gasped Betty.

'Ten whole pounds!'

Patricia pulled a single note from the till and handed it to the old lady.

'Yippeee!' squealed Betty with delight. 'I can eat tonight! The cat can eat tonight! I don't have to eat the cat tonight!'

'Congratulations, Betty!' said Patricia, yanking off her Spendapenny tabard. 'Enjoy your winnings.'

'Do you want me to throw those old tickets away?' asked Betty.

'That won't be necessary,' said Patricia, putting the winning lottery ticket in her purse and smiling at Boil. 'We're just leaving. I have an urgent phone call to make.'

Deep in the bowels of the Underworld, Nyx languished on Thanatos's throne, replacing the contents of Elliot's satchel with a triumphant laugh. She raised a glass to the sleeping Hypnos in the corner.

'I don't see what's so funny,' Thanatos rasped. 'We lost the boy and we have no idea where the stones are.'

'The stones will have to wait,' smiled Nyx. 'Our victory today was altogether different.'

'I'd hardly call that a victory.'

'You were right,' Nyx said slowly. 'The battle isn't for the boy's body. It's for his mind. Elliot

Hooper doesn't know who to trust. He is lost and confused. Exactly how we need him to be. Now we just need him to come to us. We need his weak spot. And I know exactly where to find it.'

'We've all failed to kill him,' snapped Thanatos. 'Even you.'

'Oh, my son,' said Nyx with a twisted smile. 'As you of all people should know – there's more than one way to die.' She took a deep drink from her cup and threw it across the cave. 'And now I know exactly what to do,' she said. '*This* is how we defeat Elliot Hooper . . .'

Thanatos's eyes widened as his mother revealed a plan so truly fiendish even he could never have imagined it.

'And you're sure that'll work?' he asked. 'We have to succeed.'

'I never fail,' said Nyx, unfurling her wings.

'Then it is done,' said Thanatos, raising an ebony cup to his mother. 'Victory will soon be ours. And nothing and no one can stop us.'

The two Daemons clinked their glasses and drank a deep toast, blissfully unaware that the third Daemon in the cave was just beginning to wake up.

32. Knock Knock

'I do not understand why I am consistently selected last in P.E. – I have a great deal of advice to offer either team,' said Virgo as she, Zeus, Athene and Elliot walked towards the shed at Home Farm that evening. 'Today has been highly sub-optimal.'

'You're not wrong,' said Elliot, whose mind had been whirring with ideas about how on Earth he was going to hide Mum's condition from Ms Givings.

'It's going to be OK,' said Zeus, putting his arm around Elliot's shoulders.

'How?' said Elliot.

'Because we are here to help you,' smiled Athene.

'Too bally right,' said Zeus. 'We'll think of something, don't you worry. Now let's go and pay Hermes a visit. Maybe today's the day.'

They walked into the shed where Hermes had been lying since Pegasus had brought him back from Stonehenge. Although Athene and Aphrodite had done a fantastic job of healing his visible wounds, he still hadn't woken up since that terrible night ten days previously.

'How is he?' Athene asked Aphrodite softly.

The Goddess of Love had barely moved from Hermes's bedside. Elliot looked at her tear-streaked face. It was heartbreaking. Beautiful, but heartbreaking.

'I thought his finger twitched this morning,' she said weakly.

'Well, that's progress,' smiled Zeus hopefully.

'Not really,' said Aphrodite, choking back tears. 'I showed him the *Fashion Victim* pictures in *Salve!* magazine. Dionysus was wearing tie-dye. He didn't even flicker.'

'Hi, bruv,' said Elliot quietly, fist-bumping the Messenger God's limp hand. Hermes's arm flopped off the bed. Elliot carefully tucked it back inside his blanket. This was all his fault.

Athene softly cleared her throat. 'I've been

thinking,' she said quietly. 'It's been over a week. We've tried everything. He's not going to get any better. I think it's time we accepted some difficult truths . . .'

'Don't you say it!' shouted Aphrodite. 'Don't you even think it!'

'Well, someone has to!' cried Athene, tears running down her face. 'We have to face up to it some time. He's never going to wake up!'

'We don't know that!' screamed Aphrodite.

'I think we do,' said Zeus quietly. 'We've done everything we can. Only his immortality is keeping him alive now. If you can call this living.'

'What are they talking about?' Elliot whispered to Virgo.

'No idea,' shrugged Virgo. 'But I have a feeling that this doesn't end well. Although it could be that fourth enchilada I had at lunch.'

Aphrodite grabbed her brother's hand. 'Please, Hermy,' she begged. 'Please give us a sign. Something. Anything to show you can hear us. Please.'

The Gods drew together around Hermes, hardly daring to breathe lest they missed some sign of life from the comatose figure before them.

The Messenger God lay completely still.

'This is not what he would want,' said Zeus

quietly, putting his hand on Aphrodite's shaking shoulder.

'We need to release him,' said Athene through heaving sobs. 'It's only right.'

'What do you mean?' asked Elliot. 'You said you couldn't heal him. You said you can't heal anybody.'

'We can't,' said Zeus, taking Athene's hand in his. 'But we can let him go.'

Virgo gasped quietly. 'You don't mean . . . ?' she said, putting her hand to her bare neck.

Zeus nodded, biting his lip. Athene slowly agreed.

'Aphy?' said Zeus to the Goddess of Love.

Elliot didn't understand. Where were they going to send Hermes? 'Will somebody please explain what is going on?' he said, feeling the familiar dread rise in his stomach.

'They're going to take his kardia off,' said Virgo almost inaudibly.

'But . . . that's . . . you can't . . . you just said!' shouted Elliot. 'His immortality is the only thing keeping him alive! If you take off his kardia, he'll . . .'

'If we take off his kardia, his soul will be reborn in the afterlife,' said Zeus. 'If we don't, he'll stay like this for all eternity. It wouldn't be fair.'

'You can't do that!' shouted Elliot, looking desperately for support from one of his friends. 'You can't just . . . kill him. Tell them, Aphrodite! Tell them to stop! Don't let them do this!'

Aphrodite slowly lifted her tear-stained face. She looked at her brother, lying as still and pale as the grave, then at Elliot's distressed face. Slowly, she nodded her head too.

'We have to let him go,' she choked. 'Anything else would be selfish.'

'I can't believe you're just going to turn your backs on him!' raged Elliot through his tears. 'I can't believe that you're giving up on him! What if he gets better? What if he's going to wake up? What if this has all just been a mistake? What if . . .'

Zeus pulled Elliot into his massive arms and let his mortal friend's tears run down his arm. Elliot sobbed into his shoulder.

'He needs you,' Elliot whispered between his tears. 'You love him.'

'He does and we do,' said Zeus, holding Elliot tighter. 'And sometimes that means doing what's hardest.'

Zeus turned to his daughters, who were comforting Virgo in their arms. 'So we're all agreed, then,' he said.

Aphrodite and Athene nodded. Zeus took a ragged breath, tears streaming down his lined face. He pulled his shoulders back and smiled at his family.

'Then let's get our boy ready for his final trip.'

Later that night, Elliot, Virgo and the Gods gathered outside the cowshed around Hermes's candlelit body. Hercules, Theseus and Jason had joined them to bid Hermes farewell, parachuting down from the stunt plane Hercules told them he'd organized for the wake.

It was a solemn gathering. Everyone stood in silence as the flickering light danced across their tear-stained faces. Dark storm clouds gathered above.

'I put him in his favourite shirt,' said Aphrodite, wiping her eyes. 'He always said it made his abs look "banging".'

'The *Argus* is going to publish a special tribute edition,' sniffed Athene. 'All twenty pages will be devoted to *Hermes's Timeless Fashions Through the Ages*. It's what he would have wanted.'

'I've written a song for the occasion,' said Jason, pulling out his lyre. 'It's an up-tempo number called *See You in the Next Life . . . Maybe*. Shall I—?'

'No!' said everyone simultaneously.

Zeus held out his hands to his family, who in turn held Elliot's and Virgo's hands, while the heroes kept a respectful distance. Hephaestus cleared his throat.

'Never did understand 'alf of what you said,' said the blacksmith quietly. 'You got a right funny way o' talkin'. But it didn't matter none. I always understood what you did. 'Cos it was always good. Safe travels, friend. Mind how you go.'

'Goodbye, my beautiful brother,' sobbed Athene. 'Your outer beauty reflected the inner. A star as bright as you will shine for ever. We will always carry you in our hearts.'

'We love you, Hermy,' cried Aphrodite. 'You put the fab in fabulous, the brill in brilliant and the bosh in . . . bosh. You are a one-off designer original. Big kisses.'

'Toodle pip, old chap,' said Zeus in a broken voice. 'You couldn't have made your old dad any prouder. You're a hero, son. Not. Even. Joking.'

With shaking hands, Zeus reached towards the kardia around Hermes's neck.

Elliot couldn't bear it any longer.

'Wait!' he cried, putting his arm over Zeus's. 'I just want – I just want – I just want to say . . . Thank you. Thank you for being my friend. Thank you for making me laugh. Thank you for showing me the sunrise. You really were my . . . bruv.'

Athene pulled Elliot and a sobbing Virgo into her arms.

Zeus crouched down beside his son. 'Let's get rid of this old thing,' he whispered tearfully in Hermes's ear as he reached for his son's kardia. 'It's totes last season.'

Zeus went to unfasten the golden chain from his son's neck. He held the golden heart and flame in his hand.

'Goodnight, son,' he said. 'Sleep—'

'*Hush, little baby, don't you cry . . .*'

Elliot and the immortals turned slowly. Josie was walking towards them, singing.

'Mum?' said Elliot through his tears.

'*Mama's gonna sing you a lullaby . . .*'

Josie knelt beside Hermes and took his head in her hands.

'*Hush, little baby, don't say a word,*' Josie continued, gently stroking Hermes's face. '*Mama's gonna buy you a mocking bird.*'

'Look!' gasped Aphrodite. 'He's smiling!'

'*And if that mocking bird don't sing, Mama's gonna buy you a diamond ring.*'

They all stared at Hermes. Aphrodite was right. His previously pained face had softened into a calm smile. He moaned slightly.

'He – he's still with us!' cried Athene. 'There's still hope.'

Josie sang on, filling the dark night with her beautiful voice. Hermes took a deep breath and lolled his head happily in Josie's hands.

'*So hush, little baby, don't you cry,*' sang Josie, smiling at Elliot. '*Daddy still loves you and so do I.*'

She softly kissed Hermes's head.

'Don't worry, my darling,' she whispered in Hermes's ear, cradling him in her arms as the Gods gently embraced her. 'Everything's going to be fine. There's nothing that love can't cure.'

The Gods tucked Hermes back into his bed. He was still unconscious, but at least now he looked as if he were having a peaceful sleep, rather than hovering on the brink of death.

With the Messenger God safe and snug, everyone just made it back to the farmhouse before the storm broke. Within seconds, the kitchen was full of fantastic cooking smells as Athene transformed random bits of food into a sumptuous, unburnt feast.

Everyone sat around the table as course after delicious course appeared, while the storm raged outside. Before long, everyone was in fits at

Hermes's greatest adventures.

'And then,' said Hercules, wiping the tears of laughter from his eyes, 'he said, "Mate, I don't care how many countries you've invaded. That hairstyle is war crime enough for me!" I nearly slayed a Hydra!'

Everyone around the table collapsed with laughter. Even Hephaestus snorted.

'This is more like it,' said Zeus, smiling warmly at Elliot. 'Every day should be a celebration.'

'And there is much to celebrate,' said Athene. 'We have the Air Stone.'

'We have each other,' said Aphrodite, hugging Josie.

'We have seconds,' said Zeus, plopping his third helping of mash on to his plate.

'You know what you need,' hiccoughed Hercules, his face a little rosy from the nectar he'd been drinking by the pint. 'For Hermes, I mean. You need a dose of . . . Oh, what's it called . . . I heard about it during my labours . . . It'll come to me . . .'

Virgo turned quietly to Elliot as the Gods raised their glasses of nectar to Hermes.

'Elliot,' she began. 'I would just like to say that I am pleased you haven't yet died a horrible death.'

'That could be the nicest thing you've ever said

to me,' said Elliot.

'In order to illustrate my thoughts, I have written you this letter,' said Virgo, handing him an envelope. 'It explains how I truly feel.'

Elliot felt a bit queasy. Statistically, this was going to be totally gross.

'Open it,' urged Virgo. 'Please.'

Elliot gingerly lifted a corner of the envelope. He seriously did not want to open this letter.

But before he could, the envelope flew out of his hands and burst into a cloud of confetti above the table, making everyone jump. As the cloud dispersed, a message hung in the air in colourful letters:

FLUSH THE TOILET!

Everyone exploded with laughter. Aphrodite winked at Virgo, who looked around with a satisfied smile.

'This was an excellent joke, yes?'

Elliot had to give it to her. He held up his palm for a high five. Virgo hesitated, then handed him a spoon.

Elliot sighed. Virgo still had a lot to learn.

'It's on the tip of my tongue,' slurred Hercules, throwing an arm around Jason's slender shoulders.

'C'mon – you know the thing I mean . . . it solves everything . . .'

'Death?' said Jason.

'Tell me, old boy,' said Zeus quietly to Elliot as the rest of the party returned to their happy chat. 'Have you decided what you're going to do? About your father?'

'I think so,' said Elliot.

'Good show,' said Zeus with a smile.

Elliot was grateful Zeus didn't push him to commit either way. Even he wasn't 100 per cent sure what he was going to say to his dad.

'You'll make the right choice. You always do,' Zeus added.

Elliot's heart fluttered as he thought about the choice Thanatos had offered him: was the offer still open? His mum's health for the four Chaos stones . . . Could he really be relied upon to make the right decision? There was only one way to be sure.

'Zeus,' he began uncertainly. 'There's something I need to—'

'Panacea's potion!' Hercules boomed suddenly. 'That's the stuff!'

'Panacotta's what, now?' spat Theseus through a mouth of the roast beef he was carving. 'What are you talking about, you blithering buffoon?'

'Panacea,' Hercules spelt out. 'The Goddess of Cures. Before she disappeared, I heard she perfected a potion that could cure all known ills.'

All ills? thought Elliot as his heartbeat doubled. *Including mortal ones?*

'It's just a myth,' said Athene dismissively. 'It doesn't exist. No one has been able to find it – nor her, for that matter.'

'Where is she?' asked Virgo.

Elliot tried to stay calm. He could forget Thanatos. This potion – this was the answer for Mum, he just knew it.

'She vanished,' whispered Hercules dramatically. 'Hounded from the world by men seeking the cure to their maladies . . .'

'I heard she was secretly rejuvenating former boy bands,' said Aphrodite.

'Panacea's potion doesn't exist,' said Athene firmly. 'We need to find another cure for Hermes. And we will.'

But Elliot wasn't listening. He knew in his bones that the potion was out there. His mind was made up. He was going to find Panacea and get some of her potion. He was going to heal Mum and Hermes. And no one had to get hurt. He smiled to himself. Zeus was right. He could be relied upon to make the right choice.

'What were you saying, old boy?' asked Zeus.

'Nothing,' smiled Elliot, tucking happily into his roast beef.

Amongst all the happy hubbub around the table, only Elliot heard the knock at the door. Not wanting to disturb the celebratory mood – nor alert Hephaestus to the fact that someone had left the ruddy gate open again – he made his way to the front door. The rain lashed the glass in the darkness, obscuring the face on the other side.

Elliot twisted the door handle, and an enormous gust of wind blew him against the hall dresser as the door slammed back on its hinges.

'Elly!' cried Aphrodite, running out into the hallway. 'Are you OK?'

'I think so,' said Elliot, pulling himself up off the floor as everyone came out to investigate the noise.

A glass smashed behind them and Josie screamed. Trembling uncontrollably, she pointed at the man at the door.

'You're here!' she said incredulously as the visitor removed his rain hood, revealing his face.

Elliot tried to focus his blurry vision from the blow to his head. It must have been a big bang. The man looked exactly like . . .

'I'm sorry, I don't think we've had the pleasure,'

said Zeus tentatively, standing in front of his family and extending his hand. 'And you are . . . ?'

'Home,' said the visitor, taking Zeus's hand with a broad grin and a twinkle in the blue-green eyes that matched Elliot's own. 'Hello, Elliot.'

But Elliot couldn't speak – his jaw felt frozen to the floor. He stared at the man again. It couldn't be . . .

'It's good to see you, son,' smiled Dave Hooper. 'Now come and give your old dad a hug.'

THE END

(Or is it . . . ?)

What's What

ELLIOT HOOPER

Category: **Mortal**

Realm: **Earth**

Powers: 1) **Current guardian of Earth Stone** 2) **Belching**

This unremarkable twelve-year-old boy has been prophecised to rule the world should he acquire the remaining Chaos Stones. Currently resides with Josie-Mum (optimal?) and the Olympians at Home Farm, Wiltshire. Curiously unwashed.

VIRGO

Category: **Constellation (suspended)/Mortal (temporary?)**

Realm: **Earth (formerly Elysium)**

Powers: 1) **Constellation travel (suspended)** 2) **Stationery supplies**

A former member of the Zodiac Council, Virgo is awaiting trial for gross misconduct and being something of a doughnut. Companion to ELLIOT, whether he wants her or not.

ZEUS

Category: **Olympian, King of the Gods (retired)**

Realm: **Earth (wherever licensed for weddings)**

Powers: 1) **Omnipotent former ruler of creation** 2) **Wedding planning and cancellation**

His Majesty the King of the Gods has been enjoying retirement, and multiple marriages, for over 2,000 years. Previously believed to have vanquished THANATOS, recent information suggests that his pants are, in fact, on fire.

HERMES

Category: **Olympian, Messenger God**

Realm: **Various (excl. Underworld)**

Powers: **1) Flight 2) Bosh (definition unknown)**

One of few working Olympians, Hermes has retained his role delivering information around the immortal community. His responsibilities include communication, transformation and style icon (self-appointed).

ATHENE

Category: **Olympian, Goddess of Wisdom**

Realm: **Earth**

Powers: **1) Vast knowledge 2) Transformational powers 3) Handicrafts**

Currently working as an esteemed Professor at St Brainiac College, Oxford, Athene has also enjoyed success on several mortal TV quiz shows. Can create any substance from another, but refuses to work with loom bands.

APHRODITE

Category: **Olympian, Goddess of Love**

Realm: **Earth**

Powers: **1) Ability to make anyone fall in love 2) She's just lovely . . .**

The proprietor of Eros dating agency, Aphrodite exerts a powerful draw over everyone who meets her. This may be due to her immortal powers, or possibly the fact she's a drop-dead gorgeous hottie. I love you, Aphrodite.

HEPHAESTUS

Category: Olympian, God of the Forge

Realm: Earth

Powers: Invention (esp. swear words)

The Gods' go-to man for gadgets and gizmos, Hephaestus can fix or build anything. A man of few words, most of them 'Snordlesnot'.

PEGASUS

Category: Elemental, but considers himself Olympian

Realm: Earth (usually above)

Powers: 1) Flight 2) Crosswords

The transport of choice for ZEUS, Pegasus is a flying horse with a sky-high opinion of himself.

THANATOS

Category: Daemon (of Death), King of Daemons

Realm: Underworld

Powers: 1) Strength 2) Touch of death (mortals only)

Previously believed dead, Thanatos recently escaped from his prison beneath Stonehenge. Determined to regain his Chaos Stones, Thanatos intends to cull mortalkind with natural disasters, then rule over them. Enjoys golf.

HYPNOS

Category: Daemon (of Sleep)

Realm: Earth

Powers: 1) Sleep, nightmares, insomnia, sleepwalking (with ivory trumpet) 2) Gambling

Older twin of THANATOS, Hypnos evaded imprisonment with all other Daemons by betraying his brother to ZEUS. Only being who knows location of Chaos Stones, which he hid at Zeus's behest. Currently missing.

CHARON

Category: **Neutral, immortal ferryman**

Realm: **All**

Powers: **1) Transport 2) Entrepreneur**

The founder of Quick Styx Cabs, Charon can transport immortals to any realm (restrictions allowing) via the Ship of Death on the River Styx. Also available for grocery delivery, courier work and children's parties.

CERBERUS

Category: **Elemental**

Realm: **Underworld**

Powers: **Security**

The three-headed hound of hell is responsible for security in TARTARUS. Also, for financing his extensive family.

PATRICIA PORSHLEY-PLUM

Category: **Mortal**

Realm: **Earth (whereabouts unknown)**

Powers: **1) Deception 2) Lying 3) Fraud 4) Theft 5) Embezzlement 6) Arson 7) Twin-sets**

Former neighbour of ELLIOT, Mrs Porshley-Plum is determined to acquire his abode of Home Farm to develop the land for personal profit. Seems untroubled by usual mortal concerns of kindness, generosity and not being a horse's bum.

MR BOIL

Category: **Mortal**

Realm: **Earth**

Powers: **1) Education (unconfirmed) 2) Weapons-grade bodily odour**

History teacher to ELLIOT, Mr Boil's chosen career is sub-optimal due to loathing of mortal children. Exudes a powerful aroma believed to be vegetable-based.

GRAHAM SOPWEED

Category: **Mortal (but you can Call Me Graham)**

Realm: **Earth**

Powers: **Unclear**

The headmaster of Brysmore Grammar School. It has yet to be established what Mr Sopweed's purpose is in mortal life.

———————————

Places

ELYSIUM

Heavenly home of Zodiac Council. Not accessible to Elementals.

EARTH

Mortal realm. Very dirty.

ASPHODEL FIELDS

Formerly destination of aimless souls. Now shopping centre.

UNDERWORLD

Daemon realm. Also home to TARTARUS, eternal prison for the wicked. Not accessible to Gods.

RIVER STYX

Link between realms, accessed via CHARON and the Ship of Death. Also used to swear solemn oaths which, if broken, remove immortality.

Categories

DEITIES

Kardia: Precious metals: Gold (Olympians), Silver (Gods), Bronze (Heroes)

Highest order of immortality including Olympians, Gods and Heroes. Naturally imbued with great powers.

CONSTELLATIONS

Kardia: Crystal

The thirteen members of the Zodiac Council, charged with administering the immortal community.

NEUTRALS

Kardia: Glass

Rare immortals whose special gifts render them immune to other immortals' powers.

DAEMONS

Kardia: Onyx

Immortals with individual responsibility for human experience (e.g. Happiness, Luck, Wealth, Misery etc.). Require instruments to manifest powers. Currently imprisoned in Tartarus, except for THANATOS and HYPNOS.

ELEMENTALS

Kardia: Naturally occurring substances according to class, e.g. stone, wood, rock etc. Any immortal entity not listed above. May have human, animal or fantastical form. Often used for manual labour.

Artefacts

CHAOS STONES

Four elemental gems with potent powers, given by CHAOS to her son EREBUS, Daemon of Darkness (former King of Daemons, deceased, father to THANATOS and HYPNOS). Earth Stone (diamond), Air Stone (emerald), Water Stone (ruby) and Fire Stone (sapphire). Current whereabouts of three are unknown – Earth Stone protected by ELLIOT.

KARDIA

Necklace worn by all immortals to denote Category and Class. Materials vary according to above, but all shaped like a heart within a flame.

The Thank-you Bit (The Sequel)

Given that *Who Let the Gods Out?* took longer to gestate than an overdue elephant calf, it feels very soon to be sucking up . . . saying thank you . . . for its sequel. I owe both to my incredible publishers, the mighty Chicken House. There cannot be a more passionate, inspiring and wonderful group of people working in publishing and I thank the Gods daily that we are now birds of a feather. Barry, Rachel H, Elinor, Jazz, Laura M, Kes, Nina, Laura S, Sarah, Esther, Helen, Aleksei, Nick, Daphne – you are clucking marvellous and I love you to bits.

I must again give particular thanks to the saintly patience and God-given talents of my unparalleled editor, Rachel Leyshon. She is truly a Goddess and I'd be lost without her. I fear that my previous waxing strip analogy didn't hit the mark, so allow me another go: Rachel, you are the unseen support that holds me together and makes me look better . . .

Super Ed: you are my tummy-holdy-in knickers. Better?

One of the singular joys of joining the coop has been befriending my Chicken chums, the brilliant authors who ride under the same banner. Maya, Kiran, James, Natasha, Lucy, Emma, Kate, Sarah, Chris, Ally, Dan, Cat, Louise – it's been a joy watching you soar. Thank you for all your support, words of wisdom and cracking parties while I sat out my publication pregnancy. You are the best (and cheapest) therapy imaginable and I adore you all.

Gods was very fortunate to have a lot of early support from two major book babes and I'd like to thank Charlotte Eyre and Jo Clarke for singing from the rooftops about it. Your support has meant the world, and getting to know you both has been a privilege. You totally rock.

An apology to my beloved friends, who I have largely abandoned while I make stuff up all day. A huge bolt of love to Arf, Karen, Jennie, the NCT babes, the HT crew, my musical-theatre luvvies and all you other waifs and strays. I'm sorry I've been so busy. I'm even sorrier that I will be back soon.

I have so much love for my other Mum, Mollie Grennall, whose tireless love and support has seen me and my family safely through the huge changes this last year has brought. You are one of the best mortals on this planet, Mol, and we love you so very much. And Naughty Paul – you're all right too.

My boundless love and thanks, as always, to my beautiful family, who I love more than custard creams. This book is dedicated to my youngest daughter, who has faced every labour life has thrown at her with courage, grace and the cutest smile you'll find in any realm. You're my hero, baby girl, and I'm so proud of you. Especially your burps – they are epic.

And finally, all my love to my fabulous readers. I hope you enjoy this helping of Elliot and Virgo's adventures – I'll be back with more soon.

Love, and other things that are dry-clean only,

Maz

xxx

BEETLE BOY by M. G. LEONARD

Darkus can't believe his eyes when a huge insect drops out of the trouser leg of his horrible new neighbour. It's a giant beetle – and it seems to want to communicate.

But how can a boy be friends with a beetle? And what does a beetle have to do with the disappearance of his dad and the arrival of Lucretia Cutter, with her taste for creepy jewellery?

'A darkly funny Dahl-esque adventure.'
KATHERINE WOODFINE, AUTHOR

'A wonderful book, full to the brim
with very cool beetles!'
THE GUARDIAN

Paperback, ISBN 978-1-910002-70-4, £6.99 • ebook, ISBN 978-1-910002-98-8, £6.99

THE HALLOWEEDS by VERONICA COSSANTELI

When Dan's parents don't make it back from a trip to the jungle, he, his sister Martha and baby Grub are packed off to crumbling Daundelyon Hall, where Great-Aunt Grusilla cares only about tending to her mysterious graveyard garden.

But why are Grusilla and her curious servants each missing a finger? Has this something to do with the greedy 'Cabbages' in the greenhouse? And can Dan solve the mystery, keep his family together *and* hold on to all of his fingers?

'A highly entertaining mix of mystery, adventure and gory detail.'
S MAGAZINE (SUNDAY EXPRESS)

'. . . a riot of a read.'
WRD MAGAZINE

Paperback, ISBN 978-1-910002-33-9, £6.99 • ebook, ISBN 978-1-910655-60-3, £6.99